Knights Disarmed

Also by **Geoffrey Scott**

Stealing Homer
Rascal Harbor, Book One

KNIGHTS DISARMED

A RASCAL HARBOR NOVEL

RASCAL HARBOR, BOOK TWO

GEOFFREY SCOTT

PROSPECTIVE PRESS
Winston-Salem

P R O S P E C T I V E   P R E S S   LLC

1959 Peace Haven Rd, #246, Winston-Salem, NC 27106 U.S.A.

www.prospectivepress.com

Published in the United States of America by P R O S P E C T I V E   P R E S S   LLC

TRADEMARK

KNIGHTS DISARMED
A RASCAL HARBOR NOVEL

ISBN 978-1-943419-82-1

First PROSPECTIVE PRESS trade paperback edition

Printed in the United States of America
First printing, August, 2020

The text of this book was typeset in Caslon Pro
Accent text was typeset in Belleza

CONTENT NOTICE

The following work deals with sexual violence in childhood which, while fictionalized, may disturb some readers. The author has tried to treat this issues with care and welcomes any feedback on this and other issues

PUBLISHER'S NOTE

Acknowledgments

Writing a novel means the author spends lots of private time. Conceiving, drafting, editing, re-editing, and the like is largely solitary work. At some point, however, the private work turns public as drafts are shared, read, and discussed. The private work is, by turns, exhilarating, exhausting, enervating, and enlightening. The public work is just scary, as it invariably feels like sudden and dramatic exposure.

Friends help. In addition to my wife, Anne, my most consistent and attentive reader has been Emily Cole whose interest in the Rascal Harbor series has sustained my own passion for bringing these people, places, and events to life. Others have read parts of the manuscript, listened as I talked my way through plot problems, and offered advice on character motivations. That list includes Jean Dorak, Matt McConn, my father, and my children. In each instance, their kind words and thoughtful feedback proved helpful in advancing the narrative and in calming my writer's nerves.

In addition to those named above, I single out for special thanks my editor and publisher Jason Graves. I much appreciate his enthusiasm for the Rascal Harbor series in general and for his smart and judicious suggestions around this book. Thanks, Jason.

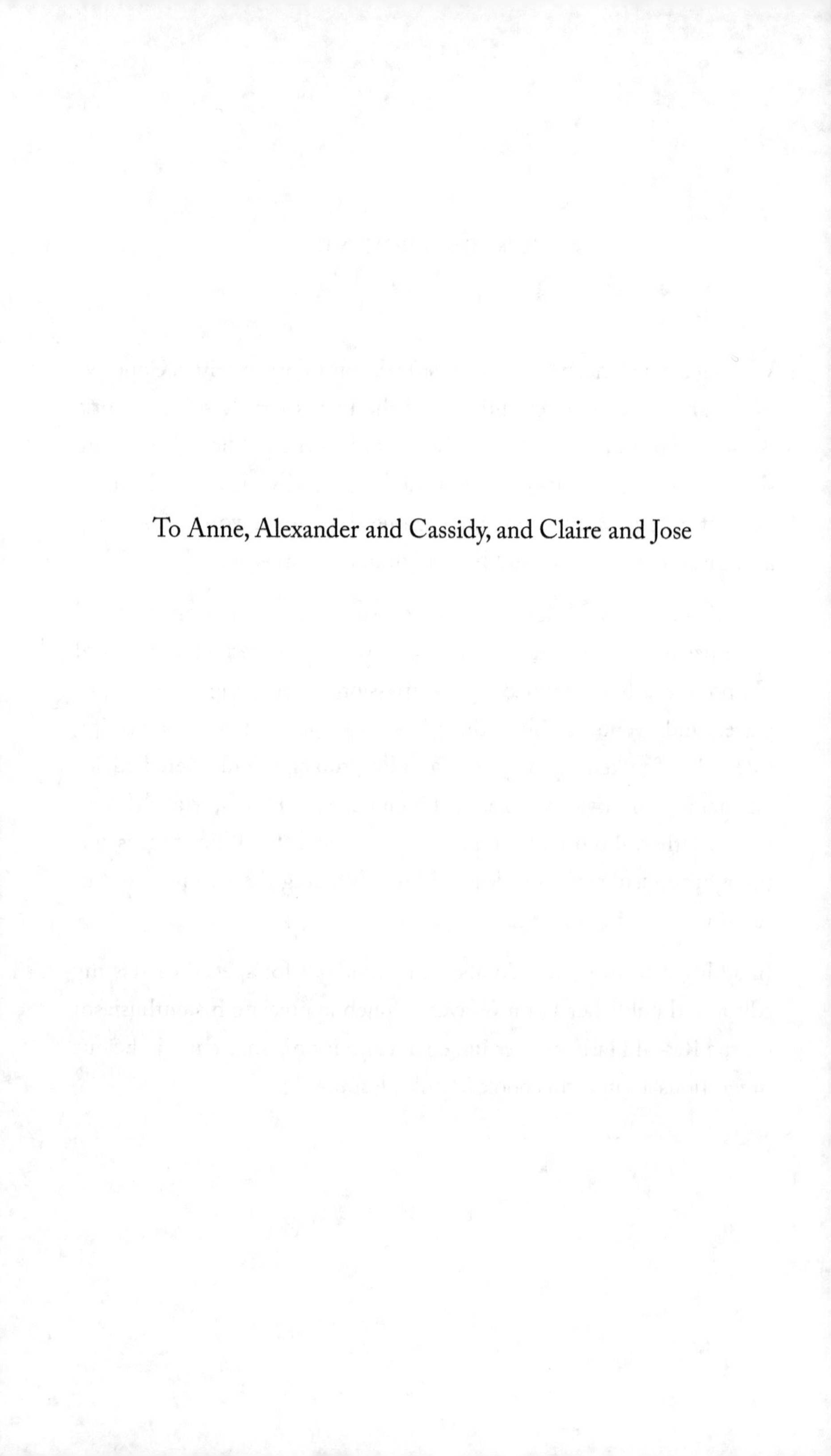

To Anne, Alexander and Cassidy, and Claire and Jose

CHAPTER 1

John Louis McTavish stopped at the service station just off I-95 in Sherman, Maine. His old Saab 9-3 seemed to be using more gas than usual. He'd filled up in Bangor and now eighty miles north, the tank was already down to a half. Not knowing where the next gas might be available or how costly it might be, he decided to fill up.

McTavish also decided to fill up on snacks. Blessed with a lanky frame and cursed with a sweet tooth, McTavish loved to nibble his way through long car trips. Although he didn't have to worry about his weight, McTavish's now-deceased wife Maggie used to chide him about his poor eating habits. He had explained that peanut M&Ms, his favorite road food, didn't count as a bad choice because the protein-laced peanut more than made up for the thin layers of chocolate and crunchy shell. "If you think about it, it's really a health food, Mags," McTavish had announced at one point. On their adventures together, he always got the biggest bag available, ate every one before the end of each trip, and was loath to share.

"It's a wonder you can stay so thin when you eat that way," Maggie had said.

"Must be my pure heart—"

"Your pure heart and your hummingbird metabolism" Maggie interrupted. "I swear that you burn up calories before you even take them in. I know ten women who would kill to be you, McTavish."

Now some two hundred miles northeast of his Rascal Harbor cottage, McTavish was on a photography and drawing expedition to The County. Aroostook County to non-Mainers, "The County" is the largest county by land area east of the Rocky Mountains; it is the size of Connecticut and Rhode Island combined. One route into The County is to continue on I-95 past Sherman to Houlton and then up Route 1 all the way up to Fort Kent. Taking the Sherman exit, puts a driver on Route 11, which is Route 1's poorer cousin. With the near-death of Maine potato growing and the downward slide of the lumber business, the economies along both routes have dwindled. But Route 11, always a hard luck story, could gain no purchase even on its hard-luck competitor.

McTavish chose Route 11. Though it had been years since he last traveled it, he expected to find several good sites to photograph and, if the blackflies weren't too bad, to do some outdoor drawings. It would also take him by what was once his family's farm. He was anxiously excited to get started on a new line of artwork; for a different reason, he was just anxious about seeing the old homestead.

Chapter 2

The drive up from the coast had taken McTavish by other potential photo and drawing sites and by farms similar to the one on which he was raised. He made notes about each for future trips.

Although he couldn't say why, McTavish aimed his Saab and his mind toward The County. He had no particular reason to do so, but ever since his involvement around the theft of a newly-discovered Winslow Homer painting during the previous fall, his thoughts kept drifting northward.

Raised on a family farm in the southern part of Aroostook county during the 1960s, McTavish had left home to attend college and he had not returned. The first on either side of his family to complete an undergraduate degree, McTavish found a home in academia in general and the University of Maine history department in particular. Good grades in his bachelor's program enabled him to get into a partially funded master's program at another good, if not great, public university. More good grades and some supportive faculty convinced him to stay on and complete a Ph.D.

McTavish had never known anyone with a doctorate before going to college and he wasn't exactly sure what to do with the one that he now had in hand. So he simply followed his advisor's suggestion and applied for academic jobs in history departments around the country. A medium-sized Indiana public took a chance on the new professor and, with only modest regret, McTavish left the east coast for the great mid-west. His Maine-bound family never quite forgave him.

Settling into a new job in a new part of the country, McTavish loved the first and adapted to the second. The adaptation was eased by a high school English teacher he met after a public lecture on Indiana schools in the mid-1980s.

McTavish specialized in the history of education and he found much to research in the waves of reform that had blown through Indiana and its neighboring states. Asked to give a talk about the Midwestern roots of the *McGuffey Readers*, McTavish focused on the notion that the books taught a method of reading on the surface and a set of civic and moral values just below.

In the audience was a tall, red-haired woman who sufficiently caught McTavish's attention that he stumbled over his remarks on three separate occasions. He looked for her at the reception afterward, but was not sure what he would do if he found her. That problem resolved itself when the woman approached him as he was leaving the building.

"I liked much of what you had to say, Professor, but I'm curious about the 'surface and below the surface' meanings you say are in the *McGuffey Readers*."

Taken with her strong and attractive face and dancing blue eyes, McTavish could muster but a single word, "Oh?"

"Indeed. It seems that you believe you've made quite a breakthrough in understanding the books."

Recovering only a bit of his brain, McTavish said, "Well, the idea hasn't been much written about…"

"But, Jesus, isn't it just common sense?" the woman said. This declaration only posed as a question. "Aren't there layers to nearly every human interaction? You know, the stuff we see easily, on first glance, and then all the other stuff that we figure out later?" These, too, seemed like propositions weakly disguised as questions.

"Well, ah, well, you make a good point," McTavish replied. "I suppose…"

"You suppose? Have you not had much experience outside the books, Professor?"

"I grew up with two brothers and two sisters on a family farm," McTavish said, more defensively than he meant to. Who in the hell is this woman? he thought.

The woman answered for him. "Well, there you go, Professor," she said. "And now you've met someone else." Sticking out her hand, the woman said, "I'm Margaret McIntyre, but my friends call me Maggie and I expect you to do the same."

And so he had. First, at the coffee shop that night where Maggie told him about herself. Later, on the several dates they undertook to popular attractions, historical sites, and the bedroom. And still later, when they married and produced a son, Noah McIntyre McTavish.

Maggie had died of pancreatic cancer one year ago this week in early May. McTavish suspected that Maggie's death was part of the reason that lay behind this trip northward. He really was seeking out new artistic inspiration. But with the anniversary of her death upcoming, McTavish also realized that he wanted to be away from the Rascal Harbor cottage that he and Maggie had filled with memories over the years.

Chapter 3

Maggie's life and death filled McTavish's thoughts in the time it took to drive from Rascal Harbor to Bangor. From Bangor north to Sherman, his thoughts shifted to the people he had come to know during his first year as a full-time Rascal Harbor resident.

Six months into his tenure there, a small, Winslow Homer watercolor was discovered in the attic of an old Victorian house. The head of the Rascal Harbor Art Colony, Robertay Harding, convinced the owners to allow the Colony to host a reception to introduce the painting to the world. A hitch or two developed during the reception, but a bigger problem occurred afterward: The painting was stolen and then recovered from the trunk of art student Jimmy Park's old Ford.

What seemed a simple theft and recovery became knotty as it appeared that Park might have been set up by an older Rascal Harbor artist, Simon Britton. The several clues pointing in Britton's direction seemed solid and he was arrested, jailed, and indicted.

The real culprit in the case, however, was Jimmy Park's best friend, Bradley Little. Park was presumed to be gay by many Rascal Harbor residents and especially by Little, who had fallen in love with his friend. Little suspected Britton, an openly gay man, of trying to steal Jimmy away from him. So he framed Britton as the thief as a way to "save" his friend Jimmy and, thus, prove his love. The whole thing came unraveled when Little then thought that Jimmy and McTavish were about to become lovers.

Recalling this crazed situation still confused McTavish whose understanding of and tolerance for what Maggie had called "the flaw" in human existence was limited. They had had many conversations before Maggie's death about McTavish's limited insights into human nature. He hadn't made much progress over their long marriage and so McTavish wasn't much surprised that their conversations continued in his mind. McTavish wanted to give himself a bit of credit for developing a friendship with Gary Park, Jimmy's dad and the proprietor of Gary's Garage. Maggie wasn't so sure he deserved any. McTavish protested, but only mildly, for he feared losing Maggie's presence if he progressed too much.

In the five months since the resolution of the Homer case, Rascal Harbor had settled back into its surface-level, small-town ways. Fish and lobster were caught, high school basketball games were played, and coffee and alcohol were drunk in equal measures. Gossipy tongues continued to wag and the principals in the Homer theft were featured players in the nattering.

Jimmy Park, though cleared of suspicion as a thief, remained the prime subject of chatter. Curiously, the fact that he emerged from the incident as an openly gay man interested townsfolk far less than the fact that he had been the love interest of Bradley Little, a presumably straight star athlete. Folks "knew" that Jimmy Park was gay, even if he didn't, and so would not have been surprised if Simon Britton had involved him in a love *and* criminal relationship. To find out that Jimmy was the unwitting center of the crime amazed and fascinated the chinwags.

But only slightly more than the fact that Bradley Little was gay. Bradley had seemed the poster boy for a hardy—and straight—Mainer. Residents professed themselves shocked that this ruggedly handsome, athletic, and hardworking boy could be "playing for the other team" as one ninny concluded.

The fact that neither boy still lived in the Harbor discouraged talk about them not one whit. Bradley was in the state penitentiary in Warren serving a seven-year sentence for theft of the Homer painting. Jimmy decided to forgo his weekends in Rascal Harbor and live exclusively in Portland where he was finishing his college degree in studio art. McTavish knew that the boys' physical absence had not made the townsfolks' hearts grow fonder; he wondered how long it would take to settle their tongues.

McTavish had his doubts that it would happen anytime soon because Simon Britton had decided to stay in town. Simon had fared poorly in the county jail. The prison was too small to have a segregation area for sensitive prisoners, so Simon had lived among the general population. There, his gentle artistic and clearly gay soul was exploited at every turn. The jailers were not indifferent to Simon's plight, but neither did they intervene at every cruelty.

The Simon who emerged after Bradley Little's confession tried on a brave face with his neighbors and friends. It didn't work. His prison travails had weakened him physically; his once erect posture was gone and his once trim frame could only be described as gaunt. Still more concerning, however, was Simon's face. His smile and his eyes, which had shone brightly before his incarceration, did not die, but they showed little sign of life and even less sign of rebounding.

Chapter 4

"Jesus, I really do need to meet some new people," McTavish said to himself after this reflection. He felt badly about the fates of Jimmy, Bradley, and Simon. He felt badly for the sour effects evident on Jimmy's parents and sister, and on Bradley's mother.

He knew people who would take it as their calling to "fix" all of these people. That wasn't him. McTavish felt empathy for others, he just didn't think it was his job to solve their problems. That unwillingness to intervene unless invited to do so bothered Maggie; it infuriated their son Noah. "A silent presence," Noah had once called him in a fit of anger at a father he could only think of as aloof.

"And I suppose that's why I'm taking this trip alone," McTavish said to himself. He'd had offers for company—his brother Mark and his sister Giselle had each said they would go with him, though not together, as had Jimmy's dad, Gary. "Might have been nice to have some company," McTavish mused. "But then I wouldn't have had the time to think about Maggie on the drive up to Bangor." Maggie could go silent at times, but he talked with her often and he missed her during times of her absence.

"Kind of a sad sack, am I," McTavish muttered.

"A sad sack of shit feeling sorry for himself, if you want my opinion," he heard Maggie say. Maybe he didn't always miss her.

As he made his way onto Route 11 with a tank full of gas and a bag full of peanut M&Ms, other memories drifted through McTavish's mind. Though he had yet to cross from Penobscot into Aroostook county, McTavish saw places familiar from his childhood trips down this road. He passed old houses and new trailers, he passed farms that were prospering and more that were not, he passed a few young people—very few young people. The folks he saw getting into cars, walking to mailboxes, coming out of sheds, and gazing out of windows had the look of the past. He didn't recognize these people—he had grown up another forty minutes north—but he recognized their lives. The big farms, lumber yards, starch factories, and plywood mills betrayed these folks on their pay stubs and through their bodies. And now those corporate entities were themselves betrayed by world-wide market forces of which their owners never dreamed. So now the bent bodies of the elderly lived next to the broken bodies of their worksites and all McTavish could envision was a great lowering, as bodies and buildings returned to the earth.

This dour reverie persisted another ten miles despite the handful of peanut M&Ms that McTavish popped steadily into his mouth. Christ, this might be a two-bag drive, he thought.

As he finished this thought and threw the crumpled bag into the back seat, McTavish came upon a familiar and favored place. A couple miles south of Pinkham was a tree farm that had been planted during McTavish's youth. The Soil Conservation Society replanted the clear-cut acreage to prevent soil erosion. From his childhood on, McTavish recalled watching for the trees every time he passed this way. It was not that McTavish had never seen trees before. Well over eighty percent of Maine is tree covered, and while maple, pine, beech, and oak predominate, there are well over a hundred species within the state borders. What McTavish had never seen before were seedlings laid out and planted in a grid. He didn't know how many acres had been given over to this effort, but he guessed no fewer than twenty as the gridded trees ran along the highway for half a mile and as far back as he could see.

As a boy, these spruce trees had gained no more than a foot in height, and under winter snows they appeared as the dimples on a basketball. When McTavish was a teen, the trees would have reached his thigh if his father had ever stopped so that his oldest son could wander this land. On his last trip home before moving to Indiana, McTavish saw what he had come to think of as his trees approaching adulthood. "Seems we've grown up together," he said to himself and to the trees.

McTavish had made a few more trips along this road as he himself moved further into adulthood. Those trips, however, were most often for hospital visits and funerals and the journeys were hastily planned and executed. The trees were still there though, and they had taken on a stolid quality that McTavish imagined as a physical link to a more vibrant past.

Rounding the turn just before the trees, McTavish smiled for the first time on this trip. "Trees…really, John? It's the trees that make you smile?" he heard Maggie say. Once again she had dressed up a declaration in the clothes of a question.

"Ayuh," he said and pulled the car to the side of the road.

Chapter 5

Happy as McTavish was to be among them, the trees presented a problem. Actually two problems. He should have anticipated the first. Blackflies, lots of blackflies. "Ah, shit," he said aloud as he entered the trees. "Forgot the fly dope."

Cursed by generations of Mainers, blackflies follow the first warm days of spring. And they follow with a vengeance. Clouds of these tiny insects can drive humans and warm-blooded animals to distraction. They bite any exposed skin, but they especially enjoy swarming around the head where reportedly they are attracted to the carbon dioxide in a human's breath. They are also attracted to the warmth of bodies and the colors of clothing, though experts disagree about whether they prefer lighter or darker garments. They like cloudy days, humidity, and still air; they don't much like repellents made with DEET, though the long-term effects of DEET may be worse than a few itchy bug bites.

Blackfly season generally lasts from Mother's Day to Father's Day. Mosquitos, the blackfly's big and nastier brother, arrive in the spring and can last through fall. On either side of the blackfly and mosquito hordes are the no-see-ums—a really tiny little biter that is more annoying than a real bother—and the deer and horse flies that can grow up to an inch and a quarter long and take a chunk of flesh with each bite. Clothing and DEET-infused fly spray help, but life in Maine during the six good-weather months of the year is to live with bugs.

It was a mixed day of sun and clouds with an intermittent breeze when McTavish stopped to visit his trees. Fine conditions for blackflies and mosquitos, they made his welcome hot and discomforting. Still, he was determined to make some sketches, take some photographs, and scout some sites for longer engagements on less buggy days.

The trees were magnificent—ruler straight, three to four feet in diameter, and heavily canopied as their upper branches interlaced forty feet in the air. The effect was that of a high-ceilinged cathedral, but one more safe, more welcoming, and more spiritual than any man-made church McTavish had ever attended. McTavish typically scoffed at new-agers who held an inflated belief in the doctrine of nature-wor-shipping pantheism. Today, however, he thought they might be on to something.

Constantly swatting away insects was problem number one; fo-cusing on the images McTavish wanted to capture was number two. He "knew" these trees, yet he could not find his artist's vantage. The individual trees, the way they stood together and apart, and the un-dulating forest floor all appealed to his eye as did the quality of the felt experience in this copse. But McTavish could find no focal point: He literally could not see the forest for the trees. McTavish wanted to laugh at this realization, but feared that doing so would invite a mouthful of blackflies.

So McTavish pulled out his camera and took a series of shots with close, medium, and long-range focal points. Doing so, he hoped would help him decide which images to put in the foreground of his draw-ings and which to place in the background. Those decisions would come later; now he dashed from the woods to his car trailing an ener-gized blackfly cloud.

CHAPTER 6

Safe in his car, McTavish killed the few flies that entered with him, scratched a couple bites, and vowed to pick up anti-itch cream and fly spray with the highest concentration of DEET allowed.

"Must have lost my Maine blood out there in Indiana," McTavish said to himself. "The bugs never used to bother this much." The thought made him think about what else of his former Maine identity he'd shed over the years. He resisted the urge to mouth Thomas Wolfe's adage that you can't go home again. Too cliché, he thought. Then he remembered a conversation with Noah the previous fall. At the time, his son had remarked that McTavish seemed to be reacquiring his Maine speech. "Ayuh," McTavish had said with his thickest Down East accent. As he now pulled back out onto Route 11, he said, "Well, sir, Mr. Wolfe, maybe you *can* go home again."

Knowing there to be no overnight accommodations in his old home town, McTavish stopped at the Biddle Inn, a bed and breakfast in Pinkham that he hoped was still in business. It was, and one of the six guest rooms was still available.

"Ain't the best room, but ain't the worst neither," the short, raw-boned man at the desk said. Though he was acting as the desk clerk, he looked like he might be more comfortable fixing a hay bailer than checking in a visitor. His flannel shirt, rolled at the sleeves, exposed hands and forearms roughened by weather and work.

"As long as there's a bed and a place to take a shower in the morning, I'll be all set," McTavish said.

"Got that all right," the clerk said. "I got the boiler goin' agin this mornin' in time for the out-a-townas to do their bisness. Be all set for you tommorra."

"Thanks much."

"Whatcha doin' back hea?"

"What do you mean?" McTavish asked, puzzled.

"Well, ain't you Malcolm McTavish's boy?"

"I am…well, I was. My father died…" McTavish started to say.

"'Bout fifteen years ago now, ain't it?"

"Yes," McTavish said, "Do I know you? Or do you know my family?"

"Well, a course I do, you simpleton!" the man exclaimed. "You're Malcolm and Nadine's boy, the one who went off ta college and then never come back."

"I suppose I am, though my brother Danny never returned either."

"Right, right," the man said. "He was a pistol, that Danny!"

"And what did you say your name was?" McTavish asked, wondering if this conversation would last until night fall.

"Don't think I did, but it's Alton Chase. Guess you don't remember me?" When McTavish shook his head, Chase continued, "I used to live upta Myron where you come from. I farmed just like your dad, but way over on the Crosby Road. Your dad, he was a fine man. He helped me out a couple different times and I weren't the only one. He was a damn fine man."

McTavish nodded. "He was."

"I come down here to Pinkham 'bout five years ago to live with my boy," Chase said. "You might remember him, Brenny Chase? Brendan, I mean, he don't like to be called Brenny anymore. He musta went to the high school with you…but now as I think about it, he was probably a couple years behind you."

"Sorry, I don't recall him."

KNIGHTS DISARMED

"Oh, he's a good boy. He owns the IGA and his wife, Lilly, she's a peach. But hell, I miss bein' on my own. That's why I'm workin' over hea at the Biddle. The Clancys, that's the Masschusetts people who own the Inn, they's good enough folks, but don't know shit about fixin' things and this old place takes lots of fixin'. So I fix stuff and take a turn at the desk when the Clancys are outa town."

Near the end of this monologue, McTavish wondered, though not for the first time, where the image of the laconic Mainer had originated. He'd only been back in the state for a year, but it seemed to him that Mainers yakked as much as any of the mid-westerners he'd lived among. The difference, he recalled, was that the latter talked endlessly about themselves as well as others whereas Mainers typically talked endlessly *only* about others.

Not willing to lose the rest of the day to Alton Chase, McTavish took his leave. He dropped his bag in his upstairs room, threw some water on his face, and counted his bug bites.

McTavish had seen the IGA on his way into town, so he now walked over with the intention of buying fly spray and anti-itch cream. After locating these items, he saw the wine and liquor section. He'd forgotten to bring a flask of Bushmills Irish Whiskey, his favorite drink. Jameson Irish was down his list. Here, it was the only option so he picked up a fifth. "Quite a chemical stew, you got there, John," he heard Maggie say. "If the fly spray doesn't work, you can always lather your skin with the Jameson!"

After supplementing his medicinal purchases with a couple of bags of peanut M&Ms, McTavish strolled around the town before heading back to the Biddle Inn.

His hometown of Myron had had little in the way of businesses—a gas station, a hair salon, a heating oil company, and a small lumberyard. Pinkham, though it had only twenty-five hundred residents, was considered a metropolis by comparison. During McTavish's youth, Pinkham had two grocery stores, a hotel and a bank, two garages, a movie theatre, and a liquor store. It also had two diners and a pizza

Geoffrey Scott

shop, a pharmacy, a hardware store, and a five-and-dime. McTavish's family, like many others from Myron, traveled to Pinkham most every Friday night or Saturday afternoon to restock their larders.

Pinkham also had a public library. If the family went to town on Saturdays, McTavish went first to the library and checked out the legal limit of books each time. He worked hard on the farm before and after school, but the family had no TV and so McTavish spent his nights reading. After the library, McTavish's next stop was the matinee at the theatre. He didn't know it at the time, but the experiences these two entities provided underscored his sense that northern Maine might not be the limit of his imagination and his life.

Disheartened, but not surprised, McTavish now saw a town seeming to fall in on itself. The library was still there as was the pharmacy and one each of the diners, grocery stores, and garages. The hotel, pizza shop, movie theatre, and five-and-dime were just gone—out of business and the buildings torn down. The building housing the liquor store was gone as well. The booze survived, however, having made its way into the grocery store McTavish had visited earlier.

A walk down Main Street told all this story at a glance—the brightly painted and well maintained buildings of McTavish's past now showed wear and neglect; elsewhere empty, abandoned lots surfaced between buildings. The effect was like that of an old man's smile—weak and yellowed choppers interspersed with voids marking spots for those teeth long lost.

The back streets of Pinkham showed a similar gap-toothed smile— decrepit and forsaken houses standing beside vacant lots where others once stood. Derelict cars and trucks sat up on blocks, broken toys littered yards, lawn chairs upended by wind and neglect—these elements both individually and in sum murmured acceptance of a final defeat.

"Just more of what I saw on the drive up from Sherman," McTavish said to himself. *Walking* past more of the same, however, seemed far worse. You *can* go home, I guess, but you might not like what you see, he thought.

Northern Maine in early May is still recovering from winter's oppression. The melting snow lingered and did so in its grimiest fashion. In the dooryards and vacant lots, gray piles of ice-hard snow drifts underscored the general dreariness.

About to turn back onto Main Street, a bit of color caught McTavish's eye. On the south side of a nondescript house, he saw the small, but vibrant purple blossoms of crocus plants. Scattered randomly, some grew in full sun while others poked through crusted snow. "Huh," McTavish said to himself. "Life."

CHAPTER 7

Back in his room, McTavish sat with a straight pour of Jameson in a bathroom water glass. No one greeted him on his arrival back at the Biddle Inn; apparently the Clancys had yet to return and Alton was off fixing something. With no ice machine in evidence, McTavish sipped his Jameson neat.

Normally, he would have grumbled; Jameson had a harsher taste than the Bushmills he typically drank and the absence of ice only magnified the difference. McTavish hardly noticed though as he could not shed the vivid image of the crocus blossoms. His general disinterest in flowers and plants faltered only in early spring when crocus and then daffodils forecast warmer days to come. He had seen both around his cottage earlier that morning, residuals of Maggie's more concerted interest in such things.

Had he thought about it, McTavish might have assumed that the snow and ice he had seen on the tree farm and around the houses and lots during his walk around Pinkham would forestall spring blooms for another few weeks. The crocus caught him off-guard. They disrupted his dour perspective on Pinkham's decline; they sparked his artist's eye. Might be something there, he thought.

As the nutritional value of his peanut M&Ms faded and the influence of the Jameson grew, McTavish realized he was hungry. With limited dinner options, but a preference for greasy food, McTavish slipped downstairs past the still unmanned desk and walked to Janey's Diner.

Walking through the door, McTavish was struck by the similarities between Janey's and Lydia's Diner in Rascal Harbor. Both places had an assortment of lighting fixtures, scarred tables with mismatched chairs, and floors with dingy linoleum tiles, only some of which seemed firmly anchored. Lydia's walls were painted yellow; Janey's appeared to be blue, though a couple of different shades were evident. Neither place sported a consistent decorating theme unless "eclectic utilitarian kitsch" qualified. Paint color—or colors—mattered little in either spot, however, as all manner of artifact was hung, nailed, screwed, or glued to the walls.

Whatever the physical differences, Lydia's and Janey's were the same place. The tang of a well-used Fry-o-Later, grill, and toaster hung heavily. The hunched shoulders of working and worn out men and women pressed against one another at tables too small for the groupings. The conversations wafted and waned, punctuated by curses of both mild and medium intensity. McTavish knew no one here and yet he *knew* everyone here.

Even though it wasn't Saturday night, McTavish ordered baked beans, hot dogs, and coleslaw. He was pleasantly surprised to see two apparently homemade yeast rolls accompany the meal.

Growing up, he had hated baked beans, but loved the yeast rolls that his mother made every Saturday night. He would eat all the rolls he could and pray that the beans would somehow disappear. They didn't, and baked beans grown cold tasted like rabbit droppings. He wasn't sure when it happened, but at some later point he'd developed a tolerance and then a love for beans baked in molasses and brown sugar. He still hated them cold.

McTavish needn't have worried. The beans and dogs were appropriately hot, the coleslaw appropriately cold, and the rolls appropriately delicious. As he ate, he tried to read the copy of the *Bangor Daily News* that he'd picked up at the gas station in Sherman. Doing so proved challenging, however, as he found snatches of conversation interesting enough to be distracting:

"Christ, you see Ronald's new skidda? Thing's so tough lookin' I expect the trees will cut themselves down."

"Didja hear Julie is getting married to Adrian Walker? That girl really must wanta go to a weddin'!"

"Goddamn school taxes goin' up again this yeah. There ain't hardly no kids left in town and the taxes is still going up? How the hell's that make any sense?"

The topic of school taxes surfaced across a table of four beefy men. They were castigating the board members who advocated the increase, when one of the table mates said, "Speakin' a old fahts, didja hear this one? What did the maxi-pad say to the faht? Without waiting for a response, the man half-sang, "You are the wind beneath my wings!"

"That's a good 'un, Nathan," another man said. "Why do fahts smell?"

"For the folks who is hearing impaired!" one of his friends replied, then added, "But I can top that one. Seems there's this old County gal gone down ta Portland and she goes inta one a them fancy hotels ta take a wee. At the mirror are these two girls gabbin' and fussin' with their hair when one waves her hand all around says all arrogant, 'Smell this. Pure Poison, forty dollars an ounce.' This other lah-di-dah says, 'That ain't nothin. This is Chanel, fifty dollars an ounce!' They's all quiet for minute when the old gal bends ova, lets out an old rippa' of a faht, and says, 'B & M Baked Beans, thirty-five cents a pound!'"

"Ah, Jesus, that's a doozy," the fourth man at the table said. Then he asked and answered his own joke: "What's the real reason women can't faht loudly in public? Because they can't shut up long enough to build a decent pressah!"

Listening in to this conversation was a table of three older women. They had been maintaining their own confab, but McTavish noticed that they laughed quietly at the jokes. After the last one, one of the women called over to the men, "I got one for ya, Tommy. Why don't little girls faht?" When no one at the men's table responded, she said, "Cause they don't got assholes till they get married." The other women, and most of the rest of the diners, burst into laughter.

Not to be outdone, the man named Tommy said, "Ah hell, Maddie, you're so damn old, when you faht, you blow dust!"

Everyone laughed again and Maddie said, "Christ, Tommy, that actually was a good one!" With that, the diners turned back into their cups and dishes and conversations.

Jesus, I'm two hundred miles away, but I'm right back in Lydia's, McTavish thought, men and women scraping on each other. Oh, and folks substituting an 'ah' for every 'r' and dropping the "g' at the end of every word. Haven't heard an 'ayuh' yet or a 'dhow' but it's just a matter of time.

By the time he finished his meal and paid his check, McTavish had registered three ayuhs, four dhows, and five wickeds, the last being the preferred adjective when expressing anything of inordinate size, shape, or peculiarity. "Well, sir, guess I'm home anywhere I drop my hat in the state of Maine," McTavish said to the long-gone and home-forsaken Thomas Wolfe.

CHAPTER 8

Dressed for a day of sketching, photography, and avoiding blackflies, McTavish left his room dressed in jeans, long-sleeved work shirt, sweater, and Bean boots. He carried his satchel of cameras and drawing materials and his old leather coat. It promised to be a sunny day, but McTavish expected to need the coat for the first couple hours of this early spring morning. "Still got a little too much of that thin mid-western blood?" he heard Maggie ask. He nodded.

Anxious to get on with the day, McTavish greeted his hosts, the Clancys, with a nod and quick hello. He picked up a couple corn muffins and a to-go cup of black coffee. He was on the road north to Myron with his coat on and with the heater blasting by seven o'clock.

The strengthening sun played over the still-white snow banks in the fields and the dew on the trees and shrubs. McTavish stopped a couple of times to take photos. He wasn't sure that he'd later be able to translate the images into drawings, but he looked forward to trying.

The houses, farms, and fields he passed told no different story than the one he had heard on the drive from Sherman to Pinkham. Once a living and working landscape, he recalled farmers harrowing the newly-tilled potato fields, laundry flapping in the spring-chilled breezes, horses and cows grazing in barely-green pastures, children playing in still-muddy yards. It was not a Boston living and working landscape;

there was no frenzy, no hum other than the blackflies and mosquitos. But then it *lived* and now it moldered.

McTavish crossed from Pinkham in Penobscot County to Myron in Aroostook with nothing by a rusted sign to indicate the transition. With his family's old farmstead still two miles up Route 11, McTavish pulled onto Brock Lane. At the end of the dirt road, the Brock farm had been one of Myron's finest. Generations of Brocks had planted, harvested, and prospered from the potatoes grown on one hundred acres of the richest soil in southern Aroostook county. McTavish had known all of the Brock kids and had chummed around with the eldest, Frank.

A couple of new Cape Cod-style houses lay interspersed among the now-abandoned homes of the Cyr, Ames, and Coolidge families. The old Kerry place still showed life signs, but the name on the mailbox was Mays.

Half a mile later, McTavish drove onto the Brock property, or what he remembered as the Brock property. That memory would have to be revised now. The once meticulously tended house, barn, and out buildings still stood, but only in the barest sense of the word.

Roofs had caved in or blown away on the sheds and part of the barn; the house roof looked mostly intact, though the chimney had begun to topple. Walls on all of the buildings showed similar damage and disrepair. Paint clung to clapboards in patches; window glass had been broken out long ago. The fields once tended with care that earned Lester Brock the nickname "the finicky farmer" had gone to weeds and alder trees and bushes of various species.

McTavish's heart drooped. His first thought was sadness, his second anger. What the hell? he wondered, how could this have happened? Then he did the calculation—he'd been gone from the area over thirty years now. The sadness returned.

Memories played through McTavish's mind as he got out of the Saab, grabbed his kit, and begin walking the grounds. As farm kids, neither McTavish nor Frank Brock had had much time to play. Yet McTavish recalled social events in the Brock home, smoking cigarettes in the barn—then getting upbraided by Frank's dad for doing so—sharing a dented can of beer with Frank under a tree in a back field. Those memories stood in sharp relief against the dreary and discarded backdrop he now saw.

And then he saw it again—the violet leaves of a bed of crocus on the south side of the house. Mrs. Brock's flower gardens had once been well-known and widely praised. McTavish suspected that neglect had neutered most of them, but the crocus had survived. He pulled out his camera, stood over them, and took several shots. Nice to see something alive around here, McTavish thought.

Walking over to another bunch of crocus, McTavish realized that it might be interesting to shoot the flowers against the stone foundation of the house. Snapping a few close and medium-range shots, he then backed up so that the crocus, foundation, and a portion of the paint-flaked house came into view. He immediately liked the artistic contrast of the violet leaves, the various grays of the stone, and the white paint and weathered siding of the house. Shooting several photos from different angles and with different focal lengths, McTavish saw a new reason to smile. The contrast of the hard-luck siding of the house, long-enduring stone, and smile-inducing crocus blossoms told an interesting story.

And then it dawned on him why he'd been so taken with the sight of the crocus next to the house in Pinkham: He was *seeing* a story of life. All the dour adjectives he'd used to describe the lives and houses and businesses on this trip north were still there…but life continued. And if it could be as bright and luminous as those crocus blossoms, then maybe the rest of what he had seen could also come back into the sun.

McTavish realized he'd have to do some more thinking about this notion of life among the wreckage. Now, however, he wanted to see if there were examples beyond the crocus plants.

And he found them. At the Brock farm, those examples were all nature bound. The large crab apple tree in the southeast corner of the house was lit up with white and pink blossoms. Chokecherry bushes, with their spikes of fragrant, white flowers, grew all along the old fence that separated the house from the road going to the back fields.

These natural examples of nature's urgency and faith in life sparked McTavish's rational and artistic minds. But he was not, by disposition, a nature-focused kind of guy. So as he leaned against his car, eating the second corn muffin, he tried to see his way back through the morning's drive. What had he seen that showed life against the drab backgrounds that had defined the trip so far? And then the images started to pop—the kid in the bright red jacket weaving in and around mud puddles on a new bike; the freshly painted Irish symbol on a mailbox; the new studding that defined the in progress shed on a house. Down is down, he thought, but down is *not* always out.

CHAPTER 9

McTavish smiled as he drove away from the Brock farm. He hadn't realized how deeply the dismal scenes he'd experienced on the drive north from Sherman could depress him. He also hadn't realized how a few bunches of early spring perennials could make him smile. He sensed Maggie about to say something but, in his mind's eye, he just saw her smile.

Pulling out on the northbound lane of Route 11, McTavish felt his stomach clench. He knew his family's farm lay only two miles away. He wondered, however, if geographic distance was the only relevant measure.

The stomach clench tightened as McTavish crested Bullock Hill and saw the farm site another quarter of a mile on the right.

Or what was left of the farm. McTavish knew that the property had passed into other hands ten or more years ago. The new owners, the Guptils, were long-time farmers, but McTavish thought he recalled his brother Mark telling him that the farm had passed through more hands. He hadn't expected that it would remain a working farm. Even before this trip, he knew that many others had passed into dysfunction. He shouldn't have been surprised to see it fallen into disuse and disrepair, but he was.

Like the Brock farm, weeds and bushes had claimed the fields, neglect and disrepair had claimed the buildings. As he slowed, however, an old house trailer sitting in the dooryard came into view.

There are old house trailers and then there are *old* house trailers; this was the latter. It sagged in the middle, rust ran down the sides, shabby curtains flattened against cracked windows. A parking area of busted cars and trucks littered the front and back yards in and among busted bikes, go-karts, and ATVs. McTavish assumed at least one usable vehicle could be constructed from the various parts, but he wouldn't have bet on it.

Though he later would wonder why, McTavish pulled into the dooryard. Two dogs, a cat, and three children ran out before he got out of the car. A cacophony of kids and dogs ensued.

"Who are you, mister?"

"What'cha you doing here?"

"Our dogs don't bite, mostly."

"What kinda weird car is that?"

"What do you want?"

This blizzard of questions and comments along with the constant barking of the dogs backed McTavish up against his closed car door. He was about to leave when a thin, young woman came running out of the trailer yelling at kids and dogs to be quiet. McTavish took advantage of the lull to open his door and start to get inside. The woman's insistent stride toward him, however, caused him to pause. "What is it you want?" the woman asked brusquely. "I ain't ever seen you before. You got business here?"

McTavish wasn't sure which question to answer first so he opted for a down-the-middle response. "I used to live here," he said. "I grew up here…when it was a farm, a potato farm. Well, we had some cows too, but it was mostly—"

"Yeah, I get it, it was a potato farm. Now it ain't. So what do you want?"

"I suppose I was just wondering how the old place had fared over the years."

"Well, open your fuckin' eyes!" the woman said and started back to the trailer.

"Okay…but would it be okay if I walked around a bit, maybe took a few pictures of the buildings?"

"No!" the woman fairly shouted. "You can't take no fuckin' pictures here! Jesus Christ, get out of here before my boyfriend comes up and beats the livin' shit out you!"

"Sorry, sorry," McTavish said. "Not a problem. My apologies."

As he turned to get into his car, the woman said, "Well, you can take your apologies and shove 'em up your ass. Just get the hell outta here."

Driving south on Route 11, McTavish looked in his rear view mirror. He saw the woman still in the yard watching him as kids and animals circled her. What in hell was that all about, he wondered.

"Just that old John McTavish charm!" he heard Maggie say.

"Ah…Christ," McTavish said shaking his head.

CHAPTER 10

McTavish was within three miles of Pinkham when he realized that he hadn't finished his trip to Myron. The town itself lie another three miles north of what was the McTavish farm. The shock of his interaction with the woman from the trailer had so taken over his mind, that he had turned south without another thought.

He gave a minute to the idea of turning around and going back, but two things stopped him. One was his expectation that Myron proper was likely to be even more down-and-out than Pinkham and he was done with down-and-out. The other reason: McTavish didn't think he could face driving past his old home and its new residents again. The woman's reactions and the desperate look of the farm unnerved him. He would go north no more.

By the time McTavish reached Pinkham, he was starving. His corn muffins a distant memory and his peanut M&Ms unsatisfying, he longed for some real food. It was mid-afternoon, however, and Janey's was closed. He remembered that tea would be served in an hour so he returned to the Biddle Inn. Once in his room, he took a nip of Jameson, then showered off the day's dregs.

Downstairs, McTavish enjoyed a blueberry scone and a cup of lemon tea. He didn't enjoy the prattle of Mrs. Clancy once she learned that he had been a college history professor and was now pursuing an art career. She professed a fascination in both, though she seemed more interested in expressing her own views than than in listening to McTavish's.

Alton Chase saw McTavish's predicament, so came over with an invented problem that needed Mrs. Clancy's attention. "Thanks," McTavish whispered to the old man.

"Ah, the old girl can get some wound up," Chase said quietly. "You're not the first guest I've had to rescue." He then said, "But I was gonna talk with you anyway. I was tellin' my boy Brenny about you being from up in Myron and he and Lily got all interested in havin' you over for suppa. That's if you ain't got any plans. Won't vouch for the food—Lily's as sweet as sugar, but she can't cook for shit. It'll be edible all right, but tasty? Well…"

"Got it," McTavish said. "I'd be delighted to come." As they worked out the details and directions, McTavish thought he could see Maggie smirk, and then nod approvingly.

CHAPTER 11

As McTavish drove to the Chase home, he reflected on two conditions of dining in Maine—language and time. "Dinner" in Maine is served at noon; real Mainers know that others use the term "lunch" for the mid-day meal, but the proper term is dinner. The Pinkham Lumberman's Museum big fundraiser is a bean-hole *dinner*. Upwards of two hundred people attend, but every year some hopefuls miss out because they arrive in the late afternoon expecting an evening meal. "Supper" is served in Maine kitchens any time after 4:30 PM, but is always wrapped up by 6:00 PM at the latest. Dining this early wouldn't fly down Boston-way, McTavish knew, but farm lives run from early morning to early evening and then to bed. Alton Chase and his family no longer farmed. Old habits are habits hard to break, however, and so McTavish wasn't surprised to learn that supper would be served promptly at 5:00 PM.

The Chase house stood out among its neighbors. Freshly painted clapboards, trim, and shutters, a well-tended yard, and a couple of relatively new cars bespoke an upscale island on a shabby street. It even had a small bed of crocus.

At the side door, Brendan Chase, a taller and fleshier version of his short-statured father, met McTavish with a smile and business-man's handshake. "John McTavish, I don't expect you remember me as I followed you in school, but I remember you. Come on in and break bread." He added quietly, "Course with Lily's cooking, breaking the bread is probably what you'll need to do."

Just inside, McTavish was met by Lily Chase. Dancing eyes and a wide smile defined her; two elementary-aged children, a boy and a girl, hid behind her and giggled. Alton Chase came out of the kitchen with three beers and handed one to McTavish. "Let's all have a drink, Mr. McTavish, I expect we'll need the lubrication."

Alton led McTavish to a long table in the kitchen as Brendan helped Lily ready the meal. "How'd ya spend your day?" he asked.

As McTavish started to tell him about his trip to the Brock farm, the rest of the family came to the table bearing food and drink. As it took a few minutes to organize, McTavish eyed the fare for signs of the dining disaster about which he'd been warned. Though the food appeared edible, McTavish was struck by the absence of any aroma. As plates were passed and food dispersed, McTavish noticed a patina over each portion. The beef, potatoes, and peas all looked as if a light gray wash had been painted over them.

Well cooked, he thought, and he was instantly reminded of all the meals his mother had prepared. In Nadine McTavish's case, the inspiration to overcook came from a magazine article that warned of the ills associated with undercooked pork. Nadine had generalized the solution—cook, and then continue to cook everything until "done." Such an approach had three results—in color, the gray cast appeared; in texture, meat became stringy, all else became mushy; and in taste, well, something had to give. McTavish vividly remembered the first time he'd eaten real Italian food. The explosion of flavor had nearly made him cry.

McTavish could see Alton and Brendan covertly watching as he began eating. Knowing well what to expect, he had taken small portions and salted heavily. His smile was less about the food than the memory of mother's cooking. It reassured Alton and Brendan, however, and they seemed to relax.

Never one to seek attention, McTavish hoped to pass the meal listening to the Chases describe their day and their lives. Nothing doing.

Lily wondered what life was like on the coast; Brendan wanted the details on the theft of the Winslow Homer watercolor; Alton pushed to hear more about McTavish's visit to Myron; the kids wanted to know why he drove that "old-timey car."

McTavish wasn't sure how to respond to Lily's question; he damned the Internet for Brendan's interest; and he had no idea how to explain his long-held love for Swedish cars. So he opted to describe his day in Myron.

As he tried to explain why the crocus and the budding bushes and trees had so excited him, he noticed Alton and Brendan exchange wondering glances. McTavish kept talking, but he suspected the two Chase men were thinking, "Jesus, what a dope. Doesn't he know that trees and bushes and plants bud out every spring?" So he shifted his narrative to talk about putting the new plant life in the foreground and the buildings in the background. That point didn't seem to inspire much interest either. So he transitioned again to report on the encounter with the folks who now lived on his family's farm.

Considerable interest ran across all the adult faces as he did. Lily expressed concern about his safety. Brendan thought the family likely worked in the burgeoning rural methamphetamine industry. Alton wondered who the family might be.

Again, McTavish took Alton's question first. "Not sure, though the name on the mailbox was Knight. I remember it because of the way she came charging out of the trailer."

"Knight, eh?" Alton said. "Seems like there usta be a Knight family over ta Briggs. Desperate bunch as I recall."

"What do you mean by 'desperate' grandpa," one of the Chase kids asked.

"Oh, thin soil, poor pasture, man was a drunk," Alton recalled. "Think his wife died young, left him with a buncha kids. Seems I remember he packed 'em off ta different places."

"Packed them off'?" Lily asked with alarm on her face.

"Think a sister took some and then a guy up northa Myron took a couple. He was a rough character, that one. Mean as a bastard…er…" Alton looked chagrined as Lily cut him a look. "…a bugger? A bad guy? Anyway, them kids probably had a rough time in that house."

"So maybe the boyfriend of the woman in the trailer is one of the Knight sons," McTavish concluded.

"Could be," Alton said. "Or a sister. Guess you ain't sure who all bought your folks' place after they died."

"No, can't say that I do," McTavish admitted. "Maybe my brother or sister would as they handled the sale at the time and I'm guessing it might have passed through a few other hands since."

"Possible," Alton said. "Too bad though. Your dad was a damn…a darn good farmer and your mom was a peach. Hard to think about how far Myron's tumbled since then if there's drug dealers on your farm."

"People are saying that it's becoming an epidemic," Lily said. "There was a big piece in the *Bangor Daily* about it."

"Desperate folks," Alton said with a shake of his head. "Desperate times."

The cherry pie that Lily brought out for dessert brought smiles around the table, especially when she said that, because she'd not had time to bake, Brendan had brought it home from the store. McTavish knew he ought to pass it up—he'd eaten upwards of a pound of peanut M&Ms over the last two days. His insistent sweet tooth prevailed, however, and he bashfully accepted a second piece after quickly finishing the first.

CHAPTER 12

Back in his Biddle Inn room at 7:00 PM, McTavish thought about having a nip of Jameson and then hitting the sack. The early hour, however, convinced him that he'd sleep fitfully. So he poured the Jameson and downloaded the images from his camera to his laptop.

McTavish smiled as he reviewed the photos from the tree farm. He wasn't sure what he might do with them drawing-wise, but the long-held memories of the site pleased him. McTavish's artist eye saw far more possibilities in his photographs from the Brock farm. The foreground/background issue that he'd struggled with in capturing the tree farm forest vanished. The figure or foreground images of the crocus and the budded bushes and trees stood starkly against the ground or background of the foundation and walls of the house and the long wooden fence. The figure-ground relationship is most clearly reflected in graphic design, but it is a central principle in the construction of all art. In simplest terms, the featured image is the figure; everything else is ground.

McTavish had given considerable attention to the principle of negative space in the drawings of human hands he had focused on during the previous fall. He had snapped a number of pencils along the way, but in the end he had liked the work. Both the *process* of learning to create finely drawn hand images and the final *products* pleased him.

A moment's inspiration led him to add rectangular shapes that framed the images. Adding these lines, McTavish realized, moved his work from drawings to *art*. McTavish's young artist friend, Jimmy Park, had praised the original hand drawings. When he saw them with the added framing lines, however, he agreed with McTavish's assessment. Pulling out the first of the revised images, Jimmy shook his head and said, "It was there before, but now it's there differently."

Figure-ground, McTavish sensed, was much the same concept as positive and negative space. The notion of the negative space created by the rectangles around the positive hand images had helped him *see* those images in a richer light. The framing lines had transformed the visual plane. Now looking at his photographs of the scenes around the Brock farm, McTavish felt the concept and language of figure-ground could prove just as useful as he contemplated the drawings to come.

"How about adding a little color this time?" he heard Maggie say.

McTavish wasn't surprised by Maggie's comment. When he had dedicated himself to building his artistic chops last fall, he'd decided to stick with pen, pencil, and charcoal in an attempt to get back to basics. He felt pretty good about the decision at the time, though the rectangular frames he had later added to his hand drawings were made with a chestnut brown Conté crayon.

As he evaluated his photographs for their potential as art pieces, however, McTavish wondered if he'd be able to do them justice in black and white images alone. There was something about the violet leaves of the crocus against the gray foundation stones, for example, that sparked him. Maybe it wouldn't be the worst thing to add a little color, he thought.

CHAPTER 13

Awake early, McTavish was on the road back to Rascal Harbor by 7:00 AM. He had a couple more of the Biddle Inn corn muffins and a large cup of coffee. He'd pick up more peanut M&Ms later in the day.

McTavish didn't dream about the figure-ground idea, but it was on his mind. He hated to think about the possibility that he'd been missing the importance of the construct all these years. He smiled at the thought that it took a crocus plant half buried in a snow bank to help him see it. He suspected Maggie would smile at this insight, too.

As he drove south, McTavish's artistic eye scanned the countryside. Shifting the weedy fields, broken houses, and junked cars to the background, he attended more closely to those signs of life that he could see in the fore. He saw lots of examples: a fresh pile of lumber anticipating a building project, a set of newly painted shutters, a young dog bouncing around a dooryard, a stiffly new American flag fluttering, and young kids lounging in a tree.

Not wanting to chance any more unpleasant encounters, McTavish didn't stop. Instead, he pulled to the side of the road, rolled down his window, and snapped a couple of quick pictures of each scene. His aim was not fine photography. He just wanted to make a record of the images so that he could later manipulate them through his pencils… and just maybe his paints.

Chapter 14

Other than the stops to take photographs, the drive south was uneventful. In Bangor, McTavish turned off I-95 and picked up Route 1A to Hampden. There, he turned onto Route 202 and drove through Dixmont and Troy to the town of Unity where he turned onto Route 220 and drove on to Waldoboro.

With his refocused eye, McTavish now clearly saw the mix of life and decay that he had missed on his drive north. More building projects, more new paint, more new buds on trees. And daffodils. McTavish didn't stop and he often only caught glimpses, but these sure signs of life caught his eye as he drove down the two-lane roads.

Along with more signs of vitality, McTavish saw fewer signs of decay. He'd heard people talk about "two Maines," the prosperous southern and coastal Maine and its economically troubled sister to the north. His tour confirmed the split, at least in terms of the natural and man-made landscapes. The hardscrabble north was not dead—neither nature nor humans had given up. But from Bangor north, the hold the humans had seemed weaker than that their peers had in the south.

McTavish's artistic and economic musings kept him occupied until he arrived in Waldoboro and Moody's Diner. Like LL Bean's, Moody's is one of Maine's commercial landmarks. Pulling into the outsized parking lot at 11:30 AM, McTavish beat the typical mid-day crush.

Taking a seat at the counter, McTavish ordered a fish sandwich and fries, knowing that both would come in outsized portions. A second cup of coffee arrived with his meal. Working his way through both, McTavish tried to recall the story the humorist Tim Sample tells about a bunch of fishermen who sat at the same counter on a Saturday night. The men filled up on baked beans and then filled the air with the odorous gas that so often follows. He couldn't remember the elaborate backstory, but the punch line came back—"If I'da known it was her turn, I'da let her go first!"

Arriving back in Rascal Harbor, McTavish immediately noticed the daffodils in bloom and the tulips in bulb all around his cottage. Crocus, daffodils, and tulips pretty much defined his horticultural knowledge. Taken together with the other signs of life that he had noticed, McTavish now felt as though he had cracked his figure-ground problem and could now pursue a clear and exciting new artistic direction.

McTavish had just finished unloading this car when he got a call from his son. Noah was finishing his junior year as a fine art major at a Big Ten university. His plan was to come to Maine in time for the next McTavish family luncheon scheduled for the end of May and then stay in Rascal Harbor for the summer.

McTavish and his son struggled to find their way into a new relationship after Maggie's death. The illusion of closeness between the two was the result of Maggie's many efforts. Her death fractured their always-thin relationship and they were only now, a year later, starting to find ways to construct a new one.

"How was the semester?" McTavish asked.

"Pretty good, though I'd like to kill my English professor. The guy is a total jerk."

After McTavish and Noah finished dissecting the jerky professor, they made plans for Noah's trip to Maine. McTavish thought he heard a bit of excitement in Noah's voice. That excitement grew as Noah inquired about the family gathering planned for a couple days after he arrived.

The McTavish siblings had felt adrift after the death of their parents and the sale of the farm. McTavish was the oldest at fifty-five; he was also the first to leave the state for school, a job, and a life. His brother Mark and sister Ruth had never forgiven him. They also blamed him for the fact that the youngest McTavish, Daniel, also left the state. Danny was doing well in his Chicago-based career, "But he never woulda had that idea if you hadn't scooted off to Indiana," brother Mark told McTavish almost every time they met. McTavish was trying to like his brother and sister. It turned out to be a trial some times.

Mark, the second oldest at fifty, had built his modest associates degree into a successful career in computer sales. His big belly and big laugh contrasted on both levels with the spare bodies and temperate dispositions of the other McTavishes. Ruth took both of those characteristics to the limit. Her sparrow-like body well matched her gray nature and her bookkeeper position. McTavish had often thought that, if Ruth every got truly excited about something, her body might just fly apart. Though as opposite as two siblings could be physically, Mark and Ruth were a matched pair in their views of the world, the family, and life. Each had married a spouse that reflected the other and they lived within half a mile of one another in West Taylor, a suburb of Portland.

McTavish and his youngest sister Giselle fell in between Mark and Ruth in most ways. Tall, trim, and quiet, they tended toward the ironic. Their career paths diverged, however. Where McTavish left for college and then never left academia, Giselle had drifted through colleges and majors until she found meaningful work restoring old houses. Her partner, Martin Mayberry, was a master plumber. They lived in a barn they were turning into a house in Sincere, a little town fifteen miles north of Rascal Harbor.

McTavish wasn't quite sure where his brother Daniel fit in. A typical youngest kid in a big family, Danny had Mark's easy laugh and feel for business, but he had the trim body typical of the rest of the family. Danny was doing well in Chicago's financial industry and Mark and Ruth touted his success to all who would listen. Why they gave Danny a pass for leaving Maine, while continuing to poke McTavish was a mystery.

Since McTavish's return, the jibes had lessened, especially as the siblings now tried to meet at least once a month for a noontime meal—"dinner" for Mark and Ruth; lunch for McTavish and Giselle. It was this meal to which Noah now expressed interest in attending.

"We're meeting at Giselle and Martin's, right? And everyone will be there?" Noah asked.

"Far as I know," McTavish replied. "You'd like to go then?"

"Of course! Jesus, Dad, you never reveal anything about yourself so I'm hoping to get the scoop from your brother and sisters. They've got to have some insights into why you are the way you are."

"Why I am the way I am?"

"Yeah, why you're so within yourself. Everybody thinks you're like this deep, sage, self-contained kinda guy, y'know? I'm curious if you've always been that way."

McTavish couldn't remember ever being any different, but he wouldn't predict what might come out if Noah started interviewing his aunts and uncle.

"I'm a pretty simple guy, Noah," McTavish said. "Your mom was the lively one."

"I know, I know, Dad. Sometimes I think I'm more like her, but other times…"

"Yeah, I know, Noah. But you'll be who you'll be…and I'll be proud of you," McTavish said quietly.

"I hope so, Dad. I really hope so," Noah said equally quietly.

Shifting topics, Noah asked, "Anything new?" McTavish took advantage of the topic change and started describing his trip to The County. With the help of Noah's questions, he talked through his stop at the tree farm, the round of fart jokes at Janey's, his photographs at the Brock Farm, and his encounter with the family in the trailer at his old homestead. Noah was curious about McTavish's excitement over the figure-ground relationship he had rediscovered. He was even more curious about the split up of the Knight family. "How could that even happen? Wouldn't social services or somebody step in?"

"Not a lot of social services in The County at that time, families tended to fend for themselves, even if it wasn't always the best for the kids."

"I'll say," Noah said. "It must have been hell for those kids to lose their mom and then get shipped off all over the place."

"Agreed," said McTavish. He and Noah then confirmed flight times, expressed their eagerness to see one another, and hung up.

CHAPTER 15

In the days before Noah arrived, McTavish worked on several sketches based on his County photographs. Some, he reproduced in ways more or less faithful to the photographs. For example, he did a series of drawings featuring crocus plants against the stone foundation of the Brock house. For other drawings, he manipulated the images to try out different combinations of figure and ground. In one instance, he took an image of daffodils and positioned it as the figure in a drawing against a background of trees. Similarly, he placed a stack of new boards in front of a decrepit house.

The drawings pleased him and he worked hard to keep up with the figure/ground possibilities that flooded his brain. His brain also flooded with color. McTavish experimented with combinations of pen, charcoal, and pencil. Each medium allowed for sharp and subtle administrations. The fine point of a #5 pen could reimagine a penciled-in section; a bit of charcoal added to another part and smudged slightly created yet another visual element. The effects McTavish was getting through the lightest grays to the darkest blacks interested and pushed him.

But color beckoned. The drawings, many of them anyway, felt finished in their white, gray, and black expressions. Yet the remembered experience of *seeing* the color evident in a patch of crocus, a set of painted shutters, and a pair of mittens hanging off a mailbox tugged at him. He resisted pulling out his paints, but he wasn't really sure why.

Noah's arrival offered a good distraction. McTavish explained his no-paint-yet decision on the drive north from the airport. Doing so, he noticed Noah looking at him askance. "Jesus, Dad, do you ever do anything without chewing it over for months?" Noah asked, and then answered his own question, "No, I don't suppose you do. If Mom were here, she'd give you holy old hell and tell you to pick up the paints before she did it for you!"

McTavish smiled because he could see Maggie nodding in his mind's eye. "You both might be right," he said, then added with a wink. "I'll give it some thought."

Noah and his father stayed up far too late and drank far too much Bushmills to get an early start to Giselle's for the family luncheon the next morning. McTavish managed scrambled eggs and bacon for the two of them—no veggie omelets for this pair—before they packed up a contribution to the family meal and headed to Giselle and Martin's house.

On the way, they stopped at a gas station so that Noah could pick up a copy of the *Rascal Harbor Gazette*, the local weekly. Noah admitted an addiction to the paper after his Thanksgiving visit. He read it online when he was at school, but he had left for Maine before the latest issue came out. Although Noah chuckled at some of the typical silliness that passes for small town news, he could not wait to read the obituaries.

Nellie Hildreth's family had produced the *Gazette* since the late 1800s. Her spinster status caused her some despair at times for fear that ownership could pass out of the family if her sister's boy, Toulouse Rustin, refused to take it up. Nellie thought the boy bright, but with a fucktard name like Toulouse and a nitwit for a mother, he had a high hill to climb.

Crustier than the crustiest Maine fisherman, seventy-year-old Nellie delighted in running the paper the way she saw fit. She didn't begrudge the society ladies—well, most of them, anyway—for publicizing their teas and garden parties and dances, especially because she had a decent reporter, Sarah McAdams, who could write that shit up and hold her nose while doing it.

Sarah, assistant editor Rich Reed, and advertising/budget director Lindy Richards took seriously the care and feeding of the paper. Doing so, freed Nellie to pursue her passion—writing obituaries.

Noah and his father had actually debated whether the term "writing" best described Nellie's process. She always based some part of her obits on the vitals of a person's lived experience, but then Nellie's inventive streak took over. "I just add a little touch of creative honesty and reflection," Nellie explained whenever anyone dared to ask her how she wrote her pieces.

Noah read the latest of Nellie's obituaries to himself as he and his father drove to Giselle and Martin's. Laughing and shaking his head, Noah then read the obit to his father:

> *David Driscoll died. He was alive, walking around town last Friday. Died the next day. What friends he had went looking for him on Tuesday. And there he was…68 and dead…when they found him on Thursday. He must have done something in his life, but damned if anyone could remember him do anything but walk around town. So now he's dead and the funeral's done. Save your flowers.*

Looking at his father, Noah said, "Jesus, Dad, I wonder what she might write about you."

"Well, can't imagine that she'll ever die, so good chance that she will. Just hope it's later than sooner."

The two continued to talk about the license a small town newspaper owner has and the toleration small town residents can have for folks who walk either side of the center line.

Home-barn-home. Giselle spent all of her working life in and amongst the wreckage of old houses. Her talent was in putting them aright, adding both structure and grace notes. Yet she lived in a barn. It was a comfortable barn—Giselle liked her amenities. Everything was second-hand, but good-quality second hand. The largely open space was filled with odd pieces of furniture, tables, bookcases, and rugs that suggested disarray. On closer inspection, however, an understated orderliness emerged. Spaces for conversation and eating, for reading and reverie could be seen if one looked. McTavish knew that every piece and arrangement reflected Giselle's enthusiasms and Martin's muscle.

All of this was lost on Mark and Ruth. The latter just shook her head; the former boomed, "Jesus, sister, you live in a furniture warehouse! Only thing missing are the 'for sale' tags!" Giselle looked over at McTavish, shook her head, and walked into the kitchen area to help organize the meal.

Mark managed to find a chair that could accommodate his girth. From there he began a running commentary on whatever ideas popcorned around in his head. No one bothered to respond:

"'Member when we went down to John's cottage and the cupboard was bare? Jesus, thought I was gonna starve that day."

"The Sox are loaded up this year. If the starting pitching doesn't tank, they'll be in the Series, for sure."

"Wonder what Dad would say about Giselle living in a Christly barn!"

"'Member that time when we were jumping off the shed room into the snow bank and John lost his boot? Never found it till the next spring. I'll never forget him stomping around all winter with one of his and one of dad's old boots on!"

Giselle interrupted Mark's musing by calling the clan to the dinner table.

Mark, Ruth, and their respective families, McTavish and Noah, and Giselle and Martin settled around a long country table piled high. As they did, Noah prompted Mark to tell more stories, especially about his father. Mark's and Ruth's kids groaned, but Mark obliged.

"Well, Noah, the boot story might be the most interesting one about your dad. He was a bookish sort so he didn't get involved in too many hijinks. Mostly I remember him being a stubborn cuss," Mark said. Looking at his siblings, he said, "Remember Saturday nights?"

As Mark, Ruth, and Giselle turned their eyes toward McTavish, he muttered, "The beans."

"Exactly!" Mark trumpeted. "The beans! Seems our brother hated baked beans and baked beans were what we ate on Saturday night. And we ALL had to eat them. Well, John would fill up on rolls and hot dogs when we had 'em, but the beans just sat there. We all loved them. I even offered to eat his—"

"Mark, you would've eaten the table cloth if any bean juice fell on it," Giselle said.

"Rightly so, sister," Mark replied. "I do love my baked beans! Well, John would just sit there and stare at those beans cause you couldn't leave the table till you'd cleaned your plate. Only thing that saved him was bedtime."

"Oh, and that one time when he fell asleep at the table and he fell face first into his plate," Ruth said. "That was quite a sight."

"And quite a mess," McTavish said. "Though it ended up convincing the folks to let me be. The weird thing is that I ended up developing a taste for beans after a time."

"Well, you are a weird dude, brother John," Mark said to chuckles all around the table.

"And a stubborn one to be sure," Noah said to nods from the other adults.

More stories followed including one about the time that Giselle and Ruth found the bottom half of a deer leg in a back corner of the barn. For the first time ever, Malcolm McTavish had killed a deer out of season to put some fresh meat in the family freezer. When he drove home one afternoon and saw his daughters waving the deer leg at passing motorists, he decided his jacking days had best be over.

The stories prompted Noah to remind the family that McTavish had just come back from a visit to The County. The eyes of the assembled turned to McTavish and their questions peppered him about the trip in general and the old homestead in particular.

McTavish chose not to describe his artistic discoveries, expecting them to create a glaze over his now-bright listeners' eyes. So he focused on his encounter with the trailer lady and her brood. His story elicited a range of reactions—sadness about the loss of their homestead, disgust that the land was no longer being farmed, surprise that the house had been abandoned for a trailer…oh, and some concern about McTavish's safety from the implied threats.

The last came, predictably, from Ruth who saw danger, malice, and peril in nearly every social situation. "Likely they are all in the methamphetamine business, John," Ruth concluded. "You were lucky to escape with your life!"

"Hell, Ruth, all John had to do was start reading from one of his books and he woulda bored them all into a stupor!" Mark said. "Hey, now there's an idea—solve the drug problem by havin' John read 'em all to sleep!"

"Let's try it out on you, Mark" Giselle said. "You'd be a good big guinea pig!"

All laughed, though McTavish wasn't sure that they were all laughing at the same thing.

As the family turned to dessert, Ruth asked McTavish about the trailer woman's name. He had mentioned that Knight was on the mailbox, though he now admitted that he didn't know if it was the woman's or her boyfriend's name. He added that, once he'd returned to his cottage after the trip, he confirmed that a Galen Knight had been involved in the murder of a man named Simpson. The crime occurred before McTavish moved to Rascal Harbor but, because murder happened infrequently, Knight's name remained in play around town.

"Think I played high school ball against a Knight kid or maybe it was Knowlen or Nicols," Mark said. "Mean little Christer as I recall."

"You played basketball?" one of Mark's children asked in an amazed voice.

"He did until he *ate* the ball," said Giselle reaching over to poke Mark's beach-ball-sized belly.

Ignoring Giselle, Mark said, "Yup, star forward for the Myron Mavericks."

"Did you *really* eat the ball?" Ruth's youngest asked. "Kinda looks like you did, Uncle Mark."

As everyone laughed, Mark said, "Why yes I did little one...and that's when I decided I'd never be a vegetarian!" Here, Mark winked at Giselle, the lone vegetarian among the McTavish clan.

"Except basketballs have a leather cover," said Martin, also a vegetarian. "Guess that makes you a 'meat and hide-a-tarian'!"

"I always wondered what happened to that old deer leg," Giselle said, looking around the table. "Guess we know now—Mark ate it!"

With that final jab, the meal ended and the clean-up began. On the old farm, Nadine McTavish and her daughters made meals; Malcolm and the boys always did the dishes afterwards. Long-practiced family traditions grip hard and so, without a word, Giselle, Ruth, and Mark's wife, Amy, moved into a sitting area while the men and Mark's oldest boy cleared the table, packed the leftovers, and washed the dishes. The ribbing continued with much of it aimed at Mark's belly, Martin's furniture moving skills, and McTavish's stubbornness. Noah seemed to be enjoying himself, McTavish observed. But then he realized that he was, too. Past family gatherings had taken more hostile turns. McTavish wasn't sure this bright cheeriness was the new normal, but he would take it.

CHAPTER 16

As they drove back to the cottage, McTavish and Noah chatted through the day. "That's your McTavish family at its best," McTavish said.

"And quite a family it is," Noah said. "I really like Aunt Giselle and Martin's cool. I still don't know what to think about Uncle Mark. I used to be afraid of him—you know, he's so big and loud. But now I see he just needs a lot of attention. He's kind of fun to be around…but maybe in small doses." Pausing for a minute, Noah continued. "Aunt Ruth is the one I don't get. She just seems so different from all the rest of you. Don't get me wrong—you're *all* different. But she is all kind of different."

"I suppose she is. I'm not sure Ruth has ever really figured out how she fits into the family."

"What do you mean?"

"Well, she's not loud like Mark or quietly centered like Giselle, and she doesn't see herself as ambitious and successful as Daniel is."

"That sounds about right."

McTavish said, "The odd part is that she's most like our mother; she even looks like Nadine. The difference is that Nadine knew deeply who she was and what she wanted. She was a farmer's wife and that was enough for her. I expect Ruth has never known that kind of assurance. I think it's made her a little timid."

"And that's why she seems to hang so close to Uncle Mark?" Noah asked in that way that Maggie had of posing a question that came out as a conclusion.

"That's what your mom thought."

"She would have been smiling all day today," Noah said wistfully.

"Ayuh."

Noah smiled. "Ayuh."

Unpacked and settled in, each McTavish pursued his individual interests. A national graphic design competition for students had caught Noah's eye a week ago. His interest in graphics ebbed and flowed, but he had a couple of ideas that might garner notice in the contest. He had worked on them during the trip to Rascal Harbor and he looked forward to getting back to them now. Noah had an art space upstairs in his bedroom, but he had started his graphics ideas on his laptop, so he sprawled on the couch and went to work.

McTavish walked to his drawing table with a bit less enthusiasm. He had started a couple of drawings based on his County photographs and was anxious to complete them. Yet the color thing kept bubbling up in his brain. He now realized that he would soon pick up his brushes. But was today the day?

"Jesus, John, just do it. Shit or get off the pot," Maggie said in his mind.

Ah, my sweet, subtle Maggie, McTavish thought. But before McTavish could act on Maggie's advice, Noah called out to him.

"Hey, Dad, that Galen Knight guy is pretty weird."

"Galen Knight? I thought you were working on your design entry."

"I got stuck, then remembered we were talking about Galen Knight so I pulled up a couple of stories. One says he went completely mum after he got arrested, refused to say a single word to anyone. But they got his DNA at the place where this Walter Simpson guy died and they found Simpson's blood on his clothes. So he was convicted even if they could never establish a motive."

"I remember hearing that about the case, that the defendant wouldn't defend himself."

"Huh, this is interesting," Noah said as he continued to surf different stories about the case. "This piece says that the cops couldn't find any relationship between Knight and Simpson. But it says Simpson was a farmer up in Aroostook county."

"Aroostook is big place."

"I guess…ever heard of town called Richmond Plantation?"

"I think it's on the eastern side of The County, somewhere north of Houlton."

"Yup, there it is," Noah said after entering "Richmond Plantation" into MapQuest. "Seems like quite a distance from Myron so unlikely that Knight knew Simpson. And they didn't play basketball against one another cause Simpson was a lot older. I wonder if it was one of the Knight kids that Uncle Mark played against."

"When he wasn't eating the basketball…" McTavish said. And they both laughed.

Chapter 17

Noah slept in the next morning, having come home late from a date with Jimmy Park's sister, Louise. They had met during the fall at a party celebrating the theft charges being dropped against Jimmy, and had kept in contact over the intervening months through email, text, and the occasional phone call.

McTavish left a note for Noah and then drove over to Lydia's Diner. For years, he resisted the molasses donuts Lydia's daughter Trudy made every morning thinking that they could not compete with those dipped in cinnamon sugar. Maggie had pushed him to try a bite, but McTavish was a loyal man—when he found something he liked, he stuck with it. And then one day, the only donuts left were molasses. McTavish's sweet tooth would not abide any healthier foodstuff so he ate a bigger piece of Maggie's donut—and discovered that donut loyalty was over-rated. He still like cinnamon sugar donuts, but the molasses variety had grabbed his heart. He typically resolved the dilemma by having one of each.

It was with that compromise in mind that McTavish drove to Lydia's.

Rascal Harbor in May is still a quiet place. Bus tours bring in tourists to the few hotels that open early, but most shops and restaurants remain closed and the sidewalks offer clear pathways through town.

As he neared Lydia's, McTavish saw a couple of high school kids walking toward him. Each had on a T-shirt with a homemade slogan written on it in magic marker. The girl on left had written "The early bird catches the worm…thats half frozen" on her shirt; the one on the right had lettered "Too wrongs don't make a right, but they do make it interesting."

I guess Jumper has clones, McTavish thought.

Jumper Wilson was a local eccentric. He showed up in town one day and soon became a fixture, though one with a mysterious past. Rascal Harbor, like many Maine towns, had a wide tolerance for human behavior. Jumper was not the oddest cat in town, but he was the only one to parade around with hand-lettered slogans on his T-shirts. McTavish's favorite was "You can't teach an old dog new tricks, but a young dog will piss on your leg."

Apparently some of the local kids were following Jumper's lead. "A for effort," McTavish thought, "A D for spelling."

Taking a seat at Lydia's counter, Julia Nisbett greeted him. Julia, Lydia's only waitress, was a thin woman with long muscles in her arms and legs. She had a lovely smile when she chose to use it; McTavish got one this morning.

"A couple of Trudy's finest, Professor?" Julia asked.

"Please, Julia. One of each today and a cup of coffee to cut the sugar," McTavish said with his own smile. When Julia returned with the donuts and coffee, McTavish said, "You're smiling today. Does that mean that the back tables haven't gotten cranked up yet?"

"You're an observant man, Professor," Julia said with a wink. "Those pissants can wind my smile back a full week." The pissants to whom Julia referred were the cluster of five or six men who gathered each morning at table in the back. A short hallway leading to the kitchen separated the men's table on the left from a similarly clustered table of women on the right.

Neither table was full yet. All or most were retirees from hard jobs, so they trickled in as soon as their tired bones and achy muscles allowed them. The men had worked the sea; the women had worked the product of the sea. Each had also worked a range of landed jobs—

truck driving, carpentry, road work, and maintenance for the men; school cafeteria serving, old age care, waitressing, and family farming for the women. "Retirement" typically meant giving up a regular paycheck. Most of Lydia's regulars still worked at one thing or another to keep busy, to keep their bills paid, and to keep their families afloat.

Rob Pownall, a lean man of considerable height and weather-beaten face, anchored the men's table. Rob had captained a shrimp boat and was looked up to by the others, most of whom worked on or below decks. Rob was talking quietly to Vance Edwards and Bill Candlewith. A still muscular man, Edwards had a low-key countenance and a sly sense of humor. Candlewith was often the subject of Vance's barbs, but they were either too sharp or Bill's brain was too dim for him to always notice. A wiry man, but barely five feet tall, Candlewith limped due to catching a fishing gaff in the meat of his left leg.

Ray Manley, Candlewith's equal in the brain department, and Slow Johnston, a side-step below those two, had yet to arrive. A sixth man, Caleb Rimes, had yet to retire so only joined the boys when he was out of work. Rimes was a lout and so made more table sessions than he missed because his mouth kept him regularly unemployed.

The ladies' table also had a couple of empty chairs. Like Rob Pownall, Geraldine Smythe tended to moor the women's area. Wearing her trademark scarf, Geraldine was a tall, solid woman of clear intelligence. She sipped her coffee and half-listened as Maude Anderson and June Pickering huddled over a day-old piece of gossip. Matched exactly in height, Maude and June varied exactly in the weight their five-two frames carried. Maude, the plumper of the two, had never been able to keep weight off; June could never keep it on. Sitting at the other end of the table from Geraldine, but matching her weak interest in their gossiping friends was Karen Tompkins. Also tall, but athletically built, Karen was the youngest of the group and the most recently retired as shift supervisor at the seafood plant.

Missing was Minerva Williams, a rangy, hard-scrabble woman of medium height. McTavish knew that the seated women's voices would never rise high enough for him to hear and understand. Once Minerva arrived, however, everyone in the diner would know.

Ten seconds into that thought, the front door opened and typhoon Minerva swept through. "Keep your pants zipped, boys," Minerva said as she walked by the men's table. "I ain't got time to take you all on this morning!" She pinched Bill Candlewith's ear, winked at Vance Edwards, and sat down at the ladies' table. "You all got your bras on girls?" she asked. "I don't wanna see your boobs fallin' into your coffee cups again! Plus it's tit-nipply out there and you don't wanna get a froze-up udder!"

"Oh Minerva," June and Maude said at the same time.

"And here we go," Julia said to McTavish with a slipping smile.

Since the theft of the Winslow Homer painting and its subsequent recovery, townsfolk had lacked a theme for their conversations. They made do with the Red Sox, lobster prices, presidential politics, and who was fucking whom, but nothing quite grabbed their sustained attention like the art crime had.

Minerva's quips about the ladies' breasts sagging into their coffee cups recalled another perennial topic—Robertay Harding's large chest. As the chair of the Rascal Harbor Art Colony board, Robertay styled herself as *the* maven of the local art crowd. She would have been an imposing woman anyway—her untamed hair, her nearly six-foot frame, and her imperious manner—all defined a woman of considerable substance. But it was her large and often free-ranging breasts that give rise to conversation at the ladies' table and to conversation and more at the men's. Bill Candlewith had once remarked that each of Robertay's boobs deserved its own zip code.

But Robertay was nowhere in sight and no other topic elevated either back table's ire so once Minerva settled down the diner talk returned to buzz level.

KNIGHTS DISARMED

Caleb Rimes—jackass, jerk, homophobe—engendered many descriptions. His behavior aptly mirrored those descriptions and, in many residents' views, toed awfully close to the line of too much. Still, Mainers' toleration for one another generally runs wide and, although he'd been booted from Lydia's on a number of occasions, Caleb had yet to be banned.

That distinction did not mean that Lydia's patrons ignored Rimes's entrance that morning. As the short-waisted, barrel-chested man sauntered through the restaurant, McTavish thought he saw some diner's shoulders sag and heads shake. The man sitting next to him muttered to his friend, "Ah, that fuckhead's here again." Julia's faded smile turned even further inward.

Caleb walked to the men's table and sat without comment. Minerva, ever alert, noted Rimes's arrival with a curt, "There goes the other table's IQ."

Bill Candlewith asked, "Where you been, Caleb? Ain't seen much of you."

"I've only seen you for three minutes and that's enough for me," Vance Edwards said.

"Been workin' ta keep you assholes in Social Security checks," Caleb grumbled.

"And I thank you kindly, 'cept you ever actually work a job where they don't pay you under the table?" asked Ray Manley.

"Often enough," Caleb said with a grin.

The tablemates laughed and circled back to their discussion about whether the town manager would hold onto her job after the next selectmen's meeting.

McTavish had eaten his cinnamon sugar donut and was finishing the molasses one. He was no stick-in-the-mud, so he liked to alternate the sequence in which he ate his treats. Savoring the tang of that last bite, he heard a commotion at the men's table. Jimmy Park's and Bradley Little's names arose and then the language of "queers," "faggots," and "homos" coming from Caleb Rimes.

"Them fags is takin' over," Rimes said, standing up and waving his arms. "They oughta all be locked up! They never shoulda let that fuckin' Park kid out of jail."

Other men at the table, notably Rob Pownall and Vance Edwards stood and tried to calm Rimes down, but his voice and remonstrations grew only louder. "I don't know why you're trying ta protect him," Rimes shouted at Pownall in particular. "You a faggot, too?"

At this point, Trudy and Julia converged on the back table and demanded quiet. Not all voices obeyed, but enough did so that Trudy could order Rimes out of the restaurant.

"You know I do not put up with that horseshit, Caleb Rimes," Trudy said as she stood inches away from him. "Get your ass out of my diner and take your mouth with it! And don't plan to come back until I tell you it's okay. You got that?"

Bluster gone in the face of this confrontation, Rimes slammed his chair on the floor and stomped toward the front of the restaurant. Seeing McTavish watching him, Rimes veered over to him, leaned in, and said, "And don't think I don't know you to be a faggot, too, Mr. Professor. You and them boys…"

Too stunned to say move or say anything, McTavish couldn't stop staring at Rimes. The latter took note and growled, "You keep eyeballin' me like that and I'll kick your—"

Before Rimes could finish his threat, he felt a powerful punch to his groin. Trudy had grabbed a broom, walked up behind him, and swung the broom end upward as hard as she could. Though the bristles cushioned the impact, Rimes's eyes bugged and he grabbed his privates, a low moan escaping his lips. He started sagging to the floor, but Trudy whacked him in the ass and kept doing so as he hobbled to the door.

"Sweepin' out the trash, are ya, Trudy?" Minerva cackled from the back of the diner. "Dumb ass'll be a falsetto for a week!"

CHAPTER 18

Two days later, Detective Dick Chambers was on his way to the state penitentiary in Warren. A tall, fit middle-aged man, Chambers had taken over the detective duties in Rascal Harbor three years ago. Coming from southern Florida after taking a bullet in a botched drug raid, Chambers brought north a small pension and a desire to live a calmer life. He was not ready to give up police work, but he was ready to do it on a smaller scale.

A year into his tenure, however, he found himself leading a murder investigation. Chambers had worked out of a narcotics unit in Florida, but many times his cases involved murders so the reality did not unnerve him. Still this was the coast of Maine and only a handful of Maine's twenty or so murders a year happened there.

Typically the Maine State Police take charge of murder investigations. And they did so in the case of Walter Simpson, but only after Detective Chambers had arrested and jailed the culprit, Galen Knight. It was Galen Knight, current resident of Warren, who Chambers drove to see.

The Simpson case qualified as one of the oddest in memory. Walter Simpson, seventy-five years of age, had grown up on a farm in Richmond Plantation, a small town buried in eastern Aroostook county. The oldest son, he had taken over the farm on his father's passing and continued growing potatoes and milking a few cattle. Simpson was known to have a temper and to spend more than he should on drink. He had had a few scrapes with the law and had even spent a night in jail, but he paid his bills and his taxes. He grumbled more about the latter than the former.

After farming into his seventieth year, Simpson put his property up for sale. Farmed out, wife dead, and only daughter long escaped to the coast, he walked away from Richmond Plantation with a decent-sized check and walked back into his daughter Dorothy's life to pass the rest of his days.

Simpson was hobbled by the usual ailments of a demanding life—arthritis, diabetes, and a heart flutter. Still, he got himself out of bed each day, walked a mile up and down the road outside the house, and helped out with the household chores. Dorothy, or Dottie as Simpson called her, was a middle-aged, single mother of two high school-aged children. Dottie was largely house-bound having been disabled in a work-related incident three years earlier. Her disability checks, her father's Social Security checks, and the proceeds from the sale of the farm allowed the family to meet their needs and a number of their wants.

Why this retired farmer would end up murdered and why Galen Knight would be the suspected and then convicted killer still puzzled Chambers. He hoped that this trip, unlike the five before it, might bring some insights.

The drive to Warren took Chambers by the Italian restaurant to which he had taken Toni Ludlow for dinner during the Homer case. Ludlow, an abstract painter, had been tangentially involved with the crime and he had not wanted their budding relationship to be judged improper by the town wags so their first date had been way out of town. Someone from Rascal Harbor had seen them anyway, and the news leaked within twenty-four hours of their return. In the end, it hadn't mattered and Chambers and Ludlow now enjoyed one another's company in the open.

Although she didn't discourage these trips to Warren, Toni Ludlow did question what Chambers got out of them. Galen Knight had said not a word to anyone upon his capture, including to his lawyer, Julian Pratt. Knight maintained his silence through the trial, even refusing to say his plea aloud. With all the guilty signs pointing at his client and with that client refusing to give him anything with which to work, Julian's defense strategy focused on getting his client the least amount of jail time possible.

In Maine, murder is in its own felony class and the sentencing guidelines call for twenty-five years to life. Maine has no death penalty so Pratt did not have to fight that possibility. Knight's continued silence, however, clearly annoyed the judge and Pratt was not surprised at the life sentence he passed down.

"Mr. Knight, your extreme callousness in the commission of this crime combined with your reckless silence convince me that you should be shown no mercy by this court," the judge announced. After reading the sentence, the judge again asked Knight if he had anything to say. When Knight stared at him mutely, the judge cracked his gavel and called for Knight to be taken away.

Chambers accepted the offered congratulations and praise on putting away the only local murderer most Rascal Harbor residents could recall. Still, Knight's utter silence bothered him. Chambers had little doubt that Knight was guilty—no other suspects had surfaced and the blood evidence was overwhelming. The lack of motive or even any evidence that the two men knew each other pecked at him; Knight's damnable silence unnerved him.

So bothered was he, that Chambers sought out Julian Pratt a month after the trial. He knew the lawyer's preference for single-malt scotches so one evening he knocked on Pratt's door unannounced with bottle in hand and with the intent to find out what was behind Galen Knight's quietude. He needn't have bothered. Though the two men spent a couple of hours appreciating the scotch, Chambers left knowing only that Knight had not favored his lawyer with a single word.

"I have never seen anything like it, Detective," Pratt said. "And no one else I've talked with has either. A completely mum client. The fact is that lawyers usually cannot get them to be quiet long enough to advise them properly. This fellow, however...I believe myself to be a decent judge of human beings. Sitting in the office with the weight of the crime hanging low, clients tend to do and say things that offer insights to the careful observer. With Galen Knight, there was nothing. In fact, he would not even discuss the weather. One of the oddest professional encounters in which I have ever been involved."

After pausing to sip more scotch, Pratt continued. "Hmmm. I would like to amend that last statement; Knight's silence actually was not the oddest thing. Instead, what struck me was the strongest, strangest feeling I had that he was innocent."

Holding his hand up, Pratt said, "I know, I know—the evidence was overwhelming. In fact, I have come to the conclusion that had I been on the jury, I too would have voted to convict. And yet..." Pratt's voice trailed off. He did not take another drink, but he did sit forward in his chair. "Here's the thing, Richard. I understand that you spent a lot of time with Knight as did I. But I suspect I have spent much more time than you have with the innocent. I can be hoodwinked; in fact, I have been. In this instance, however, I believe I am right. Galen Knight is innocent."

This last line—"Galen Knight is innocent"—prompted Detective Chambers's first visit to Warren. He doubted Julian Pratt's conclusion, but he took the assertion seriously. Equally pressing, however, was Chambers's determination to learn Knight's story.

He didn't, but he did heard Galen Knight talk. Unsure Knight would even see him, Chambers was pleasantly surprised that he did.

Led through the various check-points to the "visit room," Chambers rehearsed his opening line—"Your lawyer believes you are innocent"—in hopes of shocking Knight into talking. Giving this strategy only a fifty-fifty chance, however, Chambers prepped himself to find a mute prisoner. To his surprise, Knight greeted him with a smile and the words, "Hello, Detective Chambers. Thank you for coming to visit me."

Unprepared for this introduction, Chambers simply nodded and sat down across from Knight. Dressed in the standard prison uniform of light blue cotton shirt and dark blue denim pants, Knight looked like far more comfortable than Chambers felt.

"How are you," Chambers managed to say.

"I am doing as well as might be expected," Knight replied amicably.

Still unnerved by Knight's greeting, Chambers hesitated his way through another five minutes of small talk with the genial prisoner.

Finally, Knight asked, "Why are you here, Detective?"

"Truth be told, you're a mystery to me," Chambers said. "I've never seen an accused man so determined to put his fate so completely in the hands of the system. I've never seen a man go so completely mute. You've shown me that you are capable of speech and yet you uttered not a word in your defense in court or, apparently, even to your attorney."

"How is Mr. Pratt?"

"As perplexed as I am," Chambers said candidly. "Moreover, he believes that you're innocent. Of course, you offered him no chance to make that case for you. Nevertheless, he believes it's so."

"That is generous of him. I expect it was a difficult trial for him."

"Care to shed any light now?" Chambers asked hopefully.

Knight paused, looked Chambers directly in the eye, and said, "No, Detective, I don't believe that I do."

Chambers spent the rest of his visiting time allotment encouraging Knight to change his mind. Knight refused. He remained cordial, but he would say nothing about the victim, the murder, or the trial.

The next two visits went much the same way—after an exchange of pleasantries, Chambers would push and prod Knight to offer up anything related to the case. Invariably, Knight smiled, shook his head, and remained mute.

On the fourth visit, Chambers tried a different tact. He abandoned his direct approach and simply engaged Knight in conversation about Rascal Harbor affairs and personalities. Though a small town, Chambers found much to report and realized that he enjoyed Knight's company. Knight was interested in and insightful about the people and events Chambers described. But he shut down immediately and completely if Chambers veered toward any facet of Knight's life. Chambers took this deflection well, neither pushing nor getting upset. When it happened, however, Chambers remarked, "It's almost like you want me to think of you as a full-grown child, one whose past consists only of the time since your conviction." Chambers offered this observation without rancor; it was essentially a statement of fact. Knight responded with a slight smile and a nod.

Chambers had no expectation that he would break into Knight's silent past on this fifth trip to the prison. He was right to do so for it followed the same script. He made no progress in understanding this convicted killer, but he walked out of the facility with an odd smile on his face.

The smile disappeared, however, when he saw Caleb Rimes walking through the visitor's parking lot. Chambers had had relatively little direct interaction with Rimes. He knew the man to be a miscreant, but most of Rimes's drunk and disorderly arrests were handled by the Rascal Harbor constables. Consequently Chambers's surprise at seeing Rimes was doubled when the latter looked hard at the detective and swore.

"The fuck you doin' here, Chambers?" Rimes snarled.

Recovering, Chambers said, "I suppose the same question applies to you."

"None a your fuckin' business, asshole," Rimes said and spat as he walked by.

Maybe not, Chambers thought. But maybe it is now.

CHAPTER 19

Caleb Rimes almost didn't make it into the visit room. His agitation at seeing Chambers carried with him and the prison guards sensed a man a little too close to the edge. Fortunately, the head guard recognized Rimes and took over the process of getting him signed in. He moved Rimes through the checkpoints, but did so slowly, giving himself time to assess Rimes's capacity for getting himself under control. Reaching the final gate, Rimes was calm enough that the guard allowed him into the visit room.

Galen Knight had not left the room when Rimes entered and sat down across from him. "What's the trouble, Caleb?" he asked.

The anger that raged through Rimes on seeing Detective Chambers arose again. "I saw that fuckin' detective in the parking lot. Why do you keep seein' him?"

"He is the one who visits me," Knight said reasonably. "I guess I could ask the guards to block him, but I enjoy his company. He knows that we're not going to talk about my past and he seems okay with that."

"He's a fuckin' cop, Galen," Rimes said, his voice rising.

"Easy, Caleb. You don't want to get kicked out of here again." Pausing, Knight looked around the room, then said, "I know he's a cop and a damn sharp one, too. I have to keep my guard up all the time."

"So why do you keep seein' him? Why don't you just tell him to fuck off?"

"Because if I'm going to keep your ass out of here, then I need to know what he knows. He thinks he's here to get information about me and the crime. I'm doing the same thing with him."

The two men talked about their sister Virginia, about Rimes's latest series of under-the-table jobs, and about the dust-up at Lydia's.

"Oh, what I'd give for one of those molasses donuts," Knight said.

"Wish I could bring you one. Looking around at the guards, Rimes continued, "Course those fuckers wouldn't let me. Plus, I mighta got bounced out of Lydia's for a while."

"Your temper, Caleb…" Knight started to say.

"I know, I know. Jesus, I know."

"I know you do, Caleb. Just don't let it take you down."

Rimes nodded as he saw the guard coming over to announce that his visiting time was up. He stood, nodded once more to Knight, then turned and walked out with the guard by his side.

Your temper, brother, your terrible temper, Knight thought.

Chapter 20

Heading back to his cell, Galen Knight wondered if he would ever again taste a molasses donut from Lydia's or any other diner. With the intention of remaining mum about the case, he didn't expect to ever gain parole. Still, he found it hard not to think about the life and the simple pleasures he had enjoyed not so long ago.

Galen Knight was a medium-sized man—neither tall nor short, neither thin nor fat. His benign countenance and gentle eyes had inspired the press to dub him the Kind-Faced Killer. This placid exterior masked a powerful man made strong first by a physical career in the U.S. Navy and then by a series of laboring jobs. Knight carried himself through life and now through the Maine State Prison with a powerful grace and dignity. He cowed no one, but no one pushed him either.

Prison life offered many opportunities to break men down. Physical intimidation and abuse, isolation and confinement were but some of the means by which prisoners waned. Hardest for many was the loss of family connection. Being surrounded, tightly surrounded, by strangers only exacerbated the estrangement from wives, children, and parents.

Galen Knight's physicality guaranteed his physical safety. His choice to live a largely solitary life guaranteed his emotional health. Lovers, acquaintances, and drinking companions—yes; wives, children, and close friends—no. Knight was likeable, he could carry his end of a conversation, he felt emotions. He would help a neighbor, stop a fight, and vote when he lived long enough in a place to register. But he lived a contained, walled-in life, one that could enjoy, but did not need, company.

Knight's inner life did not include much in the way of self-doubt, but neither did it include self-deception. He knew his path was inner-driven and he knew that he could choose otherwise. Content in his interactions both within and without, he thought of himself a fully functioning human being. No sociopath was he. The fact that he had thought through and discarded this possibility gave Knight a measure of calm. "I'm just a quiet guy, making do," was his standard line when others got close enough to inquire about his demeanor.

Knight learned none of these things through self-help TV shows, seminars, or blogs. He was a reader of books—a school-taught, but self-educated man. His reading habits were shaped less by category than by availability. Whatever he found—history, fiction, philosophy, religion—he read. He approached books not as the pedant who reads to confirm his preexisting views or as the dreamer who reads in hopes of identifying a direction to follow. Instead, Knight read to build his options for thought and action. He did not have to agree with the author's point of view to find value in it. He had only to understand it deeply and then to hold on to it should it prove useful to him in the future.

In this sense, Galen Knight followed the lead of the Stoics to whom he was introduced through Tom Wolfe's opus *A Man in Full*. Knight found a copy in a San Francisco bookstore before he shipped out on a three-month naval cruise. He knew nothing of the book or the author, but the title interested him and he expected the seven hundred and forty-two pages would last through most if not all of the trip. The long work hours were more than matched by the hours off and Knight had made a good start on the book within the first week. When the character Conrad Hensley appeared and described the idea of Stoicism through the words of the Roman philosopher Epieteus, Knight found his intellectual home. He would explore other *isms* both philosophical and political—existentialism, Marxism, pragmatism, socialism—and conclude that all had their points of utility. In Stoicism, however, Knight found a set of ideas that continually held up no matter how hard he pushed them. Moreover, he just liked the idea expressed through Wolfe's character that Stoics are "Serene and confident in the face of anything you can throw at them."

CHAPTER 21

Galen Knight had practiced that serene and confident attitude most of his life. And he had had lots of practice because much had been thrown his way.

The throwing began in his childhood. Knight's father, Peter, was a better bastard than he was a farmer. Even when potato prices were high and crop yields plentiful, Peter Knight barely managed to keep his wife Cynthia and their children Galen, Virginia, Susan, and Caleb fed. A solid roof proved even harder. And when Cynthia's body, always sickly, finally gave out, Knight faced a raft of challenges. He pushed through them for six months, then he folded.

Peter Knight knew he'd have to call his spinster sister, Mavis, at some point. Mavis was always the smart and sensible kid; he was the always the social one. Peter expected that Mavis would help him sort through this mess but, before she did, she'd make him feel like a dolt. So once he realized the extent of his troubles, his first call was to Walter Simpson.

"You're fucked now, buddy," Walter Simpson said. "Totally, royally, completely fucked."

Peter Knight looked up from his nursed beer and nodded. "Fucked I am, friend. Sideways, backwards, and inside out."

Sitting at the bar in The Harding a month after Cynthia Knight's death, Simpson's condolences were quickly dispensed with. The two men were moving beyond a toot and heading for a tilt. Simpson, always the meaner of the two especially as the night wore on, tried not to jab his friend, but failed.

"You're fucked, and I can't see how you're gonna get unfucked. You got all those fuckin' kids and no woman to tend to 'em, not that she was all that much anyway."

Too drunk and too sour to take offense, Knight, head down, just nodded.

"I mean she couldna been much of a help, her bein' sick all the time. Fuckin' shame. And she couldna been much of a fuck either."

"You ain't wrong there, Walter," Knight said, finally rousing himself enough to speak. "I'm fucked, but I ain't *been* fucked for some time."

"Ain't right, friend, that ain't right. A man has needs and if them needs don't get satisfied, well…" Simpson's voice trailed off. After a pause, he continued, "I know you ain't stepped out that much on Cynthia, but it was good when you did, right?"

When Knight didn't respond, Simpson resumed, "Now take me. I got a steady pump, have for years. In fact, sometimes I've had two at once. Young 'uns, too. None of that old stuff for me."

"Yeah, you're a real fuckhound, Walter," Knight said, provoking his own nasty streak. "You got the world by the fuckin' balls, dontcha? And now you're gonna rub it right up my ass. Is that what you're tryin' to do, Walter?"

"Calm the fuck down," Simpson said, his ire rising. "Your shit luck streak don't mean you got to piss all over me."

The two men glared each other down and the bartender stepped toward the baseball bat he kept under the bar.

"Both of you better calm the fuck down if you wanna keep drinking in this shithole," he said.

"You ain't wrong about that, Barney," said Simpson, smiling now. "This is one happy fuck of a shithole."

"A fuckity fuck of shithole," Knight added.

"Yeah, but it's the fuckin' shittiest shithole you two can drink at," Barney concluded and all three laughed at its truth.

Chapter 22

Peter Knight and Walter Simpson first met on a basketball floor. Razor-thin, raw-boned boys of modest height, the two could have been half-brothers.

Both boys played the off-guard position for their respective high school teams. And both played dirty. Although they guarded each other, neither was the star player, so each would target the opposing team's best shooter and take every opportunity to throw an elbow to the belly, tromp down on an instep, or thrust a finger to the eye.

So sly were these two that they ended up in silent competition and admiration, each nodding briefly when their teammates took a hit. Most of their efforts were intended to slow down and intimidate the star players, most of whom accepted the abuse as part of the hardscrabble manner of northern Maine basketball.

On one occasion, however, Knight tripped an opponent as he broke for a lay-up and the boy had ended up with a broken ulna. Simpson rushed to his teammate's aid, but as the boy was helped to the locker room, he caught Knight's eye, raised his eyebrows, and nodded. These gestures sent two signals to Knight. One was "nice move"; the other was "my turn."

Waiting until the next time they played gave Simpson time to work through a number of options. Just before half-time, he saw his spot. As Myron's star forward started his deadly jump shoot, Simpson stepped hard on his lead foot. The boy's scream resounded as his knee hyper-extended and he crashed to the floor. As Knight passed Simpson on the way to his downed teammate, the latter simply whispered, "Even Steven."

Through their four years of play, the scoreboard totals mattered less than Knight's and Simpson's individual tallies. That neither boy was ever marked for their crimes testified to the wiliness of their actions and the expectations that Maine basketball differed only slightly from rugby.

Expecting that he would never again see his opponent and co-conspirator, Knight was stunned one night to see Simpson sitting at the bar in The Harding, the seediest of the several bars in Houlton.

The Aroostook county seat, Houlton anchors the far southeastern corner of the oddly shaped county. Then the home of Ricker College, a vibrant downtown, and tree-shaded streets of Victorian homes, Houlton had restaurants and bars on a sliding scale from lovely to The Harding. Named vaguely for the twenty-ninth President, the Harding had never reached any higher on the quality scale than its namesake. It met all the criteria of a dive—a bar with stools, a couple of cheap beer taps, potato chips in bags, and guys for whom all of this was as good as it was going to get.

Peter Knight and Walter Simpson were still relatively young men when they met again. Both had put on a few pounds, grew potatoes, raised an animal or two, and bred children. Neither would confess to unhappiness, but their talk was more of the past than the present and future. Their glory days now seemed plowed under thin soil, growing debts, unsatisfying marriages, and thin prospects. Though neither man had dreamed much beyond the life he lead, sharp disappointment trumped the possibilities for general contentment.

So they supposed scenarios of bigger farms, sexier wives, more cash, and fewer children. They met once a month or so for a toot, each one arguing that the evening out was a well-earned balm.

"Think how keyed up we'd be if we didn't get out on a toot once in a while," Knight would say.

"Christ, you ain't wrong about that," Simpson would say. "Nobody could stand us if we didn't let a little air outta the tires."

The beer was cheap and risk free as neither man's spouse dared to complain after each had delivered the first couple of smacks to the head.

Though they'd started off relatively even on the economic scale, Peter Knight's prospects continually edged downward while Walter Simpson's held steady. There was big money to be made in potatoes, but it was the big farmers—men with a hundred acres and more—who made it. And since the growing conditions and prices of the product roller-coastered yearly, it was the big boys who could best manage through a poor yield or a poor price point. Both men cursed their better-off neighbors, but Knight cursed louder and longer.

CHAPTER 23

Back home after confessing his financial troubles to Walter Simpson, Peter Knight boozily assessed his situation. He knew he was going to lose the farm one way or another and the crush of that realization along with the crush of four kids and a dead wife pushed him down further than he could have imagined.

A week and another stack of delivered bills later, Knight again arranged to meet Walter Simpson at the Harding.

"I been thinking," he said as soon as the two found stools at the bar. "I know you ain't got the money nor the need for my acreage so far from your own, but I could let you have my harvester, tractor, bailer, and some other stuff at a good price."

"What the fuck are you talkin' about, Peter? I got all that shit and mine's in a whole lot better shape than yours. Why you wanna sell your equipment? You gettin' out?"

"No choice. Can't even see the top of the bill pile now and they're predictin' piss poor prices again. I can't make it, Walter. I give it my best shot, but I'm done. Gotta get what I can and get out."

"Christ, Pete, I didn't know you was that bad off. If you're serious, I might be able to pick up a few things off you, but I mostly got what I need. And I sure as fuck don't need your acres fifty miles from my own."

"I know, I know," Knight said voice rising. "I already said that I wasn't gonna try and sell you my farm. Christ, I just wanted to know if you care to buy my equipment. I was gonna give you a good deal, but if you don't need nor want it, then fuck you."

Angered, but trying to keep his own temper down lest Barney give them the bat and then the boot, Simpson said, "For fuck's sake, back off. I said I'd buy some of that shit pile you got. Okay? Jesus!"

"Never mind," Knight said testily. "I'll just put the whole fuckin' thing up for auction and then you can pick my bones just like everyone else."

Sensing that this line of thought would not rebound, Simpson deflected to a new topic. "What about your kids? Whatcha gonna do with them when you sell out?"

"Hell, I don't know. I been so focused on the farm, I ain't really thought it through about the kids."

"Well, you don't wanna let the state take 'em," Simpson said emphatically. "They'll be fucked up forever if you do." Both men nodded at the sagacity of this observation.

"I know. "I'm fucked either way. It's gonna take me some time to get on my feet again and I ain't gonna go on that fuckin' welfare so what the fuck am I gonna do with four mouths? I mean I can't let 'em go to the state, but I ain't gonna be able to feed 'em neither."

"Well, you got a sister dontcha? Can't she take 'em till you get a new start?"

"Probably not. She's just moved down on the coast. She got a job, but she's got a tiny little house. No way she could take on four kids."

"Well, what if she was to take just a couple?" Simpson asked reasonably.

"What? You mean split 'em up? No fuckin' way! Bad enough I'd have to leave 'em off somewhere. Split 'em up? No fuckin' way!"

Still opting for reasonableness in voice and idea, Simpson said, "No, right, I get it. You wouldn't wanna split 'em up permanent anyway. But face the facts, Pete, you got no options." Letting that point sink in, Simpson continued, "Nobody said it had to be a permanent thing, splittin' 'em up. Be just a temporary measure till you get righted."

Looking at his friend full on now, Knight said, "Okay…but Mavis still can't take all four of 'em. She just can't. So what the fuck am I spose to do with the other two?"

Acting as if it just dawned on him, Simpson said, "Well, hell, Peter, if you was really stuck, then the missus and I could take a couple. But just temporary, right? It wouldn't be no permanent solution. You'd collect 'em back once you got set up, right?"

"You'd do that? You'd take a couple of my kids…y'know…on like a temporary basis?"

"I would, friend. I would. Just till you get back on them big feet of yours."

Knight's eyes moistened. He clamped a hand on Simpson's shoulder, looked him directly in the eye. "That's true blue, Walter. That's as true blue as it gets."

Drinking harder now, Peter Knight slurred, "I spose I gotta give Mavis first choice…as she's my sister and all. Hate to think I'd be givin' you sloppy seconds, Walter, but it's what I gotta do."

"Hell, I know that, Pete, family first, right?" Simpson replied convivially.

"You said it, friend, but…if you was to have your druthers, you know, if you could pick first, which ones would you take? The boys I'm guessin', but is that right?"

"Hard choice that one," Simpson said, seeming to mull the decision. "Course, I'd take any of 'em. I mean they're your kids and so I'd do right by which ever ones come my way. But…if I had a choice, guess I'd take the two youngest."

"Really?" Knight asked, surprised at this choice.

"Yup, I would," Simpson replied. Appearing to reflect on this preference, he continued. "I'm thinking about Mavis and her situation. I mean, you said she's got a small place so wouldn't seem right to saddle her up with a couple small kids. I've got the farm and lots of chores that even the little boy, what's his name…Charley?…and his sister can do. I got stuff they both can do, y'know, after their school work.

And you know a farm's a far better place to raise kids than some fancy ass coastal town." After pausing again, Simpson said, "They's probably some other reasons, too, but you get my point. If Mavis don't want 'em, I'd be happy to take the young ones."

"Well, it's a good argument, to be sure, Walter. Course I'll do whatever I can to see it come your way. But I gotta let Mavis have the say. Just no way around it...." His voice trailed off as his tongue suddenly felt thick and foreign in his mouth. After a couple of minutes, he said, "Ah fuck...if you're sure about this...I mean if you're sure you can do this for me, then let's have a shot to seal the deal."

"Done," Simpson said. Seeing Knight reach for his wallet, Simpson put up his hand and said, "No, let me do it, Pete. After all, what are friends for?"

CHAPTER 24

Peter Knight's spinster sister, Mavis, knew him to be a shit and so could generate no surprise when he phoned one night and announced his "grand plan." His mounting debts, he argued, could only be resolved by selling the farm. Whatever liquidity the family once held had gone toward the immediate bills incurred around Cynthia's last illness. Her funeral bill now sat on top of the remaining pile. Since bank loan debts also sat in the pile, Knight said he could not see relief coming from that direction. Selling the farm, he explained, was the only way clear. Mavis nodded through Peter's recounting, though she suspected that his rationale and plan aimed more directly at unburdening all of his obligations than at being financially responsible.

Unburdening responsibility became the unspoken theme as Peter revealed the next part of his plan. He hated to acknowledge it, he said, but his familial debt was an even longer-term problem. With no money and few prospects, Peter "admitted" that he had no reasonable hope of keeping the family together. Everybody knew he loved his wife and his kids, he proclaimed loudly if a little too earnestly. Mavis had had to bite her tongue. She knew Peter to be a walking drunk and that a big reason for his financial woes and, she suspected, Cynthia's health issues owed to his drinking and then pissing away too much of the money that came his way.

Peter had a gift for gab. That capacity combined with his willing-ness to stand his buddies to a round made him good bar company, but a piss-poor farmer, husband, and father. As a result, Mavis thought she knew where this wind-up was going. When Peter asked Mavis to take two of his children, she could not even feign surprise.

"You sure you want to do this, Peter? Be awful tough on the kids."

"Hell, Mavis, it ain't like it's gonna be a permanent thing. It ain't like I'm gonna be gone from their lives. And, y'know, when I'm back on my feet, then I'll bring 'em all back together with me."

Despite Peter's continued earnestness, Mavis doubted both of these last propositions. She thought, but did not say, that once Peter had shed his children, he would disappear completely.

"I'll have to think about it," Mavis said. She had moved to Rascal Harbor the previous year chasing a job as a nurse at the local hospital. She had a house that was plenty big—for her. Introducing two new bodies would make things tight in the house and in the pocketbook. These were her nieces and nephews, however, and she felt the family tug.

"Thing is, you best think quick as I promised whoever you don't take to a guy I know up in Richmond Plantation. He farms fifty acres and he needs the help. I'm giving you first choice."

The phone call ended on that dispiriting note. Mavis thought about it for an hour, but she'd needed no more than five minutes. Mavis would have taken all four Knight kids if she could have so the only real choice was which two. Mavis reasoned that the two oldest—Galen and Virginia—might need the most care and comfort. Then she reasoned her way into taking the two youngest for the same reason. She called her brother back and, flipping a coin in her head, opted for Galen and Virginia.

Peter Knight delivered his two oldest children and their belongings to Mavis's care a week later. Galen, sixteen, and Virginia, fourteen, walked into the house with brave faces, but eyes adrift. Their father's quick promises and even quicker departure cut hard, but Mavis's embrace steadied them that first night and for the weeks to come.

Harder than the move was the tear away from their younger siblings, Susan, twelve, and Caleb, eight. A sickly mother and an ass for a father had bonded the children. They could spit and spat with one another, but they stood together against the rest of the world. Galen and Virginia mourned the loss of their sister and brother. And in a world when social media consisted of posted letters and expensive long distance phone calls, the physical rift cemented an emotional one. Over the months to come, Virginia tried to keep a line open, but the vague, discouraged, and sporadic letters she got in return hurt more than helped.

Galen and Virginia quickly integrated into Mavis's home. The physical and maturity problems of their parents did not take root in their oldest children. Galen and Virginia attended school and chores and family matters with an inherent reserve, but they offered Mavis no attendant causes for concern. Instead, Galen and Virginia accepted what Mavis offered and did their best to appreciate it. Neither they nor their aunt were much for emotional or physical displays of affection. Yet Galen and Virginia responded well to the quiet safety, strength, and security that fortified Mavis's home.

CHAPTER 25

Caleb and Susan Knight fared less well. Though neither was a big talker, they soon learned that the fewer words spoken the better. Words in the Simpson home too often preceded blows.

Peter Knight had smiled when his sister had taken his two oldest kids. He felt like he had to give Mavis first choice being family and all. That she had chosen Galen and Virginia meant that he could also satisfy the interests of Walter Simpson who had expressed a preference for the youngest Knight siblings. Peter thought his friend to be nuts; Galen and Virginia could offer far more work on Simpson's farm than two pre-teens. But once Mavis opted for the older children, then Knight could truck the younger ones up to Simpson's farm in Richmond Plantation. Everyone gets what they want! he thought to himself.

With Galen and Virginia in Rascal Harbor, Peter Knight drove his two youngest children to the Simpson farm in Richmond Plantation. The young children hated to think about being separated from their siblings and their father, but he promised an idyllic life with the Simpson family. They tried to believe him.

What Susan and Caleb saw as they pulled into the dooryard did look marginally better than their place did. The house was painted a consistent if dingy white, the fences and out-buildings stood relatively straight, and the equipment was all under cover. That none of these things were true at the Knight farm gave Susan and Caleb some hope. That hope rose a bit when the Simpson family—Walter, wife Marjorie, and daughter Dorothy—greeted them in the dooryard. Walter grinned broadly; Marjorie and Dorothy, standing slightly apart from Walter, offered thinner smiles.

Susan and Caleb approached shyly, carrying the few belongings their father allowed them to bring and trying to smile.

"Dottie, help them kids with their stuff," Walter said, a bit harshly Susan and Caleb thought. Turning to their father, Simpson said, "Come on in, Pete, let's have a beer."

Taking one bag each from the Knight children, Dottie led them into the house and upstairs to the bedroom they would share. The room was small and dark, but it was clean and had two twin beds with a nightstand between them and a dresser in one corner. The single window had two cracked panes and looked out onto the barn but three feet away.

"A window with a wall," Dottie said, trying to smile.

Dottie, thirteen, was a tall, homely girl with sad eyes. Her smile might have animated her face when expressed fully, but then her two crooked teeth showed and the Knight children could sense her embarrassment.

"I'm sorry about your mom," Dottie said. "I hope you can be happy here."

Neither Knight child had spoken since their arrival. Neither did now, but they both nodded their thanks to Dottie and hoped her hope would come true.

Chapter 26

The day after their arrival, Walter Simpson registered Susan and Caleb in school. He told the principal, Mrs. Harris, that they were his sister's children and they would be staying at his place for a few months as her divorce became final. Simpson had tried to intimidate Mrs. Harris while Dottie was in elementary school and had sometimes succeeded. He didn't need to this time, however, as Mrs. Harris could read forlorn across each child's face and so she enrolled them without comment.

On the drive to school, Simpson had told the children to be quiet while he got them registered. If asked, they were to say they were from New Hampshire. He told Mrs. Harris that he'd requested their school records be forwarded and that he'd bring them in once they arrived.

The paperwork complete, Mrs. Harris led the children to their respective classrooms and what she hoped would be a beneficial school life for each. When she returned, Simpson was still there.

"I didn't wanna say nothin' in front of the kids," Simpson said confidentially. "But they been through a lot. My sister is okay, but her husband was a first-rate ass…jerk. I think they're okay, but I expect there was some bad stuff happenin' to 'em. So you might hear some awful stuff come out of their mouths. Stuff that might be true or might not. Just thought you should know."

"Thank you, Mr. Simpson," Mrs. Harris said simply and turned him to the door.

"Just tryin' to do the right thing by 'em. Poor Christers just need a fresh start."

"We'll do everything we can to make that happen," Mrs. Harris replied.

At the Simpson farm, Susan and Caleb quickly fell into the morning and evening routines since they were not all that different than the ones their father and mother had established.

Up at 5:30 AM, they dressed and made their beds and went downstairs to receive a silent good morning from Mrs. Simpson. Susan and Caleb then donned jackets and went out to feed the chickens and collect the eggs. Mr. Simpson milked the half dozen cows and then fed them. Dottie, whose jobs with the chickens had been now assigned to the newcomers, helped her mother work up a breakfast each morning that nearly satisfied the Knight children's hunger.

The group ate their morning meal in silence unless Mr. Simpson—Susan and Caleb would never think of or call the Simpson adults anything but Mr. and Mrs. Simpson—felt talkative. Susan and Caleb soon learned, however, acquiescence rather than conversation was expected. Mr. Simpson would announce what needed to be done for the day and by whom. Nodding in agreement seemed to be the correct response but, if a question arose, it was tolerated and answered. Caleb, with his father's gift for gab, tried to sit on his tongue, but his natural exuberance came through at times. Sometimes Mr. Simpson would laugh and say, "Jesus, that sounds like something your old man might say." Most times, however, he would glare at the boy and say something like, "If you got something important to say, say it, and then be quiet. We don't need none of your nonsense." Susan, more naturally quiet, rarely said a word.

After-school chores consisted of homework, which was more of a chore for Caleb than for Susan, along with feeding the chickens and cleaning out the coop and the cow stalls. Still too early to plant the family garden, there was no regular work to be done yet, though one afternoon Mr. Simpson directed Susan and Caleb to use spading forks to turn over the soil and add cow manure to it.

After supper, the family watched the TV shows Mr. Simpson favored. The waking hour came early so bedtime did too. The house and its old and new inhabitants lay quiet by 9:30 PM.

And so the first few days passed without incident. The abuse started the next week and it began with Susan.

After Mr. Simpson's big smile on their arrival, Susan and Caleb had seen few others. He was not dour-faced like his wife or daughter. Instead, Mr. Simpson seemed vaguely mad or unsettled most of the time. He was not particularly gruff and he did not shout. He went about the work of the farm with a determined effort, but not one of disdain for the life he led. Yet about him was a sense of something—the Knight children never could put a name to it—that unnerved them from the first day.

Susan was the first to experience it. She and Caleb had been cleaning out cow stalls one afternoon. Though they weren't being particularly loud, the children talked and laughed about the school day. Unexpectedly, Mr. Simpson appeared behind them. He offered a light compliment on their efforts, then told Caleb that the boy needed to collect more manure from the fields for the family garden. Starting to say that he had done so the day before, the words clutched in his mouth as he saw an angered look pass across Mr. Simpson's eyes.

"Yes, sir," the boy said, put away his broom, and left the barn.

Mr. Simpson said nothing as Susan continued to clean the stalls. She tried to think of something neutral to say to bring down the tension mounting in her mind, but nothing would come.

Finally, Mr. Simpson spoke, "You likin' living here, Susan?"

Sure that Mr. Simpson would not want to hear all her many confused thoughts, Susan nodded and said, "Yes, sir. Yes, Mr. Simpson." The man's smile discomforted the girl, but she offered a tentative smile back.

"And you appreciate the fact that I took in you and your brother in when your daddy couldn't care for you."

"Yes, sir.

"I thought you did. You seem like a 'preciative girl," Simpson said. Susan could think of no response, so she continued sweeping. "You probably ain't noticed yet, but my wife and Dottie, we show our 'preciation with hugs. Big hugs." A vague fear now crawled through Susan and she could not have spoken even had she the words. "You're part of this family now. You 'preciate bein' part of this family, right? Time you learned how to give a big hug."

With those words, Simpson grabbed Susan from behind and pulled her tightly to him. She gasped, but was too startled to struggle.

"That's what we call a surprise hug," Simpson said, holding tighter now, hands moving. As if tutoring the girl, he said, "You just come up and give 'em a squeeze and surprise 'em." As he slowly let her go, he added, "You like that kind of hug, even if it's a little scary at first, right? It's fun."

Susan could not look at Mr. Simpson. Standing mute with her arms wrapped around her midsection, what had been a vague dread now stood in firm control.

"We give all kinds of hugs," Simpson explained. "Front hugs and back hugs, but surprise hugs, those are the best." After a pause, he said, "You'd probably wanta give me a surprise hug now, dontcha? You wanta surprise me. Right?"

Mr. Simpson turned around and said, "Okay so let's have a practice. This is just practice. So here I am working and you just run over an give me a surprise hug. Ready? Do it!" When Susan didn't move, Mr. Simpson simply stood there. Then he said slowly and quietly, "Susan, you do 'preciate what I done for you and your little brother, right? You know I didn't haveta take you, you children, into my house, right? You know that. Your father, he can't take care of you, so I am. I'm your father now and so you hug me now like you'd hug your father."

Letting another minute pass, Mr. Simpson said again in the too quiet voice, "You come over here now, Susan, and give me a surprise hug and then we'll get on with our day. I won't tell you again."

Walking toward the man on legs not quite her own, Susan put her arms halfway around Mr. Simpson. At her first touch, he pretended surprise, grabbed her hands, and pulled them tightly around him. "Oh no, you surprise hugged me!" he said in mock fear. Pulling her hands down toward his crotch, Mr. Simpson said, "What a naughty girl scaring her new father! But what a nice surprise!" Pulling her in tightly and then releasing her hands, Mr. Simpson turned around and knelt down so that he could look directly into the girl's eyes.

"That was a good one, Susan, a good practice hug. We'll keep practicin' that one and all the other kind of hugs. You'll get good as Mrs. Simpson and Dottie are someday." Then reaching up and holding her chin, he stared even harder at her, "But don't go tellin' Caleb nor anyone else about our hugs, you hear me? These is just what we do, what the Simpsons do. They're our hugs, nobody else's. You understand me?" When the girl did not respond, he squeezed her chin harder, "You do understand me, don't you, girl?" Susan dropped her eyes and nodded. "Good girl. That's a good girl. I'm so happy you're part of my family now. So happy."

Mr. Simpson released the girl, caressed her cheek, smiled broadly, and said, "Okay, get your ass back to work now. And remember, a surprise hug has to be a surprise, a secret surprise."

CHAPTER 27

Well after she had left the Simpson farm and after years of counseling and stints in rehab centers, Susan came to understand, or begin to understand, that the abuse was not her fault. The lines her counselors offered her—"Don't judge yourself by what others did to you"…"Do not look for healing at the feet of those who broke you"…"Instead of saying, 'I'm damaged, I'm broken, I have trust issues' say 'I'm healing, I'm rediscovering myself, I'm starting over'"—all seemed like just so much bullshit. Susan tried believing these ideas, she really did, and on some days it felt like they took. More days, however, what took was the alcohol and the drugs and the depression.

The quote that most stuck with her was "You can't separate the mind and body. It's impossible." Although she forgot its source, she didn't forget the realization, once it arrived, that the author had it all wrong. Bodies heal, she knew; hers had recovered a year after escaping the Simpson farm. It recovered from the sexual abuse anyway; the abuse that resulted from the alcohol and drugs had just begun. What wouldn't heal was her brain. And maybe her bad brain *was* connected to the abuse heaped on her body. But it felt like it was her brain that just couldn't heal.

In the years until Susan successfully ran away at age sixteen, the author of the quote was absolutely right—her mind and her body and the horror realized on both were inseparable.

Maybe worse was that they weren't constant. Mr. Simpson's hugs progressed as Susan somehow knew they would. Within the first year on the Simpson farm, he had taken her however and whenever he wanted. But he had not taken her regularly. Sometimes weeks separated one abusive occasion from another. She didn't know, but she suspected that Mr. Simpson savaged his wife and daughter in the time when he left her alone. Those times alone helped her young body heal, but they worked even harder on her brain. Psychologists say that intermittent reinforcement of negative conditions produce stronger results than those that are constantly reinforced. Constant abuse creates a singular reality; intermittent abuse forces a duality—one condition where the cruelty terrorizes the body and mind and one that just terrorizes the mind. Knowing that Mr. Simpson could take her anytime he wanted, do with her whatever he wanted, leave her in whatever shape he wanted traumatized her brain even when her body was not. It seemed that the part of her brain that wasn't Mr. Simpson was shrinking every day and was shrinking more so on the bad days.

For the first year or so, Caleb tried to understand what was happening to his sister. Always quieter and more bookish than the other Knight kids, Susan had had the kind of soft-spoken manner that their mother did. She would take Caleb's mostly good-natured ribbing and pranks in stride. She'd just smile her little half-smile and go back to her books.

When their father left them at the Simpson farm, however, Susan had seemed to talk more with Caleb. Neither child spoke much at all downstairs, but in the hour or so after being sent to bed, they talked themselves to sleep.

The first night, Caleb had cried softly for an hour. Susan's kind and soothing words helped herself not to cry, but they had little effect on her brother. He cried himself out after a while and then Susan's words and the way that she held his hand calmed him enough to go to sleep.

He cried the second and third nights, too, but less each night and, on the fourth night, he had tried to offer Susan some comfort. They had fallen asleep nestled against one another.

The children had thought they were doing okay until the night of Susan's first surprise hug. Afterward, she feigned sickness to avoid the family dinner and asked permission to go to bed. An hour later, Mrs. Simpson brought up some dry toast and weak, honeyed tea. She sat quietly as Susan forced herself to eat. As Mrs. Simpson left, she said softly, "You'll be fine. In time, you'll be fine."

When Caleb came up an hour later, Susan assured him that she was okay, that she'd be okay.

"But you were okay when we were cleaning out the stalls, and then you weren't. What happened?"

"Nothing, Caleb. It's okay," Susan said trying to keep from tearing up. "I'll be fine."

"I hope so," Caleb said in a sleepy voice. "Cause I don't wanna catch whatever you got."

But he did. Mr. Simpson caught Caleb on the boy's twelfth birthday.

If pressed, Walter Simpson would have denied any homosexual impulses. He liked the company of other men, but he also liked having sex with women, both those inside and outside of his family. When not working and not satisfying his sexual urges, Simpson spent his time with men drinking, telling stories, talking about women. He would never have advanced on any of these men, nor on Caleb's father. But he did on Caleb.

Susan had never revealed Mr. Simpson's aggressions on her to Caleb. She was more quiet and withdrawn than before, but such was her nature before the move. Moreover, Mrs. Simpson and Dottie had seemed cowed since he and his sister had come to the farm, Caleb knew, so he thought little of it. In fact, he, too, was quieter and more subdued in the Simpson home than his naturally gregarious self would be under different circumstances. The new reality could not completely temper Caleb's energy even if the Simpsons showed little joy.

If asked, Walter Simpson could not have expressed why he took Caleb. Novelty, power, latent homosexuality, pure perversion—all real possibilities, yet the reason did not matter. He took the boy and continued to do so until Caleb himself escaped the Simpson farm.

CHAPTER 28

The natural cheeriness Caleb Knight possessed began dying with the first day at Mr. Simpson's farm. Too young to do much more than hurt at his father's abandonment, the boy pushed through as best he could. And when he couldn't, he sought his sister's calm. He didn't understand her further withdrawal soon after they arrived and he knew that her encouragement of him seemed to extract a big cost. Her assurances that, "It will be okay," were enough, though barely enough, to soothe him. He wished he could bring a smile more readily to his sister's drawn face. But he could determine no cause and so no solution appeared to him.

Susan knew.

She didn't know for sure until Caleb eventually and vaguely told her, but she knew that Mr. Simpson had stolen Caleb's brain and his body just as he had stolen hers. Caleb had opened his meager birthday present and finished his supper of hamburgers and French fries. Afterward, Mr. Simpson said that he had something else for the boy so they had gone out to the barn while Mrs. Simpson, Dottie, and Susan cleaned up the dishes.

Half an hour later, Caleb came running into the house and up the stairs and into his and Susan's room locking the door after him. Mr. Simpson came in fifteen minutes later and wondered where Caleb had gone. The women, still surprised by Caleb's behavior, indicated that he had gone upstairs. Mr. Simpson nodded, offered a slight smile, and went back into the barn.

At bedtime, Susan had to plead with Caleb for ten minutes before he relented and opened the locked door. She immediately hugged her brother as he collapsed in racking sobs.

Susan could not speak. She realized much later that it might have helped, but to help her brother now would likely mean talking about her own experience and Susan knew that she was nowhere near able to do that.

So she held her brother tighter and resolved to flee the Simpson homestead as soon as she could. She knew she should try to take Caleb with her. But she could not bear to watch Caleb lose his brain and body to Mr. Simpson and she could not save him now. In this tumble of thoughts, Susan's all-consuming thought was that the only way she could save Caleb was to try and save herself.

Susan knew that running away at sixteen carried every danger of the world. Yet, when she slipped out of the house at two o'clock the next morning, she could only think that those dangers paled next to losing the rest of her brain to Mr. Simpson.

Susan ran all the way to town and on to Route 1. She put her thumb out and quickly lucked out with a ride from a woman driving to Bangor. The hard-luck-looking, middle-aged woman eyeballed Susan, but left her to herself. The tire hum, the overly warm car, and the low-volume country radio station induced Susan to sleep despite her efforts to resist.

In Bangor, the woman agreed to drop Susan at the Greyhound bus station on Main Street. Susan knew that she didn't have enough money to get a bus ticket, but it was the only place she had heard of and she supposed there might be travelers there who could help get a ride to Portland. Miraculously there was.

Portland was her and Caleb's touchstone. Neither child had ever been anywhere close to Maine's biggest city and only vaguely knew where it was. Their mother had been there once on a school trip and would sometimes talk about it as magical place with more buildings and people and roads than could be imagined. Their father typically shut down this talk as "Puttin' ideas in their hard heads," but each of the Knight children locked the Portland ideal into their minds. So that very first night at the Simpson's, Susan and Caleb resolved that, should they be separated, they would find one another in Portland.

"But how?" Caleb asked plaintively. "Momma said it was so big."

"I know, Caleb," Susan said softly. "But they got to have a place, like a library, where we could meet up."

"But when?" Caleb whined. "We couldn't live there. How would I ever know if you was there?"

Then it came to Susan—they would each go to the Portland library at noon on their respective birthdays. They would wait an hour and, if the other failed to show, then they would know to try again on the other's birthday.

Susan knew that, at twelve years old, Caleb would never be able to break away from the Simpsons until he was older. Still, she resolved to show up at the library on her birthday three months hence.

She did, and then she did again on Caleb's birthday the next year, and for both of their birthdays three years afterward. She sometimes showed up sober, but far too often she was drunk or stoned or just getting over being drunk or stoned. But she always went and always would.

CHAPTER 29

Susan went to the library at noon on her twentieth birthday to meet her brother…and he was there. Caleb was there.

The happiest of reunions it was not, however. Caleb was only days removed from Richmond Plantation and the hellish life he had lived on the Simpson farm. He had not had Susan's travel luck.

Susan's ride to Bangor was quickly followed by a second ride straight to Portland. This driver, also a middle-aged woman, had been a talker. Fortunately her talk was all about herself and the shopping trip she had planned, so Susan did not have to invent a story about why she was traveling alone. Not knowing where else to go in the city, Susan asked to be let out at the Portland library.

"I'm guessing you mean the main library on Congress Street, right, honey?" the woman asked. "You don't mean one of the branches, right?"

Susan didn't know that libraries could have branches so she simply nodded.

"Know right where it is, dear. Have you there in a couple of hours."

Susan's travel luck had not held once she got to Portland, however. At sixteen, with no skills and only a little money, she'd wandered Portland's streets, found shelter and trouble in equal measures, and discovered drink and drugs and a way to pay for both through prostitution.

It was after a late night and an unruly john that Susan found Caleb on the steps of the Portland Public Library, main branch. He didn't look a lot better than she did. Caleb always needed sleep to be his best and it had not come during his flight. Nor had the rides, especially when it rained. So the boy who now stood to shivering in the center of Portland looked a mess.

"We're quite a pair," Susan said.

"Guess we are. But we ain't on Simpson's farm no more."

What passed for life during those early months away from Simpson's farm proved a different sort of challenge. Farm strong and willing to do most any job, Caleb had found enough under-the-table work to eat and enough flophouses to sleep. He and Susan had tried to live together, pooling their resources and looking out for one another. It didn't last though as Caleb could not tolerate Susan's drinking, drugging, and whoring, and she could not take his moralizing.

"You went through the same shit I did," she said one afternoon anger rising faster than she'd intended. "At least I'm gettin' paid for it now."

"That's just why you shouldn't be doin' it," Caleb replied. "You know better."

"I don't know anything different," she said in a tired, resigned voice. "Seems like it's all I done for my whole life. I got nothing else."

"You won't even have that, you don't get yourself together. You're stoned all the time, you look like hell—"

"Then get the fuck out, Caleb! Just get the fuck out. I'm not gonna have another man tell me what to do. Not ever again."

So he left. In Susan's blurred brain, Caleb was leaving her when she needed him, just as she had left him when he had needed her. We're even now, little brother, she thought.

Later, sober, Susan knew this reciprocity would not hold. She had *left* Caleb to his fate and now she had *pushed* that same brother away. These had felt like the same thing in the boozy moment after they last talked. Now they didn't.

Knights Disarmed

So Susan reached out, found Caleb, and they'd talked. And this time they had really talked. Susan knew that Caleb held back many or maybe even most of the details of Simpson's abuse. She knew because she did the same. But they had talked and, though it was clear that they would not be able to live together, they decided that they could live around each other.

Over the next couple of years, they lived independent, but intersecting lives. Caleb stayed employed, working hard if not always smart. Susan did much the same. Caleb handled the temptations of release through drugs and drink better than his sister. His drinking bouts were violent, but infrequent. Susan continued to struggle, though she did find jobs through which she could clean herself up for stretches of time. Her addictions would stay down only so long, however.

Lives lived take many paths. With the aid of counselors in and out of her rehab stints, Susan tried to make sense of the life she'd lived. By contrast, Caleb just lived his life forward; looking backward unnerved him. And so while one looked for answers in the past, the other could only look to the future.

And the future to which Caleb most looked forward was the day when he would drive a knife into Walter Simpson's chest and cut out his diseased heart.

That thought took root the night of Caleb's twelfth birthday and it never strayed far. When free to imagine, he took Simpson's life in every conceivable way. Though he couldn't say why, he always returned to the idea of taking Mr. Simpson's heart. For obvious reasons, the thought of cutting off Mr. Simpson's cock appealed to him. But Caleb somehow knew that it was the man's heart that drove his mind and his penis and so the idea of cutting out that malevolent organ became his goal. He would pull Mr. Simpson's heart from his chest and position it such that the then-dead body became its backdrop.

Chapter 30

The nurturing of Caleb's plan took years, yet the passing time did nothing to dampen his rage. In fact, living with that wrath and imagining how he would employ it to end Walter Simpson's life, gave Caleb a strange comfort.

Caleb's rage stuck by him when others—his bosses, his friends, even his sister—abandoned him. When alone, he nursed his ire, poking and stoking it to white-hot intensity. Sometimes he let it out on the walls of whatever house he lived in, fists burrowing through plaster board until bloody. Other times, he directed it toward those who crossed him. In those cases, however, he never attacked anyone he knew to be physically weaker than he. Instead, he typically took on the biggest, nastiest guy in the bar…and just as typically got his lights punched out. Oddly enough, beating on walls and getting beaten into pulp calmed his inner rage and he could go back to work, albeit in different locales each time. Caleb knew he had to be careful though, especially in directing his fury at other people or by causing property damage that he was unable to fix: He couldn't afford to get sent to jail before he had taken Walter Simpson's heart. Caleb needed his rage, but he needed it to stay in the background.

Picking up various hand trades after arriving in Portland, Caleb carpentered when he could, took plumbing and electrical assistant jobs when he had to, and worked as a flag man on road construction jobs when nothing else came through. New home construction, business remodeling, indoor work and out, Caleb stayed in a place until he found a better gig or he had to move on because he'd let his rage have its way.

Of all these jobs, however, it was boat building that most appealed. He'd gotten a taste as carpenter's helper at a small Portland shop a year or so after leaving Richmond Plantation. It wasn't much of a job—he mostly ran tasks for the head carpenter—but he learned the scut work quickly and did it efficiently. Slowly the carpenter increased Caleb's duties and even more slowly he taught the boy pieces of the trade and the disposition to do them right.

Although that job lasted but six months, others followed, some in boatyards, most not. But the skills Caleb was learning and, in some cases, mastering began to build his confidence.

Susan was less successful. In and out of jobs and in and out of state rehab facilities, she was trying to cobble together a life from the pieces she had left. "Trying" was the operative word and sometime trying was all it was.

Still, she and Caleb stayed in touch, their lives intersecting in ways that might have seemed desultory to outsiders, but meant something to them. Neither knew what had happened to their older brother and sister. The letters dried up not long after the children were separated and the social media phenomena meant nothing to two souls who sometimes struggled to eat regularly. Caleb and Susan were managing to get on with their lives even if, sometimes, they struggled more than others.

Unbeknownst to Caleb, however, Susan had another semi-regular contact from their past. A month or so after she fled the Simpson farm, Susan had written to Dottie Simpson through a mutual school friend. Mr. Simpson monitored the family mail and would have seen any letter from Susan to his daughter. So Susan had written to their friend and asked her to serve as go-between. The friend agreed and, communication line established, Susan and Dottie exchanged infrequent and curiously objective letters. Neither ever raised the topic of

Mr. Simpson's abuse. Instead, Dottie's letters were filled with hopeful wishes for the time when she could leave Richmond Plantation and with expressions of excitement for Susan's new life. For her part, Susan encouraged that excitement with positively tinged accounts of the new person she was becoming. She also inquired about Caleb, the real reason that she had started writing. The guilt about leaving him rumbled through her every time she gave it space. The letters did little to assuage it, but they helped.

The correspondence tailed off once Caleb ran off and as Susan's need for it dwindled. Dottie continued to write often—Susan sometimes thought that Dottie might have needed the outlet even more than she did—though the frequency of her letters declined once she, too, left the farm.

So Caleb received two surprises when he met Susan for lunch one spring day to celebrate her birthday. The first was that Susan and Dottie had been writing to one another these many years. The second was that Walter Simpson, having lost his wife and sold his farm, was moving south to live with his daughter in Rascal Harbor. Susan presented this information in matter-of-fact fashion; Caleb heard it in anything but.

Not willing to share his murderous thoughts with his sister, Caleb said simply, "I figured the old bastard was dead by now."

"Nope. Dottie says he's got the usual ailments, but he's still going."

"Huh. But why would she take him in rather than send him to a nursing home."

"She didn't really say. I wouldn't want him around either. Can't imagine she just forget how he was."

"I'll never forget," Caleb said, a little more aggressively than he had intended.

"Me either," Susan admitted. "Though I'm sure trying. I want to think about the future, not the past."

"Maybe there's not all that much difference," Caleb said enigmatically.

When the two concluded their lunch, Caleb surprised Susan by giving her a long, hard hug. During these last several years, they had hugged quickly and awkwardly with Caleb giving little to the embrace. The last time Susan could remember him holding her this way was the last night they spent together on the Simpson farm. Later, she wondered if she should have seen significance behind Caleb's act. At the time, she had simply hugged back fiercely.

With the news that Walter Simpson was alive, Caleb felt at sea. His first impulse was to find the man and kill him that afternoon. Immediately following that thought was another—slow down, plan, don't be an idiot. Caleb knew these twin impulses would fight just like the devil and angel characters he'd seen in cartoons. He resolved not to ignore the first impulse, to revel in it, but he'd act on the second.

Part of acting on the planning impulse was to take a series of actions that would, eventually, position him to take Mr. Simpson's heart. The first was to change his name.

Caleb knew enough about cops to understand that he'd need to take some precautions if he was to commit murder…and get away with it. Changing his name made sense as a good first step. He thought about changing his whole name, but concluded that a new last name would suffice. It didn't take long to determine which one he would choose. His mother's maiden name was Rimes and so Caleb Knight began the paperwork to become Caleb Rimes.

The second step was to change locations. Caleb had been working in the Portland area for the last two years. He considered staying there and doing the crime from long distance. He knew small town life, however, so he concluded that a stranger lurking around and watching Dottie Simpson's house would create neighborly suspicions. So Caleb decided to insinuate himself into the Rascal Harbor community for a period long enough, he hoped, to be considered a local. That way, if he was spotted in the area of Dottie's house, he could pass it off in any number of ways.

Caleb could think of no other preparations necessary before he relocated to Rascal Harbor. With a plan in mind, Caleb took a long sip from the beer he'd been nursing in a Portland waterfront bar. Fixing an image of Walter Simpson in his mind's eye, he said in a whisper, "Mr. Simpson, your fuckin' days are numbered."

Moving to Rascal Harbor, finding work, and settling in proved no particular problem for Caleb Rimes. Such had been his life since age sixteen. Now in early middle age, he adjusted to whatever circumstances presented themselves and made do. He decided that all the moves and jobs and settling in had been in anticipation of the opportunity to finally detail and then execute his plan.

Part of that plan was not working anywhere full-time. By taking part-time jobs, most of which paid under the table, Caleb established himself as someone who might be seen anywhere in town and at any time. A steady job would have tied him down. He needed flexibility for the time when he would act.

By contrast, Caleb found a long-term apartment rental, one where he could be known by a number of people and seen as a fixture in the neighborhood. To further that end, Caleb created an identity around town—as a semi-regular at the men's table in Lydia's, as a part of the crowd who hung out at Henry's Barbershop, and as a friend to whichever Rascal Harbor cop would have him. On this last score, he'd succeeded with Rendall Kalin. Kalin was a fuck-up, but he loved talking about police business so Caleb felt like he'd be able to monitor the investigation after he struck.

The image Caleb cultivated suited him. He once thought about building a clean-cut personality so that he would be above suspicion once he had killed Walter Simpson. The years and the hard work and hard living had toughened him, however, and he convinced himself that fashioning a goody-two-shoes appearance would be too hard to carry off convincingly. So he opted for the kind of rough character that he knew he looked like—he let his clothing go toward shabby, he let his hair and beard go toward stubbly, and he let his language go toward crass. None of these changes were a big stretch; Caleb Rimes would never be confused with a dandy. One thing that was no stretch at all, however, was Caleb's homophobia. He tried to temper it, or let it out only in contexts where he could count on others' agreement. His mixed success rate, Caleb knew, might get him into bigger trouble than he wanted. "Keep your fuckin' trap shut," he would tell himself when confronted with the opportunity to talk about "the gays." And sometimes he did.

CHAPTER 31

On one occasion Caleb Rimes didn't keep his trap shut and that lapse turned out to be pivotal. He met his brother Galen.

Jonathan Hannigan's was built to be a proper pub of Irish design, one that would tolerate the Rascal Harbor locals, but pull in the tourists in bulk. It accomplished both goals for a couple of years. A downturning national economy, however, stuck owner Hannigan with too much space too far off the easy tourist track. The net result—the tourists disappeared, locals took over, and Jonathan Hannigan's became known as Jimbo's.

Caleb Rimes had been given the boot from many of the Harbor bars and restaurants, but had managed not to get himself banished from any. After getting bum-rushed from Jimbo's the week before, Rimes was trying to stay in bounds. Then he heard a couple guys further down the bar telling gay jokes. The first two were mildly funny and he laughed to himself, the third was a rip snorter and he laughed freely. Turning to the fellow sitting a couple seats away, he said, "Didja hear that one? 'Tooth fairy!'" The seated man nodded, but kept his eyes focused on his beer.

"What the hell!" Rimes said, a little too loudly. In a quieter voice, he asked, "What, don't you think that's funny?"

"Not particularly," the man said.

"Cause you got a funnier one?" Rimes asked in challenge. "Or cause you're queer?"

"Neither," the man said, now glancing over at Rimes for the first time.

"Neither?" Rimes said, this time clearly louder than necessary.

"Caleb, take it down or take it outside," the bartender said.

"Caleb?" the seated man asked. "Is that your name?"

"You're fuckin' right it is. Caleb fuckin' Rimes!"

"You're Caleb…Rimes?" the man asked, with surprise in his voice.

"Yeah, ya dumb fuck. How many times have I gotta say it?"

"Caleb Rimes…Caleb Rimes," the man said to himself. "I'll be damned." Standing up, looking Rimes full on, and putting out his hand, he said, "I'm your brother Galen. Mighty glad to see you again."

For the rest of that evening, the two brothers talked quietly at a back table. They first focused on how each had come to be in Rascal Harbor and the fact that they lived in the same area yet had not encountered each other before. In the end, they supposed that the fates that had kept them apart had just decided to bring them together.

Knight explained that he'd retired four years ago from the U.S. Navy after serving his twenty years. Having had enough of regimented life, he had been picking up work in whatever east coast city he fancied. He had returned to Rascal Harbor only a couple of months ago. He reminded Rimes that he and their sister Virginia had lived there with their Aunt Mavis.

Rimes then gave a sanitized version of his own story. He decided he would not reveal the abuse either he or Susan suffered until he felt more comfortable around this man who claimed to be his brother. The fellow looked like their father so he could well be the older Knight boy, but what were the chances that they would meet in this fashion?

They then turned to talk of their sisters. Rimes gave a slightly rosier account of Susan's life than was true; Knight was more honest about Virginia. Neither sister had prospered. Susan's ups—steady jobs, steady rents—got a shine in Rimes's account; her downs—"some trouble" with alcohol—did too. Rimes held back his knowledge of Susan's prostitution.

Virginia, according to Knight, had not fared much better. She drifted after high school, eventually hooking up with an older man, Bernie Lamont, whose family came from the vicinity of Myron. Lamont was a meth producer who stayed a only a step or two in advance of the police. Sensing his days of living freely on the coast were limited, Lamont and Virginia and their children moved up to Myron and installed a trailer on a piece of property his father owned. Telling Virginia that they needed to stay "Off the fuckin' grid," Lamont's name appeared nowhere—not on the trailer they purchased, the pickup they registered, or the mailbox they installed. Galen didn't think that Virginia was hooked on meth, but he couldn't be sure and he wouldn't have bet a dime that she wasn't.

The brothers' shared talk, shared experiences, and shared sense of concern about their sisters generated a gradual trust. That trust then encouraged them to revise the initial accounts they offered of their sisters' misfortunes. It took longer for Rimes to offer an outline of the sexual horror that Susan endured on the Simpson farm than it did for Knight to offer additional insights into Virginia's rocky life choices. Not yet wanting to expose his murderous plans, Rimes continued to withhold the information about his own abuse. Something told him that Galen might balk at the plan to take Walter Simpson's heart, so he downplayed the details of Susan's torture and buried even a mention of his own.

Having revealed the fact that Walter Simpson now lived in the area, Rimes was not surprised that Knight wanted to join him in bracing Simpson for his misdeeds. They discussed what they would do afterward, but could settle on no single plan. They would confront the old bastard first and then decide.

KNIGHTS DISARMED

CHAPTER 32

With Galen Knight invested in, but not fully aware of, his brother's intention, the two sketched out a plan. Eight years separated the brothers in age, many more separated the experiences they had with the family split. Yet they quickly bonded over the idea of encountering Walter Simpson and their planning began in earnest.

After some individual and joint reconnoitering, the brothers discovered that Simpson was old, but far from feeble. His daughter, Dorothy, by contrast was wheelchair bound after suffering some kind of accident. There was no husband in the picture, but two high-school-aged children, a boy and a girl, tended to their mother and grandfather. Largely house bound, Dottie did go to town every Thursday afternoon to do the grocery shopping and to attend to errands.

Caleb Rimes had convinced his brother that Dorothy was not to blame, that she might even have been another victim of her father. So they decided that they would make their move on a Thursday after Dorothy and her children left for town.

"When should we do it?" Rimes asked his brother, once they had worked out the patterns of life in the Simpson home.

"Do we have a reason to wait? And should we get Susan and let her come with us?" Knight had yet to see his younger sister.

"We could wait. But I don't think we oughta bring Susan. Might be too upsettin' for her. And as for time, my thinkin' is that the sooner the better."

"You might be right on both scores. And the sooner we do it, the sooner you and Susan can get on with your lives."

"I'd sure like that, brother," Rimes said.

Chapter 33

"You nervous?" Knight asked as the brothers drove to Dorothy Simpson's house.

"Yeah, guess I am," Rimes said. And he was, though excitement and dread competed for his prime emotion. "Been a long time since I seen the old bastard. Not sure now what I wanta say."

"They say you should just speak from your heart. Seems like as good a place as any to start. Then we'll see how he reacts and decide what to do after that."

"Yup," Rimes said.

The Simpson home was three miles of twisty coastal road away from town. The brothers drove past the house fifteen minutes before Dorothy and her children typically left; the wheelchair-accommodating van was still in the driveway. The men parked off the road in a way that allowed them to see when the family left. And then they waited.

Almost as if they knew the plan, the Simpson children loaded their mother, backed out of the drive, and headed in the direction of Rascal Harbor right on time. Rimes, the driver, and his brother waited another ten minutes in case the family returned for one reason or another.

When they didn't, Rimes put the pickup in motion, drove slowly to the Simpson house, and parked at the entrance to the driveway. As they walked to the side door, Knight grabbed his brother's forearm and said, "It'll be okay, Caleb. We'll get through this together." Rimes looked at his brother and nodded.

In response to their knock on the door, the brothers heard a reedy voice call out, "That you, Dottie? Johnny? What the hell're ya knocking for?"

The two men entered to see Walter Simpson sitting in a recliner turning down the volume on a TV game show. His foggy eyes took them in coldly. "Who the fuck are you?" he asked, mustering but not quite achieving a bravado in his voice.

Rimes could tell that the old man did not recognize him, but then he seemed to be more focused on Galen. Pointing to Knight, Simpson asked, "You look familiar. Do I know you?"

"We've never met," Knight said. "But you knew my father, Peter Knight, and I suppose I look like him."

"Goddamn, Peter's boy!" Simpson said rising in his chair, a smile weaving across his lips. "I should've seen it when you first come in. Pete and I, we did spend some times together. Some good times." Turning now to Rimes, who had been standing a step to the side and in back of Knight, Simpson asked, "Who's that then, that's not Pete with ya…"

The rest of Simpson's comment and his face dropped at the same time. "Who the fuck are you?" he demanded voice rising. "Who the *fuck* are you?"

"You know who I am, you fuckin' bastard," Rimes growled. "You know very well, who I am."

Silence echoed as Simpson stared, and then smiled at Rimes. The smile broadened as he sat back in his chair. "Why it's that little fuck, Caleb. Come to see the man who made him. How's your sister…Susan? Is that her name? How's little Susan?"

Dragging a chair forward and sitting so that he could look directly into Simpson's eyes, Caleb stared at the man for a long second. Knight stood silently behind him.

"She's doin' fine. No fuckin' thanks to you."

"Is she now?" the old man said seeming to relax. "Still takin' it any way a man can give it to her? I learned that girl just right…"

"Shut up, you crazy fuck," Rimes yelled, rising from his chair. Knight put a hand on his shoulder.

"Easy, brother. Don't let this old goat get to you. Say what you came to say," Knight said calmly. "I think we know what we'll do after that."

"'Get to him'?" Simpson laughed. "I already fuckin' *got* to him. I got to him and his fuckin' sister!"

Knight took a step back. "What? What do you mean?" he asked, his voice sounding odd in his throat. "What the hell do you mean?"

"He means that he took me," Rimes said in a strangled voice. But as he did, he pulled a knife from his boot and plunged it into the center of Simpson's chest.

Too stunned to move, Knight simply watched as his brother drove the knife into Simpson's heart three more times sobbing loudly and incoherently.

Recovered enough to move, Knight pulled at his brother yelling, "Stop…stop, Caleb! Jesus, Jesus!" Rimes, however, pushed even closer to Simpson, trying it seemed, to cut open the man's chest. Blood flew in spurts and globs from the horrific stab wounds. As it covered Rimes, his sobbing transformed into a wild growling sound. Knight managed to get the knife away from his brother, but Rimes continued to pound on Simpson's chest.

Finally, Knight got his arms around his brother's chest and heaved him away from the sprawling, now dead body of Walter Simpson. Both brothers fell to the floor. Knight knew only to not let go of his brother as if to do so would mean the end of them both. For his part, once away from Simpson, Rime went limp and the racking sobs returned. He curled his body, clutched onto his brother's arms, and cried.

Knight had no idea how long he and Rimes laid on the floor. He could hear blood dripping onto the newspaper beside Simpson's chair, he could count his brother's breaths, he could make out a ticking clock somewhere in the kitchen. His brain would not make sense of any of this data, however, and so he simply closed his eyes.

Exhausted in a physical-emotional-mental fashion he had never felt before, Knight opened his eyes to see his brother staring at him. Knight could perceive no movement in those eyes nor any activity behind them. Had Caleb died? No, Knight thought, realizing that he could still feel his brother's chest moving.

"Caleb? Are you okay? Can you move?" Knight asked quietly. No response. Knight shook his brother slightly and repeated his questions. Still no response.

"Caleb, please. Please tell me that you are okay. Tell me you're okay." At this request, Rimes closed and then opened his eyes and this time, Knight could see a mind returning.

"Caleb, you've got to get out of here," Knight said decisively. "Caleb, you've got to go."

Somehow Galen Knight had come to the decision that he alone would take the blame for Simpson's murder, that he would spare his brother a trial and prison. Later, he would wonder how he came to this choice and ask himself why they did not flee together. Guilt over not pushing his father to keep the family together, guilt over not being able to protect Caleb from this monster, guilt over not being available to Caleb as he tried to make a life after running away—all of this, none of this, it didn't really seem to matter. Knight knew that this time he would get his brother away and try to keep him safe.

Caleb did not resist. Later, he would, but not now. In this moment, he dumbly followed Galen's quiet, steady voice and clear directions. He avoided walking in the blood, he washed his hands, he gave Galen his bloody outer shirt. He walked calmly to the pick-up and he drove away. He found himself three days later still half-drunk in the front seat of his pick-up parked in the middle of a small field two towns over from Rascal Harbor. Beer and liquor bottles covered the floors, but he had no recollection of how they or he had gotten there. He knew nothing to do but weep.

KNIGHTS DISARMED

As Rimes had driven away, Galen Knight's mind seemed on loan from someone else, someone calm, cool, and collected. That phrase kept repeating in his ears as he managed the mayhem. His first thought—the scene had to look as though he'd been the sole murderer. He had taken care to get Caleb cleaned up and off the property. He knew that he ought to worry about Caleb in his dizzied state of mind, but he could do nothing about it so he turned to the aftermath at the house. Shutting out all other thoughts, Knight first made sure that none of Caleb's bloody footprints remained. He cleaned the few he could see, then he covered the spots with his own bloody tracks. He cleaned the sink and the sideboard around it. He then dipped his hands into Simpson's blood, touched the sideboard and sink, and washed them carelessly to ensure that none of Caleb's fingerprints could be detected. The final task was to find the knife and make sure that his fingerprints covered any surface that his brother may have touched.

Judging that he had enough blood on him to convince the police that he alone had committed the crime, Knight walked out of the house, down the driveway, and turned onto the road back to Rascal Harbor. The words he had spoken to Caleb would be the last he would utter for months.

CHAPTER 34

Detective Chambers could not shake the parking lot confrontation with Caleb Rimes on his drive home. Nor had he done so a week later. Events in the Harbor kept him busy, but at odd moments Caleb Rimes came back into his mind.

Off duty over the weekend, Chambers decided to follow his cop's nose and see what he could find out as soon as he returned to the office. Monday morning he called the state prison warden, a man Chambers had come to know and respect.

A rarity in a system that seems to privilege warehousing goals over rehabilitation, Warden Stephen Ross was no Pollyanna. He had worked in some of the toughest institutions in New England and so knew what prisons could be and what they couldn't. Called home to care for aging parents, Ross was the hiring committee's first choice to take over the newly vacated Maine prison job. Staff and inmates alike found him a reasonable man.

Expecting to leave a message, Detective Chambers was surprised when Ross took his call. They exchanged pleasantries and Chambers gave a brief account of his last visit with Galen Knight. Like Chambers, Ross was intrigued by Knight's case and the man's behavior within it.

"Nothing all that new to report, Stephen. The guy is as pleasant and conversational as anyone I know. But he clams up as soon as I try to pierce his shell."

"I'll admit that I've never met anyone quite like him. Can't say that I've spent much of any time with him. But in that time, I've sensed that he might be the most self-contained man I've ever met. The staff says he simply takes everything at face value and reacts accordingly."

Chambers nodded. "Huh. I can't disagree with a word of that assessment. Curious guy." With that comment, Chambers pivoted to the reason for his call. "Stephen, I'm actually calling to find out about a visitor I ran into the other day. He's kind of rough character. Never any serious trouble, but a kind of tough guy. And the way he came at me in the parking lot got my hackles up. Just didn't seem to be any call for it. Fella by the name of Caleb Rimes. It's been nagging me, so I thought I'd see if I couldn't find out who he's been visiting with up there."

"Can't say that I know off-hand. But I'll check and send you an email."

"Fair enough. If I can do anything for you, just let me know."

"Still have lobster down there in the Hahbah," Ross asked, exaggerating the Maine pronunciation of the letter "r."

"You betcha, mistah. Git in your cah and come on down and I'll fix you right up," Chambers said in kind. The men laughed and broke the connection.

Early the next morning, Chambers saw an email come into his mailbox from Warden Ross. The note read: "Interesting...Caleb Rimes has visited only one prisoner—Galen Knight."

"Huh," Chambers mused.

With this new piece of information, Chambers decided to do some background work before confronting Caleb Rimes. He checked with Chief Lawton Miles, Sergeant Andy Levesque, and the two constables, Artie Long and Rendall Kalin. Chambers was particularly interested in Kalin's perspective as he knew that the Kalin and Rimes were friendly.

Kalin looked genuinely surprised to hear that Rimes had visited Galen Knight.

"No sir, Detective, I had no idea those two were acquainted. You say that Caleb's gone up to Warren several times?"

"At least a dozen since Knight was sent up three years ago. So Rimes never said anything to you about knowing Galen Knight."

"Nope and seems like he would, as he can be kind of a loud mouth. If he knew a convicted murderer, I'm sure he would have talked about it all over town."

"I'd have thought so too," Chambers said. Then remembering that Kalin was his own kind of loud mouth, he swore the constable to secrecy.

"Rendall, I do not want Caleb Rimes or Galen Knight to know anything about us discovering this connection. Do I make myself perfectly clear?" Chambers said sternly.

"Roger that. Got it loud and clear."

Knowing Kalin to be a bit slow on the uptake, Chambers said, "Okay, Rendall, tell me exactly what is loud and clear to you."

A flash of annoyance passed across Kalin's eyes, but he acceded. "It means that I do not communicate anything to Caleb Rimes about any kinda bond he might have to Galen Knight."

"Can you do that, Rendall? Can you be around him and not spill the beans?" Chambers pressed.

This time Kalin's annoyed look lasted longer. Kalin knew that Chambers was not his biggest fan. "Yes, I can, Detective," Kalin said slowly. "I'm a professional peace officer. I know how to do my job."

Chambers had seen Kalin get his back up before…and then screw up mightily. So he listened to Kalin's protest, but then stared him down. "That's good, Officer Kalin. But if Caleb Rimes finds out that we're looking into this and I get even a whiff that you're responsible, then I'll have your ass and your badge."

Chastened, Kalin retreated. "Jesus, Detective, I got it! I really do. Caleb won't get nothing from me."

Chambers nodded, but felt no great comfort. He'd had to talk with Kalin, but he now wondered if he should have.

The other person Detective Chambers wanted to check with was Julian Pratt. He didn't think he'd learn anything new given that he and Pratt had talked extensively about Galen Knight earlier. "Leave no stone," he said to himself as he drove over to see the lawyer.

Chambers found the lawyer seated in his outer office talking with his office manager, Martha Honey. Chambers knew Martha to be a cracker-jack assistant and one of the few locals who could tolerate Julian's big-city ways. She did so through patience, grace, and the occasional reminder to her boss that he walked a fine line with the townsfolk. Chambers would never forget the time he walked in to hear a classic Julian rant up-ended when Martha said, "Julian, as soon as you put your big girl panties on, I'll start listening."

"Ah, Detective," Julian said looking up at his guest. "You're just in time to settle a small matter between Ms. Honey and me."

"That's Mrs. Honey, Julian. Being married to Mr. Bob Honey is trial enough to earn the title."

"Apologies, Mrs. Honey," Julian said, smiling. Chambers knew this to be part of the office banter over which Julian never gained the upper hand. Turning to Chambers, Pratt said, "I was just explaining the finer distinctions between Lobster Thermidor, Lobster Rossejat, and Lobster Benedict…"

"And I was explaining to Lawyer Pratt that my grandfather used to feed chick lobsters to his hens. So I told him I'd bring him a bowl of chicken feed for lunch tomorrow."

"Jesus, Julian, I know you're good in the courtroom," Chambers said. "But when are you going to learn that you'll never best Martha?"

"Point noted, Detective," Julian admitted with a smile. "What might I or my more than capable assistant do for you today?"

"Had a couple thoughts about Galen Knight," Chambers said. He suspected that he could have talked through Knight's connection to Caleb Rimes in front of both Julian and Martha, but the nagging feeling that he'd goofed by talking with Rendall Kalin held him back.

"All right, Richard. Not sure what I might add, but come on in."

In Pratt's closed-door office, Chambers began tentatively. "I don't know, Julian, maybe I'm just chasing my tail, but I've got hold of something and I can't let it go."

When Pratt nodded, Chambers described his interaction with Caleb Rimes in the prison parking lot, his conversation with the prison warden, and the subsequent discovery that Rimes visited Knight regularly.

"Interesting. And what do you make of this insight?"

"That's just it, Julian. I can't make anything of it. We looked hard at Knight when we arrested him, but as far as we could tell then, he had just drifted back into town a few months before the murder. And as you know, we found out that he lived in town at some point with an aunt who is now dead. I understand that he's got a sister somewhere up in The County, but she couldn't or wouldn't shed any light. And with him taking a vow of silence, we let the evidence convict him."

"And convict him it did. He didn't have a chance in court."

"I know. So how in hell is he connected to Caleb Rimes?"

"I'm sure I wouldn't know, Richard," Pratt acknowledged. "I'll take a quick look back through my case notes but, as you know, there's nothing there. The man simply refused to say a single word from arrest to conviction. Recall that he even refused to enter his plea orally—he wrote the words "not guilty" on a piece of paper and I read them. So if there's a connection with Caleb Rimes, I'm as much in the dark as you."

"Suspected as much," Chambers said, a bit deflated. "Anyway, I needed to check. Thanks for your time." Standing and turning toward the door, Chambers turned back and said, "Still, Julian, I'd appreciate you keeping all this on the QT, even from Martha. Until I get it sorted out, I don't want to tip off Caleb Rimes that I'm looking into him."

"Good point, Detective. Not a man to be trifled with." Smiling, he continued, "Sorry for ending that sentence with a preposition, but I don't suspect Mr. Rimes would care."

Adding his own smile, Chambers said, "No, Julian, I don't suppose he would. But I shan't tell."

Chapter 35

Julian Pratt called Detective Chambers later in the day to report what he expected to report—there was no reference to Caleb Rimes in his notes. By that time, Chambers had reviewed his own notes for a second time and to the same effect. The only thing he could now think of was to visit with Walter Simpson's daughter, Dorothy, who still lived in Rascal Harbor. He called and arranged to meet her the next morning at 9:00 AM.

As he made his way to Dorothy Simpson's home, Chambers recalled how many times he had driven this road in hopes of finding a clue as to the death of Walter Simpson. He knew he ought to be satisfied with the result. After all, how could Galen Knight be anything but responsible for the crime? The blood, DNA, finger, and footprint evidence all led to a single conclusion—Galen Knight and only Galen Knight was responsible for Simpson's murder.

And yet he had questions. What was Simpson's connection to Knight and what possible motivation might the latter have had to commit the egregious crime? How did Knight get to the Simpson house? Knight was found walking to town in blood-soaked clothing. Did he walk the three miles out to Simpson's house and then expect to walk back unnoticed? The prosecutor, Lee Turcotte, had handled these questions easily when Julian Pratt raised them in the hopeless defense of his client. Still, they nagged.

Pulling into the Simpson driveway and walking to the side door, Chambers was greeted by a plain-faced young woman in a kind of uniform.

"You Detective Chambers?" she asked before Chambers could introduce himself. "I'm Hildy Wheeler, I help take care of Miss Simpson and her house couple days a week."

"Nice to meet you, Hildy. Yes, I'm Detective Chambers from the Rascal Harbor police," Chambers said, showing his badge. "I have an appointment to meet with Ms. Simpson."

"Ayuh, come on in. Dottie's expectin' you," Wheeler said. She led Chambers into the kitchen where Dorothy Simpson, frailer and more drawn than Chambers remembered, was sitting in her wheelchair drawn up to the kitchen table.

They greeted each other courteously. When she realized that Dorothy Simpson was going to be okay, Hildy Wheeler excused herself to clean another part of the house.

"Sorry to intrude Ms. Simpson," Chambers began.

"Please, Detective, have you forgotten? You can call me Dottie. Everybody does. And don't apologize for intruding. Other than Hildy and my kids, I hardly see anyone so it's nice to have company."

"Even so, Dottie, I can't imagine me being here brings you any comfort. I would guess that it offers only bad memories."

"What's done is done, Detective Chambers," Simpson said in a resigned voice. After a pause, she asked, "So what brings you out to my kitchen?"

"Two things. The first is, have you had any other ideas about why Galen Knight would have attacked your father?"

Staring directly at him, Simpson said, "No, can't say that I have. It's all a certain mystery to me."

"It's just that it's so curious. I mean we sometimes have trouble convicting murderers, but I've never had a case where we can't find any connection between the victim and the assailant."

"Wish I could help you. If only there was something I could tell you."

"Well, if you think of anything. Please do give me a call."

"I will indeed. But you said there were two reasons you wanted to talk with me. What is the second?"

"Right. Well, I wonder if you know a fellow named Caleb Rimes?"

"Caleb Rimes, no, I don't think I know anyone by that name."

"Are you sure? You never heard your father talk about anybody by that name?"

"I'm quite sure. That name means nothing to me," Simpson said calmly. "Why are you asking?"

"Just trying to clean up some loose ends."

"Well, good luck with your loose ends."

Chambers smiled and said, "I might need it." Then, standing, he took his leave. "Thanks for your time."

On the drive back to the Harbor, Chambers said to himself, "Hmmm. Just as incurious as ever." He now remembered wondering about this characteristic the first time he'd met Dorothy Simpson. Here she and her children had come across a bloodbath in her living room. Her father had been stabbed to death and yet she had shown a curious lack of curiosity. Her children had asked a hundred questions, but Chambers couldn't remember Dorothy asking any. At the time, he had put it down to stress and the fact that, while horrific situations caused some people to blather on, others became almost mum. That Simpson's seeming indifference continued suggested to Chambers that it really must be a personality quirk.

CHAPTER 36

Pulling into the station parking lot, Chambers could not shake a growing agitation. "Jesus Christ. This case is over! What the hell is wrong with me?" He now realized that what he had called a "loose end"—Caleb Rimes's relationship with Galen Knight—was starting to feel like a suffocating blanket.

With no other leads to pursue, Chambers wondered if his only option now was to stage his own confrontation with Caleb Rimes. After all, what was there to lose? No one else seemed to know anything about a bond between Rimes and Knight so what would it hurt to take on Rimes directly? Chambers had too much time and energy invested to walk away now.

Still, the thought of facing Rimes gave Chambers no good feeling. Rimes was not a big man, but he carried himself in a way that suggested a powerful build and experience using it to his advantage. Chambers was not afraid of a physical clash. Rimes would not be an easy man to put down, but Chambers was well schooled in ways to do so. That said, he always opted for negotiation over combat and that approach nearly always worked. He wasn't so sure it would this time.

Rimes was likely working now, so Chambers processed paperwork, the bane of every cop's existence, until late afternoon. Knowing something of Rimes's routines from Officer Kalin, Chambers drove over to Henry's Barbershop in hopes of catching Kalin there before he started drinking at Jimbo's.

Chambers was in luck. He saw Rimes's old pickup parked in front of Henry's, so he called in to the station and arranged for Officer Long to meet him. No sense taking any chances with this guy, Chambers thought to himself.

Artie Long had been patrolling on the other side of town so it took him ten minutes to arrive at the barbershop. Chambers could see Caleb Rimes and some of the other regulars talking and passing around a small flask. Officer Long pulled in beside Chambers and joined him in Chambers's car. They decided to wait until Rimes came out to confront him in hopes of avoiding a bigger scene inside.

Rimes obliged them fifteen minutes later. He didn't appear to be drunk, but he missed the bottom step and staggered a bit as his feet hit the ground. Chambers and Long waited until Rimes was near his pick-up to approach.

Chambers said, "Afternoon Mr. Rimes."

A hard look passed across Rimes's face. Perhaps aware that Chambers and Long might smell alcohol on his breath, a slight smile quickly appeared on Rimes's lips and he said, "Good afternoon, officers," with a forced formality. "How ya doin'?"

"We're fine Caleb. Just wanted to see if you could help me understand what happened out at the prison the other day."

"What're you talkin' about?" Rimes said, with an edge to his voice.

"You seemed to come on pretty strong, Caleb. A whole lot stronger than was called for. I'm just wondering why."

"Weren't nothin' to it, Chambers. You figured you could push me around and I showed ya you couldn't."

Not interested in continuing this dance, Chambers pushed. "Who were you visiting out there, Caleb?" he asked, with a bit of steel in his own voice.

"None of your fuckin' business."

"Well it is my business if you're out there visiting with the last person to commit murder in Rascal Harbor. Why are you meeting with Galen Knight, Caleb? What are you to him?"

"I told you, it's none of your fuckin' business what I do," Rimes said, his voice getting louder.

"What are you getting all upset about Caleb? It's just an innocent question. I'm curious is all."

"Fuck you and your fuck your curiosity, Chambers," Rimes said in full growl.

Switching topics in hopes of confusing Rimes, Chambers turned slightly toward Officer Long. He said calmly, "What you think, Officer, does it appear to you, as it does to me, that Mr. Rimes here has alcohol on his breath and is about to operate a motor vehicle while impaired?"

"I expect you're right about that, Detective Chambers," Long replied. "Soon as he gets in and turns the key, we can grab him."

"Yes, I believe you are correct, Officer Long." Chambers turned back to Rimes and said, "What do you think about that, Mr. Rimes? Are you intending to operate this vehicle while intoxicated? Shall we run a test on you right now to check? After all, you wouldn't want to be arrested if you could avoid it."

Fighting to maintain his cool, Rimes relaxed his shoulders, smiled, and said, "Well, thanks much for the offer, for lookin' out for me, officers. But I do believe I'll just walk over to Gary's. I got a question for him about my truck." With that, Rimes turned away from the officers and began walking toward Gary's Garage.

CHAPTER 37

Instead of going over to Gary's, Caleb Rimes walked to the Barlow House and sat down at the end of the bar.

The Barlow House was one of the few restaurants that stayed open year round. It was also one of the few places that had not been made over in the image of tourist chic. During the summer months, the restaurant menu catered more to the out-of-staters and the summer wait staff of college kids showed lots of tanned skin and bouncy good humor. In early May, however, the food menu turned toward the Fry-o-Later and the bar scene showed signs that more pedestrian food choices were popular.

Halfway through his third beer and still angry, Rimes looked up to see Rendall Kalin approaching him. With a seeming fake smile on his face, Kalin greeted Rimes with a too-friendly hello before asking to join him.

"Suit yourself," Rimes muttered.

"What's wrong?" Kalin asked innocently. Kalin knew that he could have trouble gauging people's moods, but Rimes typically offered no challenge.

"Your fuckin' friends is what's wrong. Who the fuck do they think they are?"

Kalin had been leaving the police station when Detective Chambers called in for Officer Long's assistance, so he suspected that they had confronted Rimes. Still, he pretended to not know the reason for Rimes's foul mood. "Don't know what you're talking about."

Rimes gave Kalin a quick summary of the encounter all the while glaring at him as though Kalin himself had been responsible.

Still pretending not to know the source of the problem, Kalin asked, "What was that about the prison? You mean the Maine State Prison?"

Looking hard at Kalin, Rimes said, "Don't bullshit me, Rendall, you know what fuckin' prison. I know you guys all talk, so don't tell me that that fuckin' Chambers didn't tell you I saw him upta Warren."

Trying and failing to maintain the pretense, Kalin said, "Well, geez, Caleb, no, Chambers didn't tell me anything about seeing you up at the prison." Hoping to gain an edge, Kalin said innocently, "What were you doing up at the prison? Know somebody up there?"

Having taken Kalin's measure, Rimes ignored these questions. "Chambers best understand not to fuck with me. Cause I will definitely fuck with him."

"Hey, hey, easy," Kalin said looking around. "Careful what you say. You don't want to be heard threatening the Detective."

"You listen to me, Rendall," Rimes slurred. "You listen to me. That fuckin' Chambers best stay away from me or I will cut his fuckin' heart out." Looking hard at Kalin, Rimes repeated in a slow, menacing tone, "I will cut his fuckin' heart out."

CHAPTER 38

As he finished filling up his truck at Gary's Garage late the next day, Caleb Rimes saw John McTavish coming out of Harbor Arts and Crafts. McTavish was laughing as he turned to say something else to the Brandon Majors, the store owner. The two chatted a bit more, then McTavish came down the steps to the sidewalk.

Though he would later claim that he didn't know why, Rimes left his pick-up at Gary's, crossed the street, and blocked McTavish's path to his car. Still thinking about his conversation with Majors, McTavish didn't see Rimes until the latter was right in front of him. In fact, McTavish was so startled, he thought he must have walked up on Rimes rather than the other way around.

"Whatcha got there, faggot," Rimes said in a low aggressive voice.

"What?" McTavish asked, still trying to figure out how and why Caleb Rimes was in front of him.

"I asked you what you had in that little pansy-ass bag, faggot," Rimes insisted.

"How is that any of your business?" McTavish said, looking down at Rimes. Rimes was five inches shorter than McTavish, but outweighed him by fifty pounds.

"I'm makin' it my fuckin' business," Rimes said, reaching for the bag that had three drawing pencils and a gum eraser.

"What in hell is wrong with you?" McTavish said, starting to get angry.

"Oh, so there's something wrong with me, is there, faggot?" Rimes said in a mocking tone. "At least I ain't no faggot. In fact, where's your little faggot friend, Jimmmmy?"

"I'm done with this," McTavish said determinedly and pushed past Rimes.

As he did, Rimes punched McTavish hard in the stomach doubling him over. Trying to grab a breath, McTavish bent down on his right knee and put his left hand down on the sidewalk. When he did, Rimes stomped down. "There, you fuck. Try paintin' with a busted hand. You're gonna need your little boyfriend to do it for you."

McTavish's anguished yelp brought Brandon Majors, Gary Park, and his daughter Louise running from their respective establishments. Realizing what he had done, Rimes ran across the street, pushed Gary and Louise out of the way, and jumped into his truck. Peeling his tires, Rimes shot out of the garage lot and headed out of town. As McTavish's friends rushed to help, a passerby dialed 911.

The pain of the two blows threw McTavish's stomach in a spasm and he vomited in the street. He took a minute more and then tried to stand up.

"Jesus, stay down, John," Gary said, panic in his voice. "Please, John, just stay down."

"Help's coming," Louise said, "Try not to move."

"Don't think that's going to be a problem," McTavish said, trying to grin, but grimacing instead.

"I saw it all, John," the elderly Majors said. "Rimes just ran over and attacked you!"

Gary asked, "Is that what happened? Me and Louise were talkin' and didn't know nothin' until you went down." Then looking more closely at McTavish's bloody hand, Caleb Rimes's boot print still visible. He said, "Christ, John, he broke your hand! Oh, Christ, is that your drawin' hand?"

Looking down as if he'd just become aware of the injury, McTavish stared at the rapidly swelling hand. Then, as if just discovering that he had another hand, McTavish held both up in front of him.

"Ah, no. No, Gary," McTavish said weakly. Then holding his right hand higher, he said, "No, this is my drawing hand….I think." Offering another fragile smile, McTavish's eyes rolled upward and he felt the lightheadedness he knew previewed a faint.

McTavish thought he'd lost no more than a minute or two, but when he opened his eyes, he saw his audience had multiplied. An EMT was taking a blood pressure cuff off his arm. His partner was putting large gauze pads, ice packs, and a lightly wrapped splint on McTavish's forearm and hand. Officer Rendall Kalin was looking on and looking a little pale himself. Kalin tried to ask what happened, but the EMTs and McTavish's friends shushed him.

"Jesus, Rendall, you can get the story later from all of us," Louise Park snapped. "Let the EMTs do their goddamn job."

Chastened, Kalin stepped back as the EMTs got McTavish to his feet and helped him into the ambulance. Trying to reassert his authority, Kalin pointed to his right and barked, "All right, all of you who witnessed this incident, stand over there so I can process you. The rest of you, go on home now. There's nothing else to see here." Resting his hand on his sidearm, Kalin watched the crowd dissipate under his steeled glare.

"Oh, for Christ's sakes, Rendall," Louise said. "Stop posing and do your damn job."

"That's enough, Louise," Kalin growled. "This is a crime scene and you will treat it like one."

"Aren't you the one who's supposed to treat it like a crime scene?" asked Louise. But then she caught her father's stern look and head shake. She quieted.

With the crowd gone, Kalin took statements from Louise, Gary, and Brandon then added that they might be called down to the station if further questions arose.

As they walked back to the garage, Louise said to her father, "Hope someone else takes over the case as that idiot's just as likely to arrest John as he is Caleb Rimes."

"I'd like to say you're wrong, girl, just because, well, you're not *always* right. Though I can't dispute you on that one."

134

CHAPTER 39

John McTavish was three hours in the emergency room of the
Rascal Harbor Hospital. A couple of x-rays confirmed that the
bones in his hand were broken.

At the end of a long explanation, the doctor concluded that broken
fingers would have been worse. McTavish thought the only way any of
this could be worse were if Rimes had crushed his right hand. The broken
bones were still in the right position, the doctor continued, so no surgery
was necessary. He cleaned McTavish's hand again, applied gauze pads, and
lightly wrapped the pads in place. Then he immobilized McTavish's wrist
and hand in a splint. To all of this, he wrapped ice packs to both side of
McTavish's hand, which now looked like a soft, white club. A sling completed the ensemble; an injection for the pain completed the visit.

"You'll want to keep your hand up. Don't let it hang down by your
side or the swelling will take longer to go down," the doctor said. Feeling a little light-headed again, McTavish simply nodded.

Gary Park arrived in the waiting room soon after McTavish was
admitted. Never a calm man, Park had paced the waiting room and the
corridors until a tough duty nurse had said, "Park it, Mr. Park, or I'll do
it for you!" Gary obeyed, but took a seat out of her view, where he could
stand up and walk a tight circle when the need arose.

Before Park drove a droopy McTavish back to his cottage, he called
Louise who drove over with Noah in McTavish's car. Once McTavish

was off to the hospital, Louise called Noah at Lane's Wharf, where he worked as a fry cook, and reported what had happened. They arranged for her to pick him up as soon as McTavish was released from the hospital.

The three of them got McTavish into the cottage and settled on the couch. Louise brought in the extra powerful ibuprofen the doctor had prescribed and a glass of water. Gary brought over three fingers of Bushmills for each of them.

Taking a timid sip, Louise wanted to know, "Jesus, how can you drink this stuff, John?"

The drama and the trauma of the day were catching up with McTavish and his normally taciturn approach to conversation was relaxing. "Nectar of the gods," he said drowsily, holding up his glass. "But then isn't that a tautology? Isn't nectar defined as the drink of the gods? So to say 'nectar of the gods' is really to say 'nectar of the gods, of the gods.'" He laughed and spilled a bit of his drink.

"I don't know about nectar," Louise said, setting her drink down on a side table. "But those gods either had strong stomachs or not much else to drink."

Gary said, "Agreed, daughter. It ain't no Budweiser." Rather than put his drink aside, however, Gary drained it.

"Guess the taste must run in the gene pool. I like it," Noah said.

"Think you'll be okay for a few hours, Professker?" Gary asked. "I'll go close up the shop, then stop by and check on you."

"No need, good friend," McTavish mumbled, the drink clearly going to his empty stomach and his woozy head. "I'm fit as a fiddle. And Noah is my fiddle player."

Noah shook his head. "Must have been a pretty potent shot they gave Dad at the hospital. He never talks this much, or this goofy."

"He probably won't be awake all that much longer. So let's get him stretched out on the couch," Gary said.

By this point, McTavish was nearly out and was even less helpful than he would have been had he been completely asleep. It took Gary,

Louise, and Noah several minutes to wrestle McTavish into a comfortable position and get his boots off, and then settle a light blanket over him.

Pausing at the door, Gary looked back at his friend. Shaking his head, he said, "Can't imagine what got into Caleb to do all that to a peaceable fella like John McTavish."

Louise said, "Asshole is what got into Caleb Rimes. And it's never going to let him loose." Gary and Noah smiled. Louise pecked Noah on the cheek, Gary shook his hand, and they left with Gary reminding Noah that he'd be back to check on McTavish after he closed his shop.

With Gary and Louise gone, Noah sat in an easy chair, and looked over at his father. "For Christ's sakes, Dad," he said to the sleeping man. "What kind of mess are you mixed up in?"

CHAPTER 40

At his wife Ruby's insistence, Gary Park ended up spending the night at McTavish's cottage. He'd intended to pick up Louise after closing his garage and leave McTavish to slumber

When he got back to the garage, however, the phone was ringing and Ruby was off her nut. Geneva Baxter, the worst of the town gossips, had told Ruby that Caleb Rimes had shattered John McTavish's leg and punched Gary in the nose. Both were at the hospital, Geneva said gravely, but likely only one would ever return.

Ruby knew that Geneva got every other fact right, still she couldn't be sure which were which. Cell phones mystified Ruby so she gave no thought to calling her daughter for an update. Instead she kept calling the garage, getting no response, and drinking more Manischewitz. By the time Gary arrived at the garage and picked up the phone, Ruby's normally tortured syntax had grown worse.

"Oh, my Jesus Lord Christ, that is Gary? Really indeed is you who I'm bein' talkin' wit? Say sometin' out loud, Gary, if you can talk through your mouth. Please, Jesus, tell me every one of you is okie dokie!"

After confirming that he was on the line, Gary knew that he would gain no purchase in this conversation until Ruby wound down, so he held the phone away from his ear and listened for a break. Once it occurred, Gary gave his own rapid-fire account of the happenings on the street and the aftermath, including the fact that Noah was home with his father. Ruby's unacknowledged deafness meant that she heard only a fraction of what Gary had to say. Still, she heard enough to decide that Gary needed to spend the with night watching over McTavish. Knowing the futility of arguing, Gary agreed, drove home to pick up a few sundries, and went back to McTavish's cottage.

By the time Noah and his father awoke the next morning, Gary had gone off to work. He left a note saying that he hoped McTavish was okay and to let him know if either of them needed anything. He also indicated that McTavish was to drop by the police station at his earliest convenience to file a report on the incident with Caleb Rimes.

Sharing a car with Noah mostly worked out. Typically, McTavish dropped Noah off at Lane's, but if he planned to work at home or wanted to walk to town, then Noah took the car for the day. Today, Noah would drop McTavish off at the police station and then his father would walk home.

"Are you sure you're going to be okay to walk, Dad?" Noah asked.

"Quite sure. And if I'm not I'll see if one of the police folks might drive me home."

As soon as he made this remark, McTavish heard Maggie said, "For Christ's sake, John, you don't need to be so damn self-sufficient all the time. Let Noah help you. He can't feel connected to you if you keep pushing him away."

McTavish suspected she was right. But then he'd assured Noah that he was fine and he didn't want his son to now start worrying about him. He wasn't sure, but he thought he saw Maggie shake her head.

Not sure he liked the plan, Noah nevertheless drove to the police station and left his father with a wave and a promise to call him if any need arose.

CHAPTER 41

Detective Chambers was finishing a conversation with Sergeant Levesque when John McTavish walked into the police station.

Detective Chambers met him. "Ah, Mr. McTavish, if you've come in to make a report, come on into my office and I'll take your statement." After exchanging pleasantries, Chambers asked how McTavish was doing.

"I'm fine, Detective. I'm just thankful it wasn't my drawing hand."

"Me too. Kalin's report didn't say, so I wasn't sure which hand was injured." Pausing a beat, he continued. "You won't have to worry about Rimes for a while. I'm not sure he's going to make bail."

This news should have proved salutary, yet McTavish's stomach rolled as the entire confrontation flew across his mind. Not wanting to reveal this hard reaction, McTavish simply nodded his head.

"So, can you tell me what happened?"

McTavish took a moment, then said, "Well, I suppose it will sound funny, but it's actually hard to recall with any clarity. I remember talking with Brandon at the Arts and Crafts and the next thing I knew Caleb Rimes was directly in front me and I was clutching my stomach where he hit me. It's been a long time since I've been punched in the gut and I guess I didn't handle it all that well. I went down on a hand and a knee. Apparently that was too inviting a target because the next thing

I recall was a blinding pain in my hand. I think I threw up after that."

"In a few minutes, I'll ask you to write all that down in a formal complaint. But I've got a few questions first. Some of them might help jog your memory."

"Okay," McTavish said.

"Did Rimes say anything to you before he hit you?"

"I, uh, remember him talking to me, but I honestly couldn't tell you what he said…well, except that he kept calling me a faggot or a faggot lover, something like that. He seemed infuriated, but I couldn't figure out why. Still can't"

"Other than the punch and foot stomp, did he touch you in any other way?"

"Hmmm. I don't think so. He was awfully close to me, but I don't think he touched me other than those two blows. They were quite enough, though."

Nodding, Chambers said, "I bet they were. Have you had any interaction with Rimes before the incident yesterday?"

"Ah, yeah, actually I did," McTavish said, reaching back to recall the incident at Lydia's. "Same kind of thing. I was sitting at the counter in Lydia's when Rimes came at me hard for associating with Jimmy Park and Bradley Little and then called me a faggot. I was too stunned to move that time, too. Trudy had to bring her broom to my rescue."

"Oh, right, I heard about that one. Trudy wields a mean broom when she gets her back up." Both men smiled at that thought. Then Chambers continued, "Just seems odd that Rimes would single you out. You've not had a beef with him in the past?"

"Not that I know of. But I've heard that he has real trouble with gay folks."

"I've heard the same. But he seems like he's coming unglued these last few days."

"What do you mean? Has he attacked other people?

"Well, in a manner of speaking." Chambers hesitated to tell McTavish about the prison parking lot confrontation, but he'd come to respect McTavish's discretion and advice. "Appears Rimes is upset with me, too."

"Do *you* know why?"

"Not really," Chambers said. "It started when I saw him in the parking lot of the Maine State Prison. His anger came out of nowhere and just seemed over the top."

"What was he doing there?"

"That was my question and asking it seemed to set him off. Later I found out that he's been visiting with Galen Knight."

"The fellow who murdered the old guy?" McTavish asked. "A couple of years ago, right?"

"Yeah, we got Knight convicted on a mountain of evidence, but the man never said a single word from the time he was arrested until he went to jail. What I can't figure is why Rimes is up visiting him. No one I've talked to knows of any connection between them."

"Huh. Well, as I said, I've got no idea why he might be upset with me. Just hope he gets over it soon."

"You and me both," Chambers said.

Five minutes after McTavish left the station, Rendall Kalin knocked on Chambers's office door.

Invited in, Kalin said, "Figured you probably should hear a report on my reconnaissance with that scoundrel Caleb Rimes—"

"Your what?" Chambers said, interrupting. "I thought I told you to stay away from him."

"Well, yes, right, you did…and I did. But, well, the other night I was at the Barlow House, you know, on my own time. And well, I saw the suspect sitting there, and he saw me, and so I just followed my police instinct and made contact with him. I mean, I already knew that the jig was up with him when you and Artie met with him over at Henry's. So…"

"Okay, okay, Kalin," Chambers said testily. "Just get it on with it. What did you learn that we don't already know?"

"Well, can't say that my investigation really paid off," Kalin said.

Chambers rubbed his forehead. "Well, but the thing I thought you ought to know. Is that it was like Caleb was threatening you."

Looking up, Chambers asked, "What do you mean he was threatening me?"

"Well that's what it seemed like, Detective."

"*What* it did it seem like?" Chambers asked in an exasperated tone.

"He said, well, he said, if you didn't back off him he was gonna 'cut your fuckin' heart out,'" Kalin said, making air quotes around the last phrase. "'Scuse my language."

"Really? Do you think he meant it?"

"I honestly couldn't tell you, Detective, but it sure sounded like he did. And, well, it was his face. You know, I've seen Caleb mad before, but this was something else. There's something else behind that anger. And the way he said, 'I'm gonna cut his fuckin' heart out,' well, it just kinda shocked me."

Sitting back in his chair, Chambers considered Kalin's report. "Well, he won't be doing any heart cutting any time soon. But thanks for alerting me to the possibility."

Kalin smiled, saluted, and left Chambers's office. "Maybe that boy does have some potential as a cop," Chambers said to himself. "Then again…"

CHAPTER 42

Lydia's Diner lit up with the news about the Rimes/McTavish incident, though what to call it—fight, ambush, mauling, dispute, struggle, brawl, argument, or scrap—proved challenging. The uncontested facts were in short supply; the interpretations grew like weeds.

Most everyone knew that the incident involved variations on "that asshole" Caleb Rimes and that "new art fella" John McTavish. Predictably, some thought Gary Park had landed a few blows; a couple others thought that it was Louise who finally subdued Rimes; still others heard that Brandon Majors had gotten in the middle. Given Brandon's advanced age and prissy disposition, this last rumor died fast. Most knew or assumed that Caleb Rimes caused the fracas, but a few wondered if the "new guy" might have provoked him somehow.

Such were the broad outlines of the talk at tables across Lydia's Diner that morning. The back tables were more animated, but the buzz was almost as high at the counter and the front tables.

Settled into their coffees, the men at the left-side back table could not get over the fact that Rimes was now facing an assault charge. Bill Candlewith said, "I mean, it ain't right that Caleb knocked down that artist fella, but someone told me he took a swipe at Artie, too. That's bad news."

"Not sure it's true that he went after Artie, but Caleb's been a dose of bad news for a while now," Vance Edwards said.

Rob Pownall agreed. "Folks have given him a pretty wide berth, but he's taking all that up and some more. You can't just go around attacking people on the street."

"Don't suppose he was aggravated somehow, do ya?" asked Ray Manley. As the group pondered this possibility, Ray added, "Not sayin' what he did was right, but the guy—ain't he a professor or somethin'?—mighta said something that just caught Caleb wrong."

"You're suggesting there could be a mitigating circumstance?" Rob asked.

"Who's migratin'?" asked Slow Johnston. "Ain't it a little early for the snowbirds ta be comin' upta the Harbor again?"

"For Christ's sake, Slow, shake the shit out of your ears. We aren't talking about anybody 'migrating,'" said Vance. "Especially not the summer folks." Slow smiled and turned his good ear to the conversation.

Pointing over to the men's table, Minerva Williams said to her friends, "I see the brain trust has assembled."

The two tables were separated by a short hallway so listening in on each other's conversations could prove challenging. Challenging, but not impossible. Depending on the volume of the voices and the positioning of those with better hearing, swaths of talk could be overheard, relayed to tablemates, and then remarked upon. The ladies often depended on Minerva's bat-like ears to keep tabs on the men's table and then to provide a lively commentary. Other than Rob Pownall, all the men were hard of hearing, with Slow Johnston being the worst. Rob fancied himself a gentleman, though so he rarely took the ladies' bait.

"Brain bust, you mean?" June Pickering said, with a laugh.

"Lord, don't say the word 'bust' around Minerva," Geraldine Smythe said dryly. "That'll set her to talking about Robertay Harding's bosom!"

"Speaking of bosoms…" Minerva said loudly enough for even Slow to hear.

"What was that?" Bill asked, leaning back in his chair so that he could peer around the end of the hallway. "Whatja say, Minerva?"

"I said you fellas are nothing but a buncha boobies over there if you think that Caleb Rimes needed any reason to jump somebody," Minerva scoffed. "The man's a right lunatic."

Murmurs of agreement arose around the women's table. The men's table went silent as they weren't sure if they had just been insulted or agreed with.

Vance said, "Well, anyway I heard Caleb's locked up for now and there's no guarantee a judge will let him out."

"The man's got his qualities, but he's got the fuse of a gnat," Ray said.

The men nodded sagely at this comment; the ladies all shook their heads as they mouthed the phrase "the fuse of a gnat?" and smiled.

CHAPTER 43

As McTavish walked down the driveway to his cottage, he saw Jimmy Park sitting on the trunk of his car.

"I didn't think you'd be too far away."

"I'll have you know that I've been to town and back today, Mr. Park," McTavish said brightly though, truth be told, his hand was throbbing and he felt fatigued.

"Bet you told Noah that you didn't need him carting you around all day. You are one stubborn fellow, John McTavish."

"You're not the first to tell me that," McTavish grumbled. "But come in anyway."

Inside, McTavish fixed a pot of coffee and, when it was done, he and Jimmy sat in the two kitchen rockers.

"What are you up to?" McTavish asked.

"Oh no, don't try to deflect me. I'm here on a mission to find out what *you've* been up to and why you're getting my father and sister tangled up in your brawling."

McTavish started to protest, but Jimmy held up his hand to head him off. "Just teasing, professor," he said laughing. "So, what happened?"

So for the second time that morning, McTavish described the details of the scuffle with Caleb Rimes. When he finished, Jimmy said, "Christ, you were lucky that he got your left hand."

"Maybe, but I guess I'd have felt luckier if I'd gotten in my car five minutes before he got there."

"I suppose you've got a point there," Jimmy said with a smile. "I'll tell you one thing though, that Caleb Rimes had better avoid my mother. She said she was 'over the sun mad' about him attacking you and she was going to give him 'a piece of her brain' when she next sees him."

"Best to have Ruby as a friend than a foe."

"Well, you've got real friends in the Park family. Anything you need, you only have to ask, though I expect that's harder for you to do than it is most folks."

Nodding to Jimmy, McTavish smiled to himself. He suspected Maggie was smiling too, though probably more at Jimmy's last comment than his first.

Lost in this moment, McTavish realized that Jimmy was standing beside him holding the coffee pot out to refill his cup.

"Where were you, John? Seemed like you just went inside yourself there for a couple of minutes."

"Just thinking," McTavish said. Then to change the subject, he said, "I was thinking about my trip up north. Come see the pictures I took."

McTavish got to his feet, found his laptop, and showed Jimmy the pictures he had taken at the tree farm outside of Pinkham. As he did, he talked through his struggle to determine what to focus on—what to put in the foreground and what to let lie in the background.

"Hmmm. In these shots, you can see the forest *and* the trees, but that doesn't make for the most interesting composition, does it?" Jimmy said.

"Not really," McTavish admitted. He then described the walk he took around Pinkham and the patch of crocus he saw coming up amidst the retreating snow piles. "It took me a while to figure out what I was seeing, but those crocus kind of jumped out at me and said, 'Here's your figure, idiot!'"

McTavish then went on to show Jimmy the pictures he took of the budding flowers and trees at the Brock farm and the other signs of life he saw along the drive back to Rascal Harbor.

"So not only have you got some interesting compositions developing, but you're working on a kind of metaphor of 'life amongst decay' or something like that. That's pretty cool."

"Probably isn't all that original, but it's interesting to me and I've been doing some work with it." He pulled out some of his sketches.

"Nice. I can see where you're going." Pausing to look back through the sketches again, Jimmy added, "Might be interesting to work some color into these."

"Might be, James…just might be."

"Well, glad Caleb Rimes stepped on your non-drawing hand… excuse me, your non-painting hand then."

McTavish smiled, then frowned.

"What just happened, John? Your face changed in an instant."

"I don't really know. I just flashed to a thing that happened while I was up in Myron." McTavish said, then described the confrontation with the woman in the trailer.

"Knight? Did you say the name on the mailbox was Knight?"

"Yeah, I thought of the connection with that local killer, though I'll admit that it took me a while."

"Jeez, I wonder if they could be related."

"It's possible. When I was in Pinkham, the folks I had dinner with told me about a family of Knights that got broken up because they lost their farm."

"I almost remember reading something about Galen Knight being adopted or raised or something by a woman in the Harbor," Jimmy said.

"I don't know anything about that. It all happened before I got to town."

"Don't imagine that it means all that much. They got the guy dead to rights."

"So I've heard. Still, if I remember, I might say something about it to Detective Chambers."

"Why?" Jimmy asked.

McTavish explained Chambers's discovery of a connection between Galen Knight and Caleb Rimes and Rimes's hostile behavior toward him.

"I didn't think Caleb Rimes needed a reason to be hostile," Jimmy sighed.

Chapter 44

Caleb Rimes was charged with assault, a Class D crime that carried a sentence of up to a year in jail and a fine of up two thousand dollars. The judge scolded Rimes and instructed him to stay away from his victim, but agreed to let him out on bail.

Rimes might have wished he had stayed in jail. After shaking hands with his lawyer, he was walking toward his pickup when Ruby Park intercepted him.

Ruby was a short woman of middle age and ample girth. Her most notable features, however, were her hair and her speech. Ruby managed her androgenic alopecia through trips to Charlotte's Hair and the miracle of hair extensions. Unfortunately, Charlotte's failing eyesight and zest for color sometimes conspired to send Ruby forth with bizarre hairdos. On the run up to Christmas the previous fall, Charlotte had woven red and silver extensions into the front of Ruby's hair and curled them in the fashion of candy canes. Ruby loved the look.

She also loved to talk. Her thick French accent made her words hard to understand, her partial deafness made her talk louder than necessary, and her malapropisms made her intentions challenging to decipher. And she talked very fast. In short, a conversation with Ruby could almost be considered an assault in and of itself. Still, her sweet temperament and her sunny disposition charmed all who met her.

Those qualities were not in evidence on this day, and Caleb Rimes was anything but charmed by the angry woman who stood in front of him.

"You is a low-down skunk of a human man," Ruby said, eyes ablaze. "Who you tink you is? You cannot be going around on the town hitting and hitting people, especially on their hand. What is a matter with your brain? Did you fall on your own head and then get them crazy thoughts people get? That man never done not one ting to you, Caleb Rimes, not one ting. And you, you…"

Ruby stopped there as this torrent had come out all in one breath and the lack of oxygen dizzied her. Rimes, stunned by this visual and auditory whirlwind, stood stock still.

Re-oxygenated, Ruby continue. "If I do ever hear about you gettin' around that man, that John McTavish, I'm gonna be very angry mad and you and me is going to have some trouble, some very big, ugly trouble. Are you hearin' my words, Caleb Rimes? Are you hearin' my words?"

"Hell, Ruby, they're hearin' your words upta Herrington," Rimes said. Noticing that Ruby's rant was drawing attention, he lowered his voice and said, "I ain't got no beef with you and I'm done with that McTavish. So go on now and leave me be." Rimes turned to his truck and opened the driver's door, but Ruby was not finished.

"De god, de bery god up there ta heaven," Ruby said, pointing skyward. "He ain't gonna be too much happy about you and your waya actin'. So get your ass together, Caleb Rimes, or some bad tings, very bad tings, they gonna come down on your way!"

Rimes nodded, got in his truck, and pulled away with a still-irate Ruby Park in his rear-view mirror. He had resisted the urge to punch the woman. Galen would be happy with that news.

News of Ruby's takedown of Caleb Rimes spread quickly across the Rascal Harbor gossipnet. Cell phone calls, tweets and retweets, instant messages, and Facebook postings carried the stories…as any such event generates more than one account. When Trudy heard, her first thought was, Jesus, *that* will wind up the back tables tomorrow! Her second was, best keep my broom ready in case Caleb comes in.

The news hadn't reached Gary and Louise Park and the two old-timers, Alan Tuttle and Clint Evans, who kept vigil in Gary's lobby, until Bill Candlewith limped in.

Gary, or "Gari" as his uniform name tag said, another result of Ruby's problem with the English language and her increasing deafness, was finishing a transmission job when Bill arrived.

Bill said, "Well, Gary, guess you ain't heard yet, but you will soon. By gorry, you'll be hearing about it soon, you will, Gary."

"We will if you get to it," Clint said. "Stop windin' up and let go a the pitch!"

"I will, I will," Bill said testily. "Didn't wanna step on your tongues if you'd already heard."

"Heard what, Bill?" Gary asked, trying to inject some calm before the old boys yakked themselves to death.

"Well, Ruby a'course," Bill said, as though those three words explained everything.

"'Ruby a'course' what," Gary said, his calm fading.

"Ruby and Caleb is what I'm talkin' about."

Holding up his hand to forestall Clint and Alan jumping at Bill, Gary said, "Let's hear the whole thing, Bill, stem to stern."

Because he'd actually witnessed the event, Bill's version matched most of the relevant actions far better than some of the accounts that would come later. Still, Bill's own deafness meant that he got only snatches of the exchange. This deficit proved no particular challenge, however, as Bill filled in any memory lapses with his own versions.

"Well, okay, Jesus, give a man a minute," Bill said, winding up again. Realizing that any word uttered now would set Bill back another couple of minutes, the group of men, joined now by Louise, waited expectantly.

"Well, so here I am walking down the street, well, not the street exactly, you know, I was on the sidewalk," Bill explained to his increasingly exasperated audience. "When all of sudden my eye spies Caleb Rimes and another guy, musta probably been his lawyer, a'comin' out of the courthouse and shakin' hands. And so I figure Caleb musta got out on bail, cause, y'know, he and the guy, did I say the guy musta been a lawyer, cause he was all dressed in a suit, well, they was both smilin' so's I says to myself, 'Hmmm, I bet Caleb just got out on bail.'"

Louise, not able to hold back, pushed. "Okay, Bill, we got it. When does Mum make an appearance?"

"I was just gettin' ta that part, young lady….So then I sees Ruby come chargin' down on Caleb like a runaway tug. Her hair's aflyin' and she's yellin' at him, callin' him every name in the book." Stopping here to squeeze out the drama, Bill looked around the group before continuing. "She called him a shit-heel skunk and a tinker's dam and a brainless fool. Then she got really mad and told him every little thing she was gonna do to him if he messed with that artist fella anymore."

Satisfied that this account had sufficiently stirred the group, Bill smiled and waited for an onslaught of questions that would allow him to keep the stage. Instead, Gary said, "Oh, okay, Bill. Thanks for the update." Louise stared at Bill for half a minute before turning back to the oil change she was finishing. Even Clint and Alan seemed underwhelmed as they resumed their conversation about the Red Sox's early season woes. Deflated that his scoop failed to incite more interest, Bill pivoted on his good leg and stomped out. Over his shoulder, he offered, "Well, guess no good turn goes underappreciated." The group in the garage looked at one another to see if anyone could made sense of the comment. Clearly no one did so they all shrugged and went back to it.

The Police Blotter in the *Rascal Harbor Gazette* carried a short blurb on Caleb Rimes's arrest:

Caleb Rimes, 34, was arrested on a charge of assault against

John McTavish on Tuesday last. The altercation occurred outside Harbor Arts and Crafts. Witness statements were taken at the time. Rimes was released on bail.

The Blotter story writer had more fun with the next item:

Rascal Harbor Officer Arthur Long offered assistance to Carlton Jeffers, 76, in retrieving his partial plate from under Bertha Betts's car. "I gave off a wicked sneeze and out popped me teeth," Jeffers said. "Thanks to Artie, they's back where they belong."

CHAPTER 45

Detective Dick Chambers walked into the office of the *Rascal Harbor Gazette* hoping to break the logjam in his head. The curious connection between Caleb Rimes and Galen Knight refused to settle down.

Chambers's plan today was to talk with Nellie Hildreth and her reporter Sarah McAdam. Both attended Galen Knight's trial and Chambers hoped to get copies of the *Gazette* stories and to see if either picked up anything that did not get reported.

After greeting their visitor, Nellie and Sarah led Chambers into the staff break room to chat.

"So let me get right to it," Chambers said. "Do either of you know of any connection between Caleb Rimes and Galen Knight?"

"Caleb and the Knight fellow?" Nellie asked. "Why do you want to know about those two?"

"I expect it will end up just satisfying a curiosity, but I discovered that Caleb has been visiting Galen Knight up at the prison a bunch of times and I'd like to know why."

Nellie said, "Huh. Don't recall seeing or hearing about them chumming together, have you, Sarah?"

The reporter shook her head. "I do remember seeing Caleb at the trial, but then a lot of folks attended. The reason Caleb stuck out is that he was one of the people I'd have expected to be working instead of showing up for a murder trial. Most everyone else is retired and was, I'd guess, looking for some entertainment."

Chambers said, "Hmm. You're right about Caleb. I can't say that I noticed if he was there every day, but I did see him at least once."

"Maybe it's as simple as one asshole needing to talk to another one," Nellie said. As Chambers and McAdams grinned, Nellie continued. "Caleb's a right asshole and on that point, there's a wide consensus. Galen Knight's kind of a mystery. He spent some time here in high school, graduated I think, but he's been gone a long time. He shows up again and a couple months later he's murdering a guy. He might not be an asshole to the core like Caleb is, but stabbing a guy in the heart is asshole-enough behavior."

"I can't disagree with you there," Chambers said.

"The other weird thing is that we couldn't find any connection between Galen Knight and the victim, Walter Simpson," McAdams said. "The randomness of the whole thing coupled with the viciousness of the act, well, it just doesn't add up."

"Agreed. Julian Pratt actually thinks Knight is innocent," said Chambers.

"Really?" Nellie asked. "Julian's a good lawyer, but I didn't suspect he believed any of the folks he represents are innocent."

The three pondered this idea for a minute, then Nellie said, "Well, I can't think of any way to tug the string between Caleb and Galen Knight. I heard you tried and got your head handed to you. So what if I tried to push on the Galen Knight-Walter Simpson thing. Simpson was from up in The County as I recall. I know a couple of the editors of newspapers up there. Maybe they know something."

"Guess it can't hurt," Chambers said.

"I know that you wanted to go up and investigate Simpson at the time and that Chief Miles shut you down," Nellie said.

"How did you…?" Chambers asked. Nellie held up her hand.

"I'm a newspaper gal from way back, you dope! I've got sources you can't even imagine," Nellie said with a cackle. "And I know what a turd Chief Lawton Miles is and will always be. He wouldn't let you go because he thought the case was airtight and he figured you might charge the department for an order of fries with your hamburger while you were up there. The cheap bastard." Nellie took a breath and continued. "So let me see if I can't scare up something from the guys up there."

"Thanks, Nellie," Chambers said. He didn't really expect to gain any ground, but he appreciated the offer. "You get anything and I'll buy you a burger, fries, and coleslaw at Lydia's."

"You'll buy me a lobsta roll, mista man!" Nellie grinned. "I'll eat half and bring the rest back to Sarah."

"Fair enough." Chambers smiled. Not sure why, he left the office thinking that this visit might end up being both the most expensive and the most productive so far.

CHAPTER 46

s they prepared the evening meal at his apartment, Dick Chambers described his meeting with Nellie Hildreth and Sarah McAdams to Toni Ludlow.

Chambers and Ludlow had been an "item" for six months. They met during the investigation into the theft of the Homer painting. Ludlow was a member of the Rascal Harbor Art Colony board, which had sponsored the reception unveiling the newly discovered art work. Because of that affiliation, they had agreed to keep their budding relationship quiet. "Quiet" isn't a typical condition in small towns and so word was out after their first date.

Even the word "date" stuck in Chambers's throat. Divorced now for ten years from his Florida-based wife, Chambers felt a little too old to have a "girlfriend." And yet, all the language and angst of teenage relationships defined his new situation. Ludlow felt some of the same thing, so they generally referred to one another as "my friend."

The language awkwardness aside, Chambers and Ludlow were a matched set. Both were tall and rangy with faces more interesting than attractive. They took their work seriously, had no illusions about the fairness of life, and had seen things they preferred to forget. Yet, they also laughed at the silly and ironic things they and others did. They enjoyed silence as much as talk. And they found themselves telling each other things they expected to take to their graves.

"We're as comfortable together as a pair of old horses," Chambers had remarked three months into the relationship. Imagining this, but not imagining saying it out loud, Chambers was shocked when he did. And was equally shocked when Ludlow, after a moment's pause, laughed.

"You sweet talker," she said, as Chambers's face colored. "An old horse am I? At least you didn't call me a nag!"

"I fear that I've dug myself a hole and the smartest thing might be to just jump in and fill it back up," Chambers said, trying and failing to smile.

"Well, Dick, if a couple old horses are gonna pull together, best they do so honestly," Ludlow said with a genuine smile. And at that point, Chambers knew he was a goner in the love department.

So they continued to build a life together. They kept separate bank accounts and residences, but they found more and more reasons to keep company at the dinner table, in front of the TV, and in bed.

Both were good listeners, practiced in the art of attending to the other's story without interruption. Once completed, though, every story took on deeper dimensions as question followed answer followed question. The story of Chambers's visit to the *Gazette* fit the pattern.

"So, what do you think the chances are that Nellie can find something useful in The County?" Ludlow asked.

"Fifty-fifty is probably optimistic, but given where I am now, those are looking like good odds."

"I don't know her all that well, but she strikes me as a tough old gal. Not one that I'd like to have tailing me. In fact, I was thinking the other day that I hope she dies before I do as I shudder to think what the obituary she would write. Might be something like: 'Old horse Toni Ludlow, aged ninety-nine, went on to a finer pasture last Tuesday....'"

"Jesus, I'd hoped you might have forgotten about that slip of the brain."

Ludlow laughed, "Not likely, my old stallion. Hmm, maybe I ought to tell Nellie that story just in case you pass away before she's done writing the paper's obits." They both smiled, sort of, at the idea of what Nellie might conjure up.

"Well, the old girl does keep things interesting. And of course she's given a new meaning to the term 'o-bitch-uary writer'!" Ludlow said.

After dinner, Chambers and Ludlow settled into their respective mysteries. Chambers liked the fast action and witty rejoinders that characterized Robert B. Parker's Spenser series. Ludlow favored the long-unfolding English mysteries of P. J. James.

Twenty minutes in, Ludlow stopped, put down her book, and said, "You know, there might be another angle to pursue. It just hit me that you might want to look through town and social service kinds of records to see if you can't find some connection between all these characters. Maybe they're all related somehow or maybe one guy's father double-crossed another guy's grandfather. Who knows?"

Putting his own book down, Chambers said, "Huh, didn't think about that. That whole investigation, well, truth be told, it wasn't much of an investigation. The whole damn thing wrapped up too quick and too tight. I didn't go up to The County because Miles wouldn't authorize it. And I didn't do my due diligence on the Galen Knight-Walter Simpson relationship because the whole thing just seemed so random. And all of that's probably the reason that having Caleb Rimes in the middle somehow has got me crazed."

"Well, I don't know if checking through a bunch of dusty records and talking with bitchy social service workers will do you any good, but it's something to do until you make up the next slightly insulting, but definitely endearing metaphor about our relationship." Ludlow's soft, genuine smile told Chambers she had not and never would take offense at his dumb comment. But it also told him that she'd never let him forget it. Since that meant she'd be around to do so, that was just fine with him.

CHAPTER 47

Chambers's first stop the next day was with the Town Clerk in the Rascal Harbor Town Office. Part of the same municipal building as the police station, the complex also housed the Town Manager's office, Selectman's Conference Room, and the Recreation, Code Enforcement, Public Works, and Taxation departments.

Mildred Sargent, the town clerk, had the name of an eighty-year-old, but was barely twenty-eight. The Sargent family was among the oldest in town and took seriously its link to the past. Mildred had a brother named Chester and a sister named Ethel. Only the prominence of the family and the knowledge of their preference for "old-timey names," as Mildred described it, prevented school kids from teasing them mercilessly.

That Mildred was also a beauty helped keep the teasing to a minimum. Short and slight as her people were, Mildred's face inspired old men to stare and young men to stutter. She took it all in stride, however, knowing that beauty fades, but a good brain and a town job last forever.

It was early, so the scrum of men who managed to find reason to check the records for this or that had yet to form. Mildred, who had liked Dick Chamber from his arrival in Rascal Harbor, greeted him warmly.

"I did not steal that car," Mildred said immediately on seeing Chambers enter her office. "I found it alongside the road with the keys in the ignition."

"Ah, Mildred, someday your charms will disappear and I'll have to lock you up," Chambers said with a smile. "Course I'd be lynched by half the male population by nightfall, but I'd have done my job."

"Sounds like a plan!" Mildred replied enthusiastically. "In the meantime, what do you need today?"

"Can you help me find out anything about Galen Knight's time here in the Harbor? I know he graduated from the high school and that he lived with an aunt, but not a whole lot more."

"Now that's an interesting request given Mr. Knight's current residence. Of course I'm dying to know why you're asking but, being as I'm a professional, I'll simply process your request and ask only what is absolutely necessary."

"If we could clone half a dozen of you, Mildred, every office in town would be a model of grace and efficiency."

With a smile hiding the fact that she'd already found the information requested, Mildred said, "Okay, Detective, here's what we've got. Galen Knight co-owns the house once owned by Mavis Knight, now deceased. He owns it with a Virginia Knight, who I believe is his sister. If I pull up their school records, we can see how the brother and sister are related to Mavis." With a few keystrokes, Mildred had the school records of Galen and Virginia Knight in front of her and she learned that Mavis Knight, no husband listed, was the siblings' aunt. "Says Mavis was a nurse at, I'm guessing, the Harbor Hospital," Mildred clicked through some other screens, and found that Mavis had purchased the house only a year before Galen and Virginia enrolled in school.

"So she bought a house and then a year later she gets two kids. Not sure where they came from or if she adopted them and, if she did, what their last names might have been before she adopted them." Looking up at Chambers, she said, "Jeez, I might have created more questions for you than I answered."

"Maybe, but you've got me thinking about this adoption angle. Maybe there's something there I can grab onto." Thinking, Chambers asked, "Can you get into the state's adoption records?"

KNIGHTS DISARMED

"No way. And I'm not even sure you can. I know they're more open to the adopted kids, but I'm not sure who else can access them. You'll have to check with someone up in Augusta." Pausing for a minute, Mildred added, "I do remember there's something about a new birth certificate that gets issued with an adoption. One of my aunts adopted a little boy and I recall she said he'd get a new birth certificate with her and her husband's names on it as the adoptive parents."

Chambers, taking all of this in, said, "So I should be able to figure out *if* Galen Knight was adopted by getting a copy of his birth certificate. Be good to know that at least." Pausing, he asked, "You wouldn't have a picture of Galen Knight, would you? Like a school picture?"

"Not on the computer, but we've got all the old high school yearbooks, so I bet we can find one. You want his sister too?"

"That would be great," Chambers said. Mildred went into a back room and emerged five minutes later with two yearbooks.

"Here's Galen's," she said, opening to his senior picture. "And here's Virginia's. You can see a family resemblance."

Nodding, Chambers said, "They've got the same eyes." Still looking at the photographs, Chambers asked, "Could you make me copies of both pictures?"

"Absolutely, Detective," Mildred said with a smile.

"Oh, but before you do that, could you check for anything you've got on Caleb Rimes?"

Surprised, Mildred said, "Caleb Rimes? Is he connected with the Knights?"

"To tell the truth, I'm not sure, but I think he might be."

Frowning, Mildred said, "Okay…let me see what I've got." Less than ten minutes later, Chambers knew that Caleb Rimes had not gone to school in the Harbor and that he'd only been a resident for a few years. He lived in an apartment and owned a pickup. Galen Knight, by contrast, had not registered a vehicle with the town, though Chambers recalled that he had owned an SUV with Massachusetts plates. Mildred had no information about Virginia Knight's current whereabouts.

Again apologizing for seeming not to offer much in the way of help, Mildred said, with a devilish grin, "Well, I guess I won't have you hanging outside my door, Detective."

"Mildred, you'd never know if I was for the clutch of fools who wait here just for a glimpse of your smile."

"Ayuh, they are some fools, and you can be sure that a glimpse is all those guys are ever gonna get!"

Chapter 48

Knowing that Chief Miles would never accede to an official trip to Augusta on behalf of the Galen Knight case, Detective Chambers planned to take a half-day of personal time. He thought his physical presence might help his case in dealing with the legendary thorniness of the Maine state bureaucracy. Turns out, he didn't make it.

Before he could get out the door, Detective Chambers received a phone call from Nellie Hildreth. "I got a little inside dope on Walter Simpson from my County contacts, if you'd like a cup of weak coffee, come on by and I'll give you both."

Deciding that he would take the former and pass on the latter, Chambers walked over to the *Gazette* office. On the way, he caught a glimpse of Jumper Wilson coming out of Village Hardware. Jumper had shed his winter parka in favor of a lightweight sweatshirt. Layered over the sweatshirt was Jumper's latest T-shirt announcement. He had written "Slow and steady wins the race" on the front of his shirt. On the back, he had lettered, "Though not always…cause someone else is usually faster." Chambers supposed that any thinking person might see in Jumper's adages an insight into whatever issue bothered him or her. After all, that was the benefit of an adage—it could be widely interpreted as relevant. Still, he couldn't help but think that he only saw Jumper when he was tangled up in something. Today he wasn't sure what meaning to take away from Jumper's shirt. On the one hand, it might mean that he ought to stop wasting time on the Galen Knight—Caleb Rimes—Walter Simpson mystery. On another reading, though, it might be that he needed to hurry up and get this thing untangled.

Entering the *Gazette*'s lobby, Chambers saw Rich Reed, the paper's assistant editor. "What you do suppose Nellie would write for Jumper Wilson's obituary?" he asked.

Before Reed could respond, Nellie poked her head out of her office and said, "He was one clever motherfucker."

Chambers choked on his laugh. Reed rolled his eyes, and said, "She would too."

Nellie had already moved into the staff room with a sheaf of notes. "C'mon, Detective. Let's get to it." Chambers followed obediently and the two sat down.

"Don't know if any of this will help you, but I got a couple of bites. They don't mean much to me, but they might to you." Positioning her notes in front of her, Nellie continued. "I got hold of a couple of the old guys who haven't died yet. They aren't working anymore, of course, but they haven't lost all their memory yet." Chambers nodded for her to continue.

Doing so, Nellie said, "Okay, so headline number one. Walter Simpson was a nasty fuck." Chambers tried not to think about the fact that this woman, likely old enough to be his grandmother, had used the word "fuck" or a variant on it twice in five minutes. Nonplussed, Nellie continued, "Simpson was a drunk of the second order, meaning that he managed his farm and his affairs such that he paid his bills and even sold his place for a small profit. But he was a drunk when he could be. He never got into any serious scrapes, but he tumbled with enough guys to get the reputation I alluded to in the headline."

"Interesting. Course he wasn't around the Harbor all that long and wasn't really social so hardly anyone in town knew him or anything about him."

"What about the daughter?" asked Nellie. "I thought about send-ing Sarah out to interview her, but decided against it since the case concluded so quickly. But you must have talked with her."

"I did, but I can't say that I got all that much out of her. I put it down to shock, but she gave mostly noncommittal answers. Said she didn't know Galen Knight and couldn't imagine what he would have against her father. Just kind of threw up her hands about the whole thing."

"Curious. Maybe it was the shock, but you never know. But then that leads me to the second headline—did you know that Simpson had other kids at the farm?"

Startled by this news, Chambers raised his eyebrows and said, "No, far as I know the daughter, Dorothy, was the only child."

"And she might have been, but the guys both said something about a couple other kids—maybe a boy and a girl—they couldn't be sure and they didn't remember much of anything other than some-times Simpson would have other kids with him besides the daughter."

"Huh," Chambers said, clearly surprised by this news. "You'd have thought the daughter would said something about that when I talked with her. But I've checked my notes and I would have seen something like that if it was there. Guess I'll be making another visit to Ms. Dor-othy Simpson."

"Well, don't get your hopes up too high, Detective," Nellie cau-tioned. "After all, they could have been some neighbor kids or cous-ins. Those old coots I talked with were sharp on some things, but I wouldn't bet the farm on anything they said. Still, I thought I'd let you know what I discovered and hope that it might help."

"I don't see an 'aha' in what you've told, Nellie, but I've a couple more things to look at, so I thank you much."

"Happy to help, if I have. Oh, and, by the way, when can I expect to be printing your wedding announcement?"

Stunned again, Chambers looked bale-eyed, "What?"

"Oh for Christ's sakes, Detective! You've been keeping particu-lar company with that Ludlow woman who, by the way, I quite like.

So just wondering when you'll stop that scandalous co-habitation and marry the girl." Seeing that Chambers was either not going to respond or was too dumbfounded to do so, Nellie smiled and said, "Get on with your business, Detective Chambers. I'll just ask the brains in the family when I see her next."

As Chambers left the room, Rich Reed walked up beside him and said, "Don't let it get to you, Detective Chambers, she does this with everyone. If we were living in the 1600s, she'd probably be burned as a witch."

Still taken aback, Chambers walked back to the station to see Sergeant Levesque holding out a phone. "Call for you, Detective. I'll transfer it into your office."

Realizing that he hadn't asked who it was, Chambers answered tentatively. He recognized the greeting as coming from John McTavish. "What can I do for you, Mr. McTavish?"

"Probably nothing, Detective. In fact, I'm probably just wasting your time," McTavish began. "But it's been on my mind so thought I'd give you a call."

"Okay, what have you got?"

Suddenly even more unsure about why he had called, McTavish offered up a much abridged story of his encounter with the trailer woman, the mailbox with the name Knight on it, and the story about a family broken up over the travails of farming in northern Maine. On top of these facts, McTavish added the bit of speculation that had been haunting him—the possibility that Galen Knight might be related to the unseen meth producer with whom the trailer woman had threatened him.

"So I thought, well, if the meth guy and Galen Knight are related, that might be an angle for you to work on. I mean, it doesn't help you with the Caleb Rimes thing, but it might be something." After a pause, McTavish said, "But then again, I can't say that any of this makes much sense or much difference." After another pause, McTavish said, "Since you told me that you're working on a connection between Caleb Rimes and Galen Knight, I can't get any of this out of my head. Guess I thought I'd pass it along and see if you could make any sense of it."

"Huh," said Chambers wondering if he should reveal Nellie's findings about Walter Simpson. In the end, he decided to take a different tack. "I've got a whole lot of stuff afloat in my own mind," Chambers admitted. "I wonder if you could try to track down any of the stuff you've told me. Could you talk with the fellow up in Pinkham and see if he recalls anything else about the Knight family?"

"I could do that," McTavish said with a twinge of hesitation. "He seemed like a pretty sharp old bird and I guess it's possible that he thought about the family after I left and could recall some more details now."

"Anything you do might be a help," Chambers said, and the two men hung up.

"Huh," said Chambers.

CHAPTER 49

McTavish planned to pass along the information to Detective Chambers about the idea of a family being split up and the coincidence of two people named Knight as a way to get it all off his mind. He didn't expect to get a homework assignment.

In the moment, he agreed to make the call to Alton Chase and probe the matter a little further, but he was now having second thoughts. Did he really want to get any more mixed up in this mess? It really wasn't his nature to meddle in such matters. For a long time, Maggie had accused him of being uninterested in the people and events around him. McTavish had tried to explain that there was a difference between interest and involvement—he was *interested* in people, he argued, he just didn't think he always needed to *involved* in their lives. Ultimately people needed to make their own decisions, he said, so counseling, giving advice, and the like, seemed counter-productive.

"You are one odd duck, John McTavish," Maggie had said.

"Maybe, but maybe I'm a *right* duck." They had agreed to disagree then and that détente continued until Maggie died.

"So *now*, you're going to get involved, John?" he heard Maggie push. "A detective asks and now you're considering jumping into a bunch of people's lives?"

"Seems like it. Are you mad that it's taken me so long?"

"Absolutely not!" he heard Maggie say. "From the minute I met you, I knew you were going to be a long-term project. Course I kind of expected to see progress a little faster, but I'll take what I can get."

McTavish smiled.

"What are you smiling about," Noah asked. He had just come downstairs to see a kind of bemused quality in his father's eyes and half-formed words on his lips. The first few times he had noticed McTavish in this state, he'd been concerned. Was his father getting Alzheimer's? Was this what early stages of dementia looked like? Noah left his concerns unspoken, but he watched his father more carefully now trying to see if there was any sort of pattern in the behavior and whether there were indicators that something serious was about to occur. His observations had yet to pay off.

"Oh nothing, really," McTavish said. Noah *could* have predicted this response; this kind of non-answer answer was standard McTavish. He was stunned, therefore, when his father continued, "Well, that's not quite true." This time, when McTavish seemed content to let the conversation go, Noah decided to push.

"What's not true, Dad?" he asked, trying to keep the exasperation out of his voice.

"Well, I'm wondering if I should get involved in something. I said I would, but now I'm having some doubts."

"Spill it!" Noah said, a little sharper than he intended. "Jesus, why is it so hard for you to talk about anything except for stuff like history and art?"

"Your mother asked…uh, used to ask me the same thing," McTavish said. Noah thought he saw his father's eyes momentarily drift back into that bemused state he had witnessed earlier. Maybe it's a mom thing, he wondered to himself. Rather than push or argue with his father, Noah decided to just wait him out. That decision paid off this time.

"So I'm not sure I told you about my encounter with the 'trailer lady,' that's how I think about her anyway, up in Myron," McTavish said.

Noah again resisted the urge to bite back, he asked simply, "What happened?"

McTavish offered the story he told Jimmy Park a few days ago and Detective Chambers just hours ago. Noah listened attentively.

"Jeez, Dad, sounds like a bunch of coincidences, but not a whole lot more."

"I expect you're right, but when I gave my report on the thing with Caleb Rimes, Detective Chambers told me that he's working on a connection between Rimes and the murderer, Galen Knight. And, well, I just keep turning all this stuff over in my head, so I told him the story I just told you, and he wanted me to call the fellow I met up in Pinkham, the old guy who told me about the family being split up, and, well, I agreed to do it."

"And now you're having second thoughts because that's not something you do. You watch people really closely and you figure out stuff about them, but you don't get involved. Right? That's what Mom always said about you."

"She sure did."

"Well, in this case, I'm going to disagree with her. I don't think you should get involved either, especially if that nutcase Caleb Rimes is anywhere near it. Jesus, he sucker punched you and then broke your hand! If he thought you were digging around this Galen Knight guy, he might come after you again."

"The thought has crossed my mind," McTavish admitted, in a way far too casual for Noah.

"Crossed your mind? For Christ's sake, Dad! Jesus! You have to be careful."

Surprised by the vehemence in his son's response, McTavish said, "Well, yes, I do, but if Caleb Rimes is really as unhinged as Detective Chambers thinks he is, then I guess I do need to get involved so that he doesn't keep acting this way."

"That's very noble, Dad, but this guy is a psycho. And Jesus, don't you remember how close you came to being knifed by Bradley Little?"

Noah said, his voice rising. "Hell, maybe you've been right all along about staying away from people. You try it and look at the shit you get into!"

"Fair point, Son."

Noah stared at his father. "You're gonna do it, aren't you?"

"Yup."

McTavish didn't make the call that afternoon, but he did the next morning. He gave himself the rest of the afternoon and the evening to consider Noah's objections. Of course, Noah didn't know this because he had left the cottage in a huff and had gone over to talk with Louise Park.

Having come up with no other reasons not to, McTavish placed the call to the Biddle Inn. Alton Chase was again on the front desk and seemed interested to take McTavish's call.

"Nice to hear from you, Professor," Chase said. After hosting McTavish for dinner, Brendan Chase had done an internet search and told his father that McTavish used to be a history professor. "Interested in another reservation?" Chase asked.

"No, not today, Mr. Chase. I'm calling to see if you might have remembered any more about the Knight family," McTavish said, trying to get right to the point.

"The family we were talking about over supper that night you was up here? How come you're interested in them?"

"It's kind of a long story and the whole thing might be a waste of time, depending on what you can remember," McTavish said in confession.

"Well, then, guess I best crank up the old memory units." Chase laughed. "As it turns out, I *did* recall a few more things after you left."

Not wanting to push too hard, McTavish simply said, "Oh?"

"Yup. I remembered that there was four kids altogether in Peter's family, that's Peter Knight from over ta Briggs. Can't recall his wife's

GEOFFREY SCOTT

name, nor all the kids, but I remember one was Galen. He mighta been the oldest. And then there's his sister Ginny. The other two kids were younger as I recall, Clarence and hmm, can't come up with the other name, a girl I think."

McTavish made some notes as Chase talked. He said, "I think you told me that the children had been dispersed after the family lost their farm. Is that right?"

"Yup on both counts. Peter lost the farm and then packed his kids off to others. A couple went to his sister as I recall, I think she was livin' somewhere down on the coast. Mighta been a nurse or somethin'. The other two, again, I'm not sure which ones went where, but the other two got sent off to a guy way up in The County. Can't recall his name either." After a moment's pause, he said, "Jesus Christ, don't get old, Professor, your brain just turns to shit."

"I suspect mine's already on the way," McTavish admitted. Not sure he would get much more, but wanting to be thorough, he asked, "Okay on the second guy's name, but do you recall where he lived? And did he adopt the children?"

"Don't know about any adoption, but I think the guy was from up around Richmond Plantation and I think he was a farmer as opposed to a businessman or something. I might be wrong about that, but I think that's right. Sorry I weren't more help."

"You may have been more help that you know, Mr. Chase. And if it turns out to be the case, I'll let you know."

"Fair enough. I'd be happy to see you again."

As McTavish hung up the phone, he scowled. "Shit, I wasn't thinking about an in-person report," he said aloud. And then, before Maggie could say anything in his ear, he thought, Well, I suppose I could make another expedition up north assuming that Caleb Rimes doesn't do me in. He resolved to tell Noah about the call to ease his son's mind, but expected not to tell him this last thought.

CHAPTER 50

The next call McTavish made was to Detective Chambers. McTavish wasn't sure which was the biggest piece of news so he just laid it all out. Galen Knight, it turned out, was from The County. In fact, he came from Briggs, the town next to the one in which McTavish had grown up. He hadn't known the Knight family, but he had learned that Knight's father's name was Peter, and that he must have been one of the kids that Mavis Knight had taken in after the dissolution of the family.

"Oh, and I almost forgot, the fellow I talked with wasn't sure, but he thought that some of the kids were packed off to a farmer in Richmond Plantation. That's up in The County, too."

Sensing some coherence starting to gel, Chambers asked, "Did he give you a name? Could it have been Walter Simpson?"

"Don't know," McTavish admitted. "He couldn't remember a name and wasn't even all that sure that it was Richmond Plantation. Why? Does any of this fit with what you're learning?"

"Could be," was all that Chambers would offer.

"Okay, Detective, good luck."

"I'll take any I can find," Chambers replied.

After hanging up with Detective Chambers, McTavish went to work on what he had begun calling his "new life" work. He had culled the best of the photographs from his trip, printed the ones he wanted to work from first, and organized them into working piles. He found all this sorting and categorizing to be useful, but McTavish knew that he was delaying the inevitable decision about the medium in which he would work. For nearly a year now, he had worked exclusively in drawing mediums—pencil, ink, and charcoal. He quite liked the work he'd produced and, until his trip north, had expected to continue with drawings only.

And yet something about that decision unsettled him. Resolving the figure/ground issue pleased him, though he felt a little silly to have taken so long to see it. What still unsettled him, however, was whether to push himself to pull out his paint box. He'd made drawings with crocuses peeking through dingy-gray snow piles and highlighted against crumbling foundations. He made other drawings where he foregrounded a new human touch against a hard-luck background. For example, he had done several sketches based on the picture he'd taken of a small addition added to a house that was far more in need of structural work and painting than extra space. He experimented with more and less white space around the images and with a range of light gray to the darkest blacks. The resultant images captured most of the dynamism between the evidence of life set against the background of decay. But not all.

"Oh, for Christ's sakes," McTavish said to himself. "What's the big deal? Add some goddamn color and be done with it!" And yet he stalled—which drawing to start with? How much color to add?

McTavish concluded that a cup of coffee would help him decide. As he prepped the coffee maker, it hit him—he would commit to adding color to one of his drawings as a test run *and* he would use a color marker rather than his paints to do so. "A fine compromise," he said to himself.

"Seems kind of weaselly to me," he heard Maggie say. But before he could respond, his phone rang.

KNIGHTS DISARMED

"Mr. McTavish?" Detective Chambers asked. "I wonder if you'd like to take a trip with me tomorrow."

Chambers went on to propose taking McTavish with him to the state prison to meet with Galen Knight. A little surprised and very wary of this request, McTavish asked why.

"To be honest, I'm not sure," Chambers admitted. "Part of it is that you're the only person I know from The County and I'm wondering if you might pick up on something when I confront Galen Knight about the fact that I now know he is too. The other part is that, like it or not, you and I are both in Caleb Rimes's cross hairs and he's become even more unglued since I saw him in the prison parking lot." Hesitating for a moment, Chambers continued. "I know there's not a lot holding these threads together, but frankly there's something here that I can't let go of so I'm going to keep pushing. And I'm hoping you might be willing to help."

"Hmm. I don't know, Detective. I figured that I would try flying under the radar for a while…"

"I can't blame you," Chambers said. "Rimes likely put a scare into you."

"It's not really that, it's more that I tend to stay outside of other people's lives. I'm happy to lend a hand if someone needs one, but I figure people don't need to me to be muddying up their personal waters."

"Huh. Sounds like you're a self-contained man. And understanding that about you gives me another reason to want you to accompany me. The prison warden described Galen Knight just that way. I'm thinking that you might be able to gain some useful insights into him." Chambers quickly added, "You don't even need to talk with him. Just listen to him and watch him and see what you think. You artist types are supposed to be good at observation, right?"

"I don't know. If you want a real artist to go with you, you ought to take Robertay Harding."

"Jesus, I'd shoot myself before I'd do that," Chambers said and laughed. "And then I'd have you shoot me! And that's assuming that

Robertay didn't shoot me first. And all of that would be a pity, because then I wouldn't be able to read the obituary that Nellie Hildreth would write."

"Well, I suspect that last part's going to be a problem anyway, though I suspect we'd *all* like to see what Nellie would write about us!"

"Indeed. So can I pick you up around 8:00 AM tomorrow morning?"

Although he would later wonder why, McTavish decided that he would go…and that he would not tell Noah.

CHAPTER 51

Detective Chambers picked up McTavish promptly at 8:00 AM. Noah was still asleep so McTavish left a note simply saying that he'd be out for the morning. I'll likely catch hell when he finds out where I've been, McTavish thought. The fact that he didn't hear anything from Maggie, though both surprised and comforted him.

On the drive to Warren, the two men talked about the earlier case involving the theft of the Homer painting and its aftermath. They talked about Chambers's other cases in Rascal Harbor and in Florida. Chambers talked more than McTavish, but the latter held his own even if he revealed little about his own life. The two men talked amiably and sporadically; neither was uncomfortable with silence.

As they pulled into the prison parking lot, Chambers said, "Okay, let's go through how this is likely to play out. I've contacted the warden and let him know you're coming with me, but it'll still take us a little while to go through all the checkpoints. We'll meet Knight in what's called the 'visit room.' It's not like in the movies where there's a little booth and Plexiglas wall with a telephone. We'll be sitting at a table and he'll not be shackled so don't let that throw you off. I plan to do all the talking, but if you see an opportunity to ask a question or make a comment that you think will help, go ahead. Even though you're not a people person, I trust your judgment. But if you just want to observe, that's okay with me."

"How will you introduce me? Won't he want to know why I'm with you?"

"He will. I'm going to introduce you as a consultant. I don't think he'll object, but, if he does, then we'll leave immediately. I think he likes my visits, so I'm hoping he'll want us to stay." After a pause, he added, "If Knight asks about your hand, just make up a story. I'm expecting to bring up Caleb Rimes at some point either at this visit or the next so I don't want him to know that you two have a history."

"But what if he already knows?"

"He doesn't. I checked with the warden and Caleb hasn't visited and hasn't sent Knight any mail since he attacked you."

With a sigh and a nod, McTavish said, "Okay."

McTavish thought he knew what to expect. Like most Americans, he had seen the inside of prisons through TV dramas, documentaries, and movies. What surprised him was the heat. For whatever reason, he thought of prisons as cold places so he was unprepared for the warm, humid air that began to envelop him as he made his way through the checkpoints. It wasn't uncomfortable nor was the air foul, though the heavy presence of disinfectant took away his breath at first. Instead the air was languid as if, he imagined, a signal to the inmates to stay calm and tranquil. McTavish needed cool air to keep his brain and body moving; if he were incarcerated here, he knew he'd spend most of his time asleep.

"Planning to get yourself sent up to the big house, are you, John?" he heard Maggie say. McTavish ignored her and tried to focus on why he was there.

McTavish had looked up images of Galen Knight earlier that morning so that he would know the man on sight. Still, meeting him, shaking hands with him, and sitting across from him in chairs and at a table bolted to the floor unnerved him. The words "I'm sitting across from a stone-cold killer," ran across the front of his brain like the crawl at the bottom of a TV news show. He tried to keep his face impassive and hoped he was succeeding.

Chambers, by contrast, seemed to perk up as the visit developed. He greeted Galen Knight warmly, introduced McTavish as he said he would, and inquired as to Knight's health and well-being since his last visit.

Knight, for his part, started to inquire about McTavish, but then seemed distracted by Chambers's steady patter. McTavish thought he saw something pass across the convict's eyes. He imagined Knight thinking—So, what game are you playing, Detective Chambers, bringing this fellow along?—and then deciding to see how the intrusion played out.

After some polite talk about the weather, the Red Sox, and events in the Harbor, Chambers switched the conversation to Knight's family.

"Have you heard from any of your siblings lately," Chambers asked casually. Knight's expression turned instantly. His face went from pleasant and open to a blank mask. McTavish paid most attention to Knight's eyes. He wasn't sure what a killer's eyes looked like, but he didn't think they looked like these. Instead of seeing rage or insanity, McTavish thought he saw a deep sadness flicker before Knight turned an impassive stare toward Chambers. And that impassive stare matched the drawn mouth on Knight's face. McTavish had heard of people shutting themselves down. He had just witnessed it.

Ignoring Knight's reaction, Chambers continued. "I'm asking because I've uncovered a few things. I'd like to chat them through with you if you don't mind." Knight had not moved since Chambers's initial question and he did not do so now.

"For example, I've learned that you were born up in The County, in Briggs I believe, and that your father's name was Peter," Chambers said all of this slowly as if trying to recall the information exactly. McTavish assumed he was doing so in order to gauge Knight's reactions. Yet, there was nothing to gauge as Knight's stone face remained in place.

Geoffrey Scott

"I've also learned that you have siblings, three I think." Chambers continued. "There's Ginny and Clarence and I'm forgetting the last girl's name. Maybe you can help me with that?"

Just as Knight showed no reaction, Chambers showed no impatience. The fact that this conversation consisted of a monologue registered on neither man's countenance. Chambers resumed. "No? Well never mind. There's more. You see, I've also learned that you and your brother and sisters were split up. I knew that you'd lived part of your life with your Aunt Mavis in Rascal Harbor. I mean that part was fairly easy to figure out. What I've learned lately, however, is that you had these siblings and that, maybe after your mother's death, your father shipped you all off.

"That must have hard. I can't even imagine. I lost my dad when I was young, but my mother took me with her to Florida and raised me there. She didn't abandon me." As Chambers made this last remark, he looked long and sympathetically at Knight before looking down at the table.

The indictment of Knight's father hung heavily. And yet McTavish could see no change in Knight's eyes; they continued to stare just beyond the right side of Chambers's head. But McTavish thought he saw a slip in Knight's tight mouth line.

"No, Galen, my mother didn't abandon me," Chambers continued. "I mean, sure, it's a lot easier for a single parent to take care of one child than four, but still, to abandon your children? It's hard to imagine."

Pausing again, Chambers looked at Knight before saying, "Abandoning one's kids is one thing, but it's quite another to split them up. That must have been rough. To lose your mother and have your father send the kids off is bad enough. But to split up the kids so that you didn't even have each other. Well, I can't imagine what kind of man does that…

"Galen, I hoped that we'd be able to talk through some of these findings, you know, so I could better understand you and your circumstances. And here, I want to be completely honest with you. I want to apologize to you for not learning about all these facts until now. I mean they didn't come up because all the facts of the murder pointed directly and exclusively at you. There was no need to investigate your background because it was clear—you murdered Walter Simpson. And the fact that you wouldn't talk about why you did what you did, well, all the investigating that I should have done into your background, I just didn't do. I'm sorry for that. If I had known any of this stuff about your background, it might have made a difference…"

"Don't let it bother you, Detective Chambers," Galen said, his voice steady, but a little sad, McTavish thought.

"Well, thank you for that, Galen," Chambers said, with a touch of emotion in his words. "Won't you help me to help you now? If I knew the whole story, maybe there's something I can do about your sentence…"

"No. Thank you for your concern. I appreciate your interest, but I think I'll return to my cell now."

Chambers tried not to show his disappointment, but it was obvious to McTavish, and McTavish thought it was probably was to Knight as well.

Knight stood as did his two visitors. They all shook hands and then Knight walked slowly out of the visit room.

McTavish started to look at the detective, but when he heard Chambers mutter, "Fuck," he looked away.

As the two men cleared the last checkpoint and walked through the prison lobby, McTavish asked Chambers, "Did you notice his hands?"

Chapter 52

"What are you talking about?" Chambers asked McTavish as they walked to the detective's car. "What do you mean did I notice his hands?"

"Did you notice Knight's last two fingers on his hands?" McTavish asked.

"No, not really. What the hell are you talking about?"

"Maybe it's because I'm working at being an artist, or maybe I'm just more sensitive to people's hands since mine was broken, but I noticed that the last two fingers on Galen Knight's hands are significantly shorter than his other ones."

About to open his car door, Chambers stopped and held out his two hands. "Well, so are mine. My little finger in particular is quite a bit smaller."

Holding his hands out too, McTavish said, "Right, same with me. But notice how your ring fingers are almost as long as your middle fingers? That's not so for Galen Knight—both of his last two fingers are noticeably short and smaller than the others."

"Huh. Now that you say it…"

McTavish continued, "You know who else has fingers like that?"

"I assume you're going to tell me."

McTavish nodded. "Caleb Rimes."

The two men speculated their way through the entire trip back to Rascal Harbor. First, they debated McTavish's observation that both men could have the same hand formation and, if they did, what it could mean. Neither Chambers nor McTavish thought they had seen any scars or other indications that Knight's and Rimes's hands had been injured or maimed. The only reasonable conclusion then was that their hands were the result of a birth deformity or some sort of genetic situation, though neither man had ever heard of anything like that. McTavish wondered aloud about the possibility that the deformities were the result of a dietary deficiency. Chambers agreed that all of these avenues were worth investigating.

As they considered the possibilities, however, each man individually kept coming back to the idea that, if it were a genetic trait, then Knight and Rimes were most likely brothers. And if they were brothers, then at least one piece fell into place: Caleb Rimes might attend his brother's trial and visit him in prison, but each brother would likely want to keep the relationship quiet for fear that Knight's actions would blow back on Rimes.

A bunch of other things could also fall into place, once Chambers knew more. For example, was it Caleb and an unnamed sister who were sent to the farmer in Richmond Plantation while Galen Knight and a sister named Ginny were sent to live with their aunt in Rascal Harbor? And if all of this was true, was the County farmer Walter Simpson? Establishing a link between Simpson and Caleb Rimes seemed helpful, but then how did Galen Knight figure in? If Simpson was known to be a brute, it wasn't hard to imagine that he had mistreated Rimes and maybe his sister. If that were the case, then did Knight murder Simpson in long retaliation for that mistreatment? Lots of *ifs*, Chambers and McTavish concluded, but it all seemed like something.

All those *ifs* would collapse if certain other questions were answered. McTavish found a piece of paper and jotted notes as Chambers worked through the "little problems with our theory."

First on the list was the problem with names. Alton Chase had offered up the name Clarence Knight. He might confused Clarence for Caleb, but where did "Rimes" come from? The chance of having two names off the mark worried Chambers. The second issue was Dorothy Simpson. Chambers had talked with her on several occasions at the time of the crime and once again a day ago. Never had she volunteered information about one much less two children coming to live with the Simpson family. And if her father had mistreated Rimes in some fashion, wouldn't she have said that Rimes posed a bigger threat than Galen Knight? Talking it through, Chambers argued that Dorothy may not have known that two other Knight children existed. So it was possible, he reasoned, that Galen Knight as the clear and convincing murder suspect disabled her sense that anyone else could have committed the crime. But then why not acknowledge Rimes's and his sister's presence on the family farm? The Dorothy Simpson problem was going to nag him, Chambers thought.

And yet there was one more problem that seemed only to grow in importance: Could Galen Knight have taken the action against Walter Simpson without Caleb Rimes's knowledge, consent, and participation? The last was the easiest to dismiss: The evidence at the scene confirmed a single killer. True, they had not been looking for Caleb Rimes after the murder so Chambers had no idea where he had been or what he had been doing. He did know, however, that nothing at Dorothy Simpson's house and nothing about the crime itself gave any indication that another person was involved in general or that Caleb Rimes was involved in particular.

After talking through this point, Chambers said, "Shit."

"Shall I write that down, Detective?" McTavish asked in mock innocence.

"Don't be a smartass, McTavish," Chambers said with a smile. "Shit, shit, shit. How does it seem reasonable that Caleb Rimes could have been mistreated by Walter Simpson who is then murdered by Rimes's brother and Rimes doesn't participate somehow? If he knew

about his brother's intentions and he agreed with them, can you imagine he wouldn't have been involved?"

"Not really. But then, if all the ifs turn out to be true, it makes a
whole lot more sense for Caleb Rimes to be the killer than his brother."

"You might be right," Chambers acknowledged. "But how in hell
would I ever prove that?"

CHAPTER 53

Detective Chambers could not wait to get to work that afternoon. The visit to the Maine State Prison might have gone better if Galen Knight had let even a crack show in his stony façade. Still, Chambers now had, for the first time, a real possibility of a connection between Knight and Caleb Rimes. There was much work to be done, but he knew how to work.

First on his agenda was a phone call to the Office of Vital Records. Lucking out, he got a helpful clerk who promised to expedite his receipt of the records requested if he faxed the request on department stationary. He agreed to do so.

As he composed the note, thoughts of the earlier incomplete investigation led Chambers to make a list of all the birth, marriage, and death records he could imagine. He first asked for the information on Peter Knight, his wife (name unknown), and their known children, especially those with the names Galen Knight and Caleb Knight. Just to be sure, he also asked for any records involving a Caleb Rimes. He didn't expect the office to have a record of a Ginny Knight, though he wrote that name and all the proper name possibilities he could think of—Regina, Virginia, and Geneva. Chambers hoped that the name and records of the fourth Knight girl would surface under the live births records attributed to Peter Knight.

Chambers requested a similar set of records for the family of Walter Simpson, his wife (name unknown), and daughter Dorothy. He thought about trying to investigate whether or not Caleb Knight/ Rimes and his sister had been adopted by the Simpsons, but decided it could wait. He could follow that lead, if it was one, once he had the other, more important records.

The next item on Chambers's to-do list was an internet search for hand deformities caused by birth, diet, or genetics. He expected to spend a few minutes on this task with a result that either confirmed or undercut his and McTavish's hunch that the same deformity had the same familial source.

Many minutes later, Chambers realized that he had had no idea there were so many possible causes of and problems with one's hands. He was able to eliminate one cause—dietary problems. Chambers could find nothing to support the idea that the issue with Galen's and Caleb's hands could have been caused by something that the brothers' mother ate, and he could not yet think of the latter as Caleb Knight, but he intended to try.

Hand-related birth defects or "congenital anomalies" proved a longer slog. He learned that potential problems in the development of hands included club hand, failure of the fingers to separate culminating in a kind of webbed hand, duplication of digits creating hands with six fingers, and undergrowth of fingers. This last defect seemed promising. Chambers read that fingers could be small or underdeveloped. The problem was that the thumbs and first two fingers of the Knight men were normal in appearance; it was only the last two fingers on each hand that were affected.

So Chambers now turned to Google to search for hand deformities that were genetic. Though it had not come up in his earlier search, Chambers now learned that having six fingers could be a genetic deformity. He also learned of a whole raft of other hand defects caused by genetics or genetically inherited diseases. He couldn't pronounce the names, but he learned that people could have generally normal hands but with shortened or deformed thumbs, they could have "trident" hands where the fourth and fifth fingers canted off to the side, and they could have fingers so excessively long that making a fist was challenging.

And then he found it. Pseudohypoparathyroidism. As he read about this inherited, parathyroid gland-related issue, he grew more and more excited. In Type 1a of the anomaly, the fourth and fifth fingers are short, sometimes as much as half the size of the adjacent digits. Chambers smiled—he had it. And then he smiled again when he realized that, with a few pauses, he could even say the name of the condition— pseudo-hypo-para-thyroidism. Goddamn, he thought, we got 'em.

After he had dropped McTavish off at his house, Chambers tried to convince himself that the reason he hadn't spotted either the deformity or the fact that both men had it was because it affected only part of their hands. He wasn't sure he would succeed. But with this discovery of a possible genetic reason for the deformities, he thought he might save some face.

The win represented by the discovery of the genetic connection between Galen and Caleb Knight began to fade as soon as Chambers remembered that it, and the brothers' prison visits, still answered none of the pressing questions about if and how Caleb was involved in the murder of Walter Simpson. "One step at a time," he cautioned himself. Then he heard himself say, "Bullshit, Chambers, just finish this god-damned case."

McTavish faced a different kind of challenge as Chambers dropped him off. Noah was standing at the doorway, arms crossed, face set in a decidedly angry cast. Oh, shit, McTavish thought.

"He doesn't look happy, John. Think you need police protection?" Chambers asked.

"No, he doesn't," admitted McTavish. "And maybe if would be best if you just shot me." They both smiled and McTavish got out of the car to face his son.

McTavish's protests that "I left you a note" went by the boards with Noah.

"It was a note that didn't say anything," Noah said in protest. "It was the vagueness that surprised me and so, when I realized that you left your cell phone here, I started to get worried."

"Ah, but I was safe with the Rascal Harbor police," McTavish tried to joke.

"Is that supposed to be funny, Dad? Is my being worried a joke to you?"

"I'm sorry. I'm not trying to make light of your concern. I just—"

"You just what, Dad?" Noah said, an edge in his tone. "Jesus, you almost got killed by that Caleb Rimes guy and now you're off somewhere and I can't find you and…" Noah's eyes brimmed and he turned away from his father.

"Noah," McTavish began. "I really am sorry. I left the note that way so you *wouldn't* worry. And now I see that it had the opposite effect. And for that I apologize."

"Well, where in hell were you? And why were you with the police?"

"I've had a most interesting morning, but I'm not sure you're going to see it that way. Let's make some coffee and I'll explain."

As he prepped the coffee maker, McTavish described how Chambers had convinced him to make the trip to the state prison. He expected Noah to interrupt with a hundred questions and accusations about the foolishness of such an adventure. Instead, Noah rocked quietly in one of the kitchen rockers, accepted the cup of coffee from his father, and listened with his head down. At first, McTavish wasn't sure that the boy was listening, but he saw Noah nodding after particular points. He guessed that Noah wanted to hear the whole story before telling his father how reckless he had been.

Noah surprised him. Instead of lashing out as he had the other day, once the tale was told, Noah looked at McTavish and asked plainly, "Do you think this thing with the hands will crack the case? Will it mean that Caleb Rimes goes to jail?"

"Hard to say. I'm not sure that Detective Chambers even knows what it means yet." Letting a minute pass, McTavish continued. "You do understand why I had to go, don't you?"

Letting his own minute pass, Noah said, "Yeah, I do, Dad. You don't really get people, but you don't let things go, and maybe you don't really let people go either. You're gonna do what you think is right."

"I try, Noah. I have to live with myself and, within myself, and sometimes that means I do things that I know are going to annoy you. They did your mother."

"You got that right," Noah said with a hint of a smile. "I used to think that her favorite expression was 'your father'! But she loved you completely and she wasn't going to let you go either."

"What do you mean she wasn't going to let me go 'either?'"

"I don't know, Dad," Noah said weakly, with eyes averted.

"Noah? What do you mean?" McTavish said, a bit stronger than he intended.

"It's just, well, it's just that," Noah faltered. Looking now directly at his father, he said, "I wonder if you're ever going to let Mom go. I mean, well, I guess you kind of have to at some point. You might meet someone else and wanna get married. And I guess I'll be happy for you to do so, because I want you to be happy and everything. But are you ever gonna let her go, like let her completely go?" Noah's eyes brimmed again.

"No, Noah, I'm not going to let her go."

Noah hesitated. "That's what I mean. You know, about not letting people go either. I knew that's what you'd say. And I guess, well, I guess part of me wants to want you to let her go so that you can get on with your life and not seem so sad. But, honestly, another part, another big part of me doesn't because…well, if you let her go, then it will be easier for me to let her go. And I don't want that. I want her, Dad, I want her back and I know, goddamn it, I know I can't get her back. But that's what I want. And so I just want to tell you how important it is to me for you to not let her go. I—"

KNIGHTS DISARMED

"I'm not going to let her go, Noah, and I'm not going to let you go, either." And then McTavish got up from his chair, pulled his son to his feet, and hugged him hard.

Noah hugged back equally hard. Before he let go of his father, he whispered, "I think you still talk with her."

McTavish whispered back, "I do, son, I do."

CHAPTER 54

oni Ludlow was pleasantly surprised to see Dick Chambers smile when he came over to her apartment that afternoon. Chambers was not a big talker, but the Galen Knight case bothered him. He had received kudos for the quick and decisive end to the case so she knew that the doubts he now had were troubling.

So the big smile on Chambers's face both pleased her and put her on guard. Had something good finally happened with the case, or did the smile manifest from a different source?

"Did the sun shine on you today, Detective?"

"It did indeed," Chambers said, smile broadening. "Sorry to say though that I'm in love with yet another artist."

"Oh?" Ludlow said, not sure what to think.

"Oh, yes. I'm in love with John McTavish!"

"Indeed," Ludlow said, her own smile broadening. "Do tell, lover boy."

Over glasses of red wine, Chambers recapped the three segments of his day—the visit with Galen Knight, the drive back to Rascal Harbor, and his subsequent discovery of a genetic link between Knight and Rimes. Ludlow listened patiently through each installment, asking a few clarifying questions before Chambers began the next chapter.

Once Chambers had finished, Ludlow leaned back in her chair and asked, "So how do you feel now?"

Chambers looked at her for a long minute, "I'm not really sure, Toni. I suppose I'm happy to have a nice set of leads to work. It's a whole lot more satisfying that walking around wondering what the hell is going on. Still, I'm not all that much further along than I was before McTavish and I drove up to Warren. I've just about confirmed a familial relationship between Galen and Caleb Knight, but I already knew there had to be something between them. And I still only have evidence to support the one-killer theory. So I'm happier than I have been, but I've got a whole lot of happy yet to go."

"I'm not sure that last part is supposed to make sense, but it does in its own way."

"Hmm," Chambers hummed. "But then that's kinda been the way with this case from the beginning. It's made too much sense to make sense." Reflecting for a minute, he continued. "That's exactly the opposite of what you just said, but somehow it seems just as appropriate."

At that point, Chambers snapped his fingers. "Christ, that's what McTavish was talking about!"

"McTavish again?" Ludlow said, with mock jealously in her voice. "You boys might need to get a room."

Laughing, Chambers said, "No, no… But I just realized that this is what McTavish was talking about when he was describing some art problem he'd just resolved."

"Art problem?" Ludlow said. "Hmm. Maybe *I'm* in love with the guy."

"You can have him, but only after I'm done with him," Chambers said. He then related a bit of the conversation he and McTavish had had about the latter's figure-ground problem.

They had run out of conversational topics about half an hour before arriving at the prison. To be polite, Chambers had asked McTavish how his artwork was going. Expecting a perfunctory response from this most understated fellow, Chambers was surprised when McTavish talked for several minutes about his trip to The County, his long frustration trying to determine what artistic angle to pursue, and then the breakthrough moment when he realized that he was battling a figure-ground dilemma.

"Do you know what that is? Have you heard of that before?" Chambers asked.

Ludlow stared at him with a kind of "Are you serious?" look on her face.

"What?" Chambers asked, genuine surprise in his voice. "Seriously, I wasn't sure if he was just making shit up, though now that I think about it, he really isn't the type, is he?"

"No, he's not," Ludlow said seriously. "And no he's not 'just making shit up.' And why would you think that I wouldn't know anything about one of the fundamental principles of art—the figure-ground relationship?"

Back on his heels now, Chambers said, "I, well, I, the way McTavish described it, the figure is the image that you want the people to focus on, the kind of main idea of the painting, and the ground, well it's like the background, what's behind the figure. Is that right?"

"It is," Ludlow said coolly. "So why would you think I didn't know about it?"

"Well, you know, the kind of art you do, the abstract stuff," Chambers scrambled, vaguely aware that he may have insulted Ludlow yet again, and unsure how to stop making things worse. "I guess I assumed, that it didn't really matter."

"I see," Ludlow responded, a bit of ice still in her voice. "Wrong on both counts, Detective Chambers. First, anybody who's ever been to art school learns about figure-ground from the very beginning. It's kind of like perspective, it's a fundamental concept. So, yes, I know what figure-ground is."

Holding up his hands in surrender, Chambers hoped for a bit of mercy, but Ludlow was only halfway through her point. "As for whether I ignore it because I do abstract paintings, I can understand why you might say that," Ludlow said, her voice softening. "After all, Jackson Pollock's drip paintings don't seem to have any central focus and some of Matisse's work actually reverses the figure-ground relationship."

"Right, right," Chambers said, thinking that Ludlow was making his point for him.

"Well, not really. What is the figure and what is the ground is pretty easy to see in most figurative paintings. In short, you know what you're supposed to focus on because the artist has used all kinds of implicit and explicit tricks to draw your attention to it. She or he has also done things to push other elements of the picture into the background. That doesn't mean that those things are unimportant; they are. But their role in the picture is to support, to back up the image intended to be the figure. Make sense?"

"Yeah, I get it," Chambers said, clearly interested.

"So how can there be a figure-ground relationship in an abstract picture? Two ways, I think. One is use color or form or some other visual element to attract the viewer's eye. The figure might not be a person or a dog or tree, but if you do more than glance at the painting, you'll see the piece of the painting to which the artist wants to draw your attention. And that's what I do in my work.

"The other way to represent figure-ground in abstract art is to leave it up to the viewer. That's the thing with Jackson Pollock's work, for example. Those drip paintings look completely random, but if you look at them, your eye will be drawn to one section after another. When that happens, you, the viewer, are creating your own figure-ground relationships. That part up the upper left corner, for example, becomes the figure for you while the rest of the painting becomes the background. And then if your attention shifts, so does the figure-ground relationship. See what I mean?"

"Actually, I think I do, and turns out this is exactly what I meant when I said that McTavish's figure-ground problem was like mine."

This time it was Ludlow's turn to look baffled. "What do you mean?"

"Well, I've got all these pieces of this case. And right now they're all competing equally for my attention. I can't figure out what's the figure and what's the ground. McTavish told me that when he stood in a tree-farm forest, he got kinda disoriented because he couldn't figure out what to focus on. He said, 'It's like not being able to see the forest for the trees even though you're standing in a forest.'"

"Huh. That seals it, I'm in love with John McTavish, too."

"Okay," Chambers said, his face brightening again. "I guess we can share him."

After supper, Ludlow and Chambers settled into the chairs each preferred in her house. Before picking up their books, Ludlow asked, "When will you run all of this past the Chief?"

"Soon. He knows I'm working on something related to Caleb Rimes, but he doesn't know about the connection with Galen Knight. Once I get the vital record confirmations I need, then I'll probably explain it all to him. He likely won't care until or unless I can prove that Caleb had something to do with Simpson's murder. He'll tell me not to waste my time on it, but he won't interfere either as long as I keep up with my other work."

As he opened his book, Chambers said, "And thanks for the art lesson. I suspect that I'll be looking at paintings with a different eye now."

Ludlow smiled. "You're welcome, though I'm guessing that I came on a little too strong and probably went on a little too long."

"Not at all. It helped me see even more clearly this figure-ground problem I'm dealing with."

"So you won't be leaving me for John McTavish?" Ludlow asked playfully.

"No, but since he brought up the idea initially, maybe I should ask him to move in with us."

The pillow she threw narrowly missed his head.

CHAPTER 55

"You didn't sleep well," Toni Ludlow said to Chambers the next morning. "Tossing and turning isn't like you."

Looking the part, Chambers thought about brushing away his restless night. Instead, he said, "Yeah, sorry. Hope I didn't keep you awake."

"What was eating you?"

"Not sure I can say. Weird dreams, miscellaneous thoughts and images. None of it makes any real sense." After a pause, Chambers continued. "It was almost like a kaleidoscope, you know. Peoples' faces, like yours and McTavish's, but also Caleb Rimes and Galen Knight, and images like some of your artwork came in and out of focus… Jesus, I just remembered that I saw Jumper Wilson at one point… Any insights, Dr. Freud?"

Scratching her chin in imitation of the stereotypical German psychiatrist, Ludlow said, "Vell, let me see… Vun tink is for sure. De patient needs more of de sex with de veddy attractive artist."

"I have to have sex with John McTavish?" Chambers cried out with a laugh.

"Good lord, Dick, that man has captured your head and your heart!"

As they both laughed, Ludlow continued. "I'm not sure, but I've got to think that all those images mean that you're still trying to sort out a coherent scenario in which all those people fit."

"Yeah, that makes sense as far as the people go, but what about all the other images?"

"Well, I'd guess the whole figure-ground thing we talked about is behind that. I mean you said that you saw images of my paintings coming into and out of focus. Doesn't it make sense that you're trying to figure out what what's figure and what's ground in your case?"

Looking out the window as if trying to see the answer, Chambers muttered, "Hmm. I guess."

Watching him for a minute, Ludlow said, "The solution might be out that window, Dick. But I'm wondering…if your head's not going to cooperate, then is there anything in your heart that speaks to this case?"

Drawn in by this seemingly odd comment, Chambers asked, "Do you mean my emotions?"

"Maybe. What do *you* think it means?"

Looking at her askance, Chambers said, "Jesus, Toni….Don't tell me I'll figure this out if I get in touch with my feelings…"

"No, just saying that if you can't make any progress with your head, you might try your heart."

And then it hit him.

Chapter 56

When the thought struck him, Chambers forced his face to remain impassive. Keep it together, Chambers, he thought. You can't tell Toni about this yet. So Chambers shrugged said, "I'll give it a try," and hugged Ludlow hard.

Chambers now had two destinations in mind. He drove first to the station to see if the Office of Vital Records had faxed the information he'd requested. If it had and if it confirmed his suspicions, then he intended to take another trip to the state prison. This trip, he knew, needed to be off the clock so as to not alert Chief Miles. He didn't feel like explaining the situation now, especially to a nitwit who might order him to stay at his desk.

Though he wasn't sure why, Chambers decided to adopt a casual approach to discovering if the Vital Record fax had arrived. He needn't have bothered. As he walked into the station lobby, Rendall Kalin rushed to him with a sheaf of papers in his hand. "Detective, Detective, these faxes have got your name on 'em. I was passing by the machine and I saw that your name and the Office…."

Realizing that Kalin was likely to blurt out the subject of the records, Chambers grabbed them and said, "In my office now, Kalin."

"Sorry, did I do something wrong?" Kalin said, looking worried.

Knowing that he'd just dodged a gossip bullet and hoping to forestall another one, Chambers reacted coolly. "No, no, Rendall, you didn't do anything wrong. It's just that the subject matter of the faxes is very sensitive."

"Aha! You've got a lead!"

"I might, but it needs to simmer a bit before I can act on it." He now looked at the pages in his hand. His fear was that Kalin had seen copies of Caleb Rimes's or Galen Knights's birth certificates and would start leaping to conclusions. He relaxed when he saw that the cover sheet simply indicated that the following pages had come from the Vital Records office. So unless he had thumbed through them, Kalin didn't know of his interest in linking Rimes and Knight. I mean Knight and Knight, he reminded himself.

"Okay, I understand," Kalin said, a little crestfallen. "But I want you to know that, if you need back-up when it all goes down, you know, when the heavy shit, er, action happens, you can count on me."

"I do realize that, Officer," Chambers said with more assurance than he meant. "When the action happens, I'll want you beside me. But until then we need to keep a lid on this."

Kalin beamed, stood, saluted, and strutted out of the office. The fact that he hadn't asked what needed keeping a lid on confirmed the idea that Kalin hadn't looked at the documents…and that he actually might be dumber than Chambers had thought.

When Kalin left, Chambers rose and closed his office door. He hoped he had guessed correctly about Kalin's ignorance of the fax, but he wanted no more interruptions.

Key details surfaced as Chambers reviewed the records. He first scanned the material on Walter Simpson. Chambers learned that Simpson had married a woman named Marjorie Lindon and that they produced a single child, a girl named Dorothy. Simpson may have had other children at his farm, but they were not his offspring. Simpson's and his wife's death certificates were at the end of this stack.

The next set of several documents pertained to the Knight family. Peter and Cynthia Knight had birthed four children—Galen, Virginia, Susan, and Caleb. Chambers thought, ah, Ginny is Virginia and the missing child's name is Susan. Cynthia Knight's death certificate was in the pile, but all the other Knights were apparently alive.

These revelations helped nail down some of the information on Chambers's list, but it was only when he realized that there was no record of Caleb Rimes that he began to be excited. After confirming that he had asked for records about a man with that name, he smiled. Caleb Rimes was Caleb Knight.

And then his smile faded. "Where the hell did the "Rimes" come from then?" he said aloud. A quick look back through the birth record of Caleb Knight answered the question. His father was Peter Knight; his mother was Cynthia Knight, *nee* Rimes. The smile returned.

The thought that hit Chambers at the end of his conversation with Toni Ludlow and now inspired his drive to Warren was the memory of Rendall Kalin's Barlow House conversation with Caleb Rimes. More particularly, it was the threat that Caleb Rimes delivered at the end—"I'm gonna cut his fuckin' heart out."

And now Chambers knew why the images of Ludlow's paintings flashed through his dreams—several of them featured large, amorphous, red shapes. They weren't heart shaped in the reality of Ludlow's painting, but Chambers now realized that they were in his dream. And the connection that had struck him that morning, the one he could not tell Ludlow about, was the distant thought that Walter Simpson's killer had tried to cut his heart from his chest. Jesus, he wondered, could that be the tip-off to Caleb's involvement?

CHAPTER 57

As he made the drive to the state prison, Chambers let his mind float. He had long ago realized the power of *both* focused and unfocused thinking. He generally favored the former as it seemed more like real work. But progress on several cases had come when he let his mind drift. He trusted the strategy, even if he didn't always understand it.

Ten minutes outside of Warren, it became clear to Chambers that Caleb and Galen Knight were both involved in the murder of Walter Simpson. True, the evidence trail led only in Galen's direction, but the connection between Caleb's threat and the nature of Simpson's injuries convinced Chambers that the brothers Knight were in it together.

But how to approach Galen Knight? A couple of minutes of thinking resulted in the realization that nothing he had done in the past had worked. Friendly banter, subtle questions, direct confrontation—nothing had jarred Knight into revealing anything about his personal and family background or about his motivations and actions in commission of the crime.

Probably a waste of time driving up here today, he thought, suddenly depressed at getting close to something only to see it slip away. "Fuck it," he said vehemently. "I'm here. Might as well see how this plays out."

Warden Ross met Chambers as soon as he checked in at the front desk. "Going to give it another whack, Dick?" Ross asked sympathetically. "Got any reason to think it might go differently this time?"

"It's a good question. Haven't had a lot of luck in the past. I've got a couple of hole cards this time, but Galen Knight is as tight as they come." Chambers then laid out the various insights he had gained since his previous visit, including his strong sense that Caleb had joined his brother in the murder.

"Never know what's gonna to shake a guy," Ross said patiently. "I wouldn't put any money on your effort today, but I also won't be surprised if he cracks open. Worth a try."

Chambers nodded, shook hands with his friend, and walked toward the first checkpoint.

His first impression on seeing Galen Knight was that the man looked tired. Not sleepy-eyed tired, though his eyes betrayed Knight's weariness, but soul-tired. This man who had defined stoicism in expression and attitude throughout his arrest, trial, and incarceration, suddenly seemed to be showing the effects. Whatever strategy Chambers might have formed for approaching Knight with his new information was abandoned. As he sat down, Chambers focused only on Knight's appearance.

"Jesus, Galen, you look wrung out," Chambers said, honest concern echoing through his words. "Are you okay?

Knight seemed as taken aback by the subtext of Chambers's comment as the words themselves. "Thank you for coming and for your concern, Detective Chambers. I always enjoy your visits," Knight said, ignoring Chambers's question.

Chambers considered engaging Knight in their typical opening banter; he also considered probing to see if some specific incident had occurred to produce this result. He rejected these options thinking that a direct approach might just work this time.

"Galen, if there is anything I can do to help you, I hope you'll ask me." Knight's weak smile and small nod suggested that he understood this to be a genuine offer.

When Knight did not respond further, Chambers pushed on, "Galen, I've continued to investigate your background and I've turned up some interesting things. I'd like to share them with you and hear what you think." Not expecting a response, Chambers continued. "For example, I learned about your brother, your sisters, and your folks. I had some solid information the last time we talked, but I've got more and more accurate information now.

"I know that your parents Peter and Cynthia Knight had four children, you, your sister Virginia, another sister Susan, and a brother Caleb. I think I called him Clarence last time, but now I know his name was Caleb, Caleb Knight, and that he's the baby of the family. So it was Susan and Caleb who your father sent off to live with Walter Simpson, a farmer up in The County. They lived with him, but apparently he didn't adopt them. That means there's really no official record of them going to him, but I think that's what happened. I'll come back to that point in a minute.

"I also know that your mother's maiden name was Rimes. I'm not sure where the Rimes folks were from, though I suspect they were County people like your father and you and your siblings. Good County folks.

"But here's what threw me. I know a fellow named Caleb Rimes from Rascal Harbor. He looks to be the same age as your brother Caleb Knight would be and, well, he got the same hands that you do."

Knight had taken in all of the information in typical silent and non-expressive fashion. But with the mention of his hands, Chambers thought he saw a weakening in Knight's resolve, as if it took more effort than it had in the past to say mum. He pressed on.

"I noticed your hands and this Caleb Rimes's hands share the characteristic of smaller and shorter than normal third and fourth fingers," Chambers said matter-of-factly. He noticed that, for the first time, Knight's eyes moved off Chambers's face. They went to his hands and then quickly back to Chambers's eyes as if he'd been caught in a verbal lie. Chambers decided to simply keep talking.

"I expect you know what I'm talking about, Galen. Those shorter fingers must have gotten notice in school and we both know how awful kids can be when they sense a difference in others. There's a name for that condition, did you know that? It's called pseudohypoparathyroidism and it's a genetic condition, passed down from parents to children.

"There's one more thing, Galen. There is no Caleb Rimes, there's only Caleb Knight. And he's your brother…" Chambers stopped here and looked at Knight directly. "And I think—in fact I'm pretty sure— that Caleb was involved in the death of Walter Simpson." Pausing again, Chambers looked down before looking again at Knight, "I don't know all the details yet, Galen, but I'm going to find out. I'd like you to help me."

With that, Chambers folded his hands, laid them on the table, and leaned back in his chair. He studied Knight who seemed to draw even further inward. Knight would not or could not meet Chambers's gaze. He sat huddled forward, head down, shoulders hunched, hands in his lap. Chambers resisted the urge to comfort and reassure him, to tell Knight that everything would be okay, to put his arm around Knight's shoulders, to show Knight a measure of human understanding.

Chambers resisted these urges because to do so might enable Knight to draw strength from the comfort as a way to maintain his silence. So Chambers waited. If he was to help this man he had grown to like, then Knight had to open up. All the reassuring words and gestures in the world, if they produced no confession, would be wasted. Sitting in wait discomforted Chambers, but he suspected it was the only way forward.

The visit room was large and institutional and loud. Close to a hundred men and their visitors sat, talked, laughed, cried. The din that Chambers had always been able to ignore now surrounded him made Knight's strained silence even harder to watch. And yet it continued. Chambers would later think that he could see Knight drawing strength from each moment he stayed mute. It was as if the prisoner's resolve that seemed so close to breaking, now became the source of his rebound.

And then he was back. The amicable, pleasant-faced Galen Knight who had greeted Chambers on each of the previous meetings sat in front of him. Chambers thought he saw a lingering hurt in Knight's eyes, but in every other way, the man appeared to be unaffected by Chambers's informational assault. Chambers had never seen the like of it. Though he had been unsure how to initiate the conversation, he felt as if he could not have delivered his findings in any better fashion. He sensed Knight weakening, he'd have bet that Knight was weakening. And yet, the slight cast to Knight's eyes aside, Chambers realized he had failed.

Chapter 58

"Goddamn it, Toni, I thought I had him. I thought…." Realizing that she had no words, Toni Ludlow reached across the table and simply took Chambers's hands.

Ludlow had called Chambers before she came over to his apartment. She'd been worried. Chambers always let her know when he arrived at the prison, when he left, and when he'd gotten home. Such checking-in was not part of Chambers's past. Cell phones made it easier, but Chambers had sensed Ludlow's discomfort with his prison visits, so he'd made it a practice of letting her know. This time there had been no call when Chambers left the prison or when he returned home. Ludlow had sat on her fear all day. At five, a mixture of anxiety and impatience overcame her reluctance and she'd called him. She managed to keep all of the impatience from her voice and a good part of the anxiety, still Chambers picked up on it and quickly apologized.

"Ah shit, Toni, I'm sorry. I should have called. I just…"

"It's okay. I'm just glad you're okay."

"Well, there's okay, then there's *okay*. I'm not exactly sure what that means, but it about sums it up."

"Okay… would you like company?"

"I'm not sure how much company I'll be," Chambers admitted. "But I'd like to see you."

"I'll bring Chinese," Ludlow said and they disconnected.

Two hours and several half-started and awkward conversations later, Chambers made his frustrated declaration. "I thought I was getting to him, Toni, I really did this time."

Chambers then laid out the whole series of events, ideas, reactions, and non-reactions. Ludlow listened attentively, still holding Chambers's hands. When she sensed he had finished, she waited a moment, then asked, "So what did you do when you realized that he wasn't going to talk with you?"

"I just left. I couldn't even say goodbye to him. I know it's going to sound weird, but it was like I was leaving him for the very last time, like he was going off to his death with his secret unrevealed. Of course, Maine doesn't have the death penalty, but I'm not sure it would matter to him. He seems absolutely resolved to stay mum."

"Did you talk with the warden?"

"No," Chambers confessed. "Probably should have. Bad form. But I just had to get out of there and drive."

"Where did you go?"

"Not sure, to tell the truth. I was aware that I was driving, I wasn't driving recklessly, but I didn't know where I was going either," Chambers said plaintively. "I found myself down in Cushing."

"Cushing?"

"Yeah," Chambers said with an embarrassed smile. "I wasn't sure how I got there, but when I realized where I was, I remembered John McTavish saying something about Andrew Wyeth—is that his name?—doing some painting around there. So I just drove around some more. Then I turned on my MapQuest and drove home. I thought about going over to the station and laying it all out for Miles, but I couldn't face seeing the smirk that he'd have all over that fat face of his. So I came home and you called just as I was coming in. Thanks for that call by the way."

Ludlow smiled for the first time, "Well, you know I can't eat an entire Chinese dinner by myself and I hate leftovers…"

"Glad to be of service," Chambers said in his most gallant voice. He sighed, "Goddamn it. I thought I could help him."

Later that evening, Chambers had still not settled down. He'd tried reading only to find himself continual looking at the same page. He'd tried working the crossword puzzle in the *Gazette* only to erase one answer too hard and rip the paper.

"Shit, goddamn, shit," he muttered.

"Are you still thinking about Galen Knight?"

"Ahhh, some I suppose, but now I'm stuck on Caleb Rimes, or Knight, or whatever the hell his name is. The thought of him being involved in Simpson's murder and still walking around free and creating havoc as he does… Jesus, it's getting to me."

"Oh, right. I see your point. But is there anything you can do now?"

"No, nothing I can think of, nothing legal anyway," Chambers said, his voice rough. He then held up his hand, "No, Toni, I'm not going to go all vigilante on his ass, though I'd—"

"Like to. Yeah, I get it. But then it would be your rusty ass in prison and then Caleb would be visiting you and his brother." Seeing Chambers slump deeper in his chair, she continued, "What are the chances that Caleb Rimes isn't going to end up in jail sooner than later, and then you'll have him."

"It's a fair point. But how many more folks like John McTavish are going to get hurt before that happens?"

At his cottage, John McTavish was experiencing his own set of frustrations. Though his hand showed signs of healing, those signs were few and the prognosis for an immediate recovery was dim. McTavish could still do his art. Nearly everything else, however, was either awkward, painful, or impossible. Noah had stepped up, taking on chores such as chopping wood and washing dishes. McTavish tried to express his appreciation; Noah had waved it off. "You'll be back in the dishpan soon enough. I know it's probably killing you to have to rely on someone else, but get over it."

And so McTavish tried. The worst thing was that the splinted hand prevented him driving…or driving very often. He'd tried it a few times only to earn a severe scolding from his son. Like it or not, McTavish realized that he'd have to accept some help until his hand was healed.

Fortunately, he could still brew coffee, pour a measure of Bushmills, and draw. And paint, or at least, color. McTavish was right—moving into paint was too big jump. So he'd dug out a large box of permanent markers of various hues and found himself enjoying the experience of applying color in limited amounts and to selective areas of his crocus drawings. He liked the yellow varieties, but it was the various purples, ranging from the lightest lavenders to the most intense blue-violets, that pulled him in. The way sunshine had created lighter and darker contrasts in the leaves and in the highly saturated yellow-orange of the stigmata made him smile.

As he worked, especially on the various crocus drawings, McTavish kept the figure-ground relationship ever-present in his mind. He'd done drawings with crocuses coming out of snow banks, blooming against sun-drenched house foundations, about to bloom next to shaded fence posts. In some drawings, there was but a single flower image. In most, however, there were small groupings, single flowers intermingled with small and larger patches. He had been experimenting with single colors from his marker set; today he'd tried layering colors to increase the intensity and the range of hues.

McTavish was working on one of these multi-flowered images in front of a field stone foundation when it struck him that it might be interesting to color the leaves and stigmata of one of the crocus plants, but leave the others and the background textured in whites, grays, and blacks.

"Huh," he said to himself. "If I do that, then does the colored plant becomes the figure and rest of the flowers part of the background? Or is the foundation the background and the uncolored flowers a kind of middle ground?"

As a historian, McTavish had been a man of words—spoken or print—but words nonetheless. Working as an artist, he had long ago realized that language often failed him. His brain, his eyes, and hands knew what to do, or what to try to do, but articulating that plan or the effect of the outcome came hard, and often he would give up, shrug, and smile. His discovery on this day seemed in this vein—foreground, middle ground, background—did the words even matter? Was it important that he try to name purpose, procedure, and effect or just turn off the word part of his brain and commit to doing the work?

"You are one weird cat," he heard Maggie say.

CHAPTER 59

As Detective Dick Chambers was driving around aimlessly after leaving the prison, Caleb Rimes was driving to see his brother. He wasn't looking forward to it. It was his first visit to Warren since beating up that artist and being jailed. He didn't expect Galen to be happy.

Rimes tried to inure himself as he drove to the prison by anticipating Galen's reaction to this news: "What were you thinking, Caleb? What caused you to act in this way? Did you consider the consequences? You have to stay out of jail, Caleb, I need to see you." These and other questions and demands bubbled around in Rimes's brain. His brother would not hit him or yell at him or call him stupid. Instead, Galen would lock eyes with him and talk quietly with him and, in doing so, would make him feel like an idiot. He knew he was an idiot for stomping that artist prick. What had it gotten him? Galen would ask that, too. Rimes knew that Galen was right to chew on him, still… if he could anticipate most of the things that Galen would say, maybe they would sting less.

He thought he'd come up with most all the questions by the time he neared the prison. But then he realized that the artist attack was the biggest dumb thing he'd done since Galen went to prison. The other scrapes he'd gotten into were bad; this one was far worse. Would Galen really snap at him this time? For a few minutes, Rimes reconsidered telling his brother anything about the incident. A moment's reflection convinced him to forget that plan—Galen could always tell what was on his mind. His brother would see something in his eyes or his face and he'd lean back, look hard at Rimes, and just say, "What is it, Caleb?" Rimes would try to deflect, but invariably he would cave; he'd explain, he'd listen to Galen's questions and advice, and he'd feel better. Rimes hoped that pattern would still hold true on this day.

On this visit, however, it was Caleb who first noticed that something was wrong. His brother's normally placid face and warm eyes seemed off; not angry off or psychotic off, but off nonetheless. Maybe tired, but more than tired. Not depressed, but definitely sad. Caleb knew there were probably bigger words that more accurately described his brother. He didn't know them, however, so he settled on sad.

But why would Galen be sad? Jesus, Caleb thought, does he already know about the thing with the artist? Who could have told him? As soon as this last question entered his mind, he knew it had to be that fucking Detective Chambers. Had he been up here casting his shit all around, badmouthing him to Galen? I *will* kill that fucker, he thought.

These thoughts darkened Rimes's face as he sat down with his brother. And true to form, Galen smiled, or tried a smile, and asked, "What wrong, Caleb?"

"What's wrong?" Rimes said, a little louder than he'd intended. "What's wrong with you? You look like shit."

"I'm fine, Caleb. *Your* face tells me that something's happened. What is it? Are you all right?"

Rimes did not even try to deflect his brother this time. "You know," he said, in a slightly accusatory tone. "I bet you already know. I bet that fucking Chambers told you."

A vague look of fear mixed with a more definite look of concern crossed Knight's face and he pushed forward in his chair. "Tell me, Caleb. What do you think Detective Chambers told me?"

"I bet he told you about me bein' involved in an attack, about attackin' a guy. I bet that's how he said it, 'attack.' Didn't he, that bastard."

"Caleb, are you talking about Walter Simpson? Are you asking me if Chambers talked with me about your involvement in that murder?"

Looking at sea, Rimes stammered, "Simpson? No, I'm not talkin' about Simpson. I'm talkin' about that artist guy, the faggot who helped that Park kid."

Looking just as confused, Knight said, "Caleb, maybe you should start at the beginning. I don't think we're talking about the same thing."

At that point, Rimes gave his account of the "thing" with that "faggoty artist," a version similar to that given by the observers only in the most obvious ways. Knight tried to find out the cause of the conflict, but to no avail. Rimes would only say that McTavish had "Pushed my buttons" and "Looked at me the wrong way." Knight eventually gave up and turned to the more important matter of understanding if Rimes had encouraged Chambers to think he was involved in the Simpson murder.

"All right, Caleb, I understand," Knight said quietly. "But you've got to keep your cool around this fellow, whoever he is. I need you to stay out of jail."

"Okay," Rimes said sullenly. He began to brighten, however, when he realized that his brother was not going to press him hard on what he had done and why he had done it. Wrapped up in that realization, he had missed Knight's next question.

"Caleb? Caleb? Are you listening to me?" Knight asked, a bit of urgency in his voice.

"Yeah, yup, sorry, Galen."

"Caleb, I want you to think really hard about this next question. Have you given Detective Chambers any cause to think that you were involved in the murder?"

Surprised at this turn in the conversation, Rimes shook his head vigorously. "No, Galen, nothin'. I ain't said nor done nothin' ta give him that idea." Still confused, Rimes took a minute, then asked, "Why? What's he sayin' about me?"

"It's what he's saying about *us*, Caleb," Knight began. "He knows that we're brothers. He got our birth certificates and he tracked us to our parents. Somehow he found out that our hands are the way they are by genetics." At this, Knight pushed his hands up against his brother's. The shorter and ill-formed fingers were readily apparent. "I forgot what the name is, but our fingers show the same defect and it only comes from our dad. Remember, he had the same thing."

Rimes did remember and he remembered being taunted by school kids for the affliction. That Chambers would discover this and point it out, that he would make something of this, angered Rimes even more than the fact of the sibling connection being discovered. "That fuckin' Chambers," he muttered. "Always stickin' his nose in. Always pushin' on us. I bet he's got stuff he ain't so proud of neither. But I don't go tellin' about it all over."

"Caleb, please understand, the point is that Detective Chambers knows that we are brothers," Knight said insistently. "He also knows that we were separated as kids. And he's pretty sure that you and Susan were sent off to live with Walter Simpson while Ginny and I were packed off to Aunt Mavis." Taking a breath and waiting until he had his brother's full attention, he continued. "All that is bad enough, but I think he's got something else. I think he's got something that ties you directly to the murder."

"What the fuck could that asshole have on me?" Rimes asked, sputtering and earning a hand gesture from his brother to quiet down. Rimes lowered the volume, but continued to rumble, "What the hell is that guy tryin' to do to me? Is he tryin' to pin the murder on me?"

Before Knight could respond, Rimes continued with a scowl, his voice rising again, "What the fuck? Is he tryin' ta make a deal with you? Is he tryin' ta get you off by framin' me?"

Knight let the absurdity of the last comment go and tried to get Rimes to focus. "Caleb, calm down," Knight said quietly. "We've got to think this whole thing through and do so calmly."

"Think it through or kill the motherfucker!"

Taking a breath before responding, Knight said, "Caleb, please… Look, I can do the time for you. I can. But we've got to keep you out of here. And we can't do that unless we know what we're up against. So I want you think hard. Is there anything you said or did that would lead Chambers to suspect you?"

Before Rimes could respond, Knight continued. "Chambers knows we're brothers and he knows you got sent up to live with Simpson. He may know that Simpson was a prick and even that he mistreated you and Susan. We don't know that he knows that, but he might suspect. Right now, though he's got no way to prove you were involved. Right? Think hard, Caleb, is there any way that Chambers could *know* that you're involved?"

Rimes heard his brother talking, but his attention had only one focus—eliminating Chambers. He really didn't have any idea why Chambers might suspect his complicity in the murder, but Chambers was a threat and Rimes knew no subtlety in dealing with threats.

Sensing that his brother was only half listening, Knight repeated his question, "Caleb, *is* there any way that Chambers could *know* that you're involved?"

"No, fuck no. He's just tryin' to pin it on me and I'm not gonna let the fuck do that. I'm not, Galen!" Staring now at his brother, Rimes said, "You can't help me, Galen, you couldn't help me with that fuck Simpson…" Here, Knight could see his brother's eyes start to redden. "You didn't help me with that fuck Simpson. And now you can't help me with that fuck Chambers. So I'll have ta do it myself."

Hearing these words, seeing his brother's contorted face, and knowing all too well the violence he could inflict, Knight's mind flashed to the scene in Walter Simpson's living room. The memory of Caleb driving the knife into Simpson and then trying to cut out his heart caused his breath to catch.

Before Knight could speak again, Rimes said, with an eerie smile, "Ah, fuck it, Galen, don't worry about it." Pushing his chair back, he continued. "I got it, Galen, don't you worry. I got it."

Rimes rose, nodded, and left the room. Knight wondered if it would be the last time he saw his brother. And his reddened eyes wept.

KNIGHTS DISARMED

Chapter 60

Galen Knight stopped crying. He wasn't exactly sure what it was that kept the worst of his prison peers from bothering him, but he knew that if they saw him cry, it might embolden them. He put his head down on the table pretending sleep and dried his eyes. Once he'd regained his composure, Knight straightened up and left the room.

"You didn't help me with that fuck Simpson," Caleb had said. Knight could not get these words to stop echoing in his ears and flashing in front of his eyes. He felt his eyes brim again and he ducked into a bathroom to flush them with cold water. The weariness that both Chambers and Caleb had detected earlier felt magnified by a factor of a hundred.

"Can I carry this burden?" he asked his mirrored self. He saw no answer to that question or to the others that now circulated through his mind.

Could Caleb really blame him for not preventing Simpson's abuse? Even expressing the question caused his heart to quiver. He knew it was unfair, he knew Caleb was just thrashing about, but he also knew that Caleb had named a deep guilt that he himself had not been able to face. He knew Caleb's accusation was wrong and yet knowing that offered no solace.

Knight knew there was nothing to do about this guilt. He would bear it and bear it and bear it until he died. The more immediate problem was his inability to learn what Caleb may have said or done that led Chambers to conclude he'd been involved in Simpson's murder. There really could not have been any evidence to speak of, so maybe Chambers was just fishing. Still, there was something about the way that Chambers had talked about Caleb's involvement that told Knight he had something and wasn't about to let it go. What that thing was, Knight couldn't imagine and his guess was that Caleb did not know either.

As if these two points were not prickly enough, Knight realized he sat squarely on the horns of a dilemma. One horn was protecting his brother. He may not have been able to protect Caleb from Walter Simpson, but he had protected him from the charge of murder against Simpson. He was willing to do that for the remainder of his life. It might not be fair and it didn't even ease the guilt of not protecting his little brother, but he would do it.

But it wasn't that simple anymore. Knight had been troubled by Chambers's previous visits. The man was smart, and if he or Caleb made any mistakes, past or present, Knight was convinced his efforts to shield his brother would implode. Discovery of any mistakes was beyond Knight's control now, so he could worry, but it would do no good.

Caleb's visit, however, had set the other horn in place—Knight's sense that he needed to protect Detective Chambers.

Given a clear choice between helping his brother or Detective Chambers, Knight knew he would choose Caleb. But his brother's brash words and unambiguous threats against Chambers roiled any choice. Put simply, if Caleb sought out and killed Chambers, Knight would end up losing both men, for he knew Caleb would be caught and imprisoned and that would be the end. Another man might have welcomed his murderous brother into the same prison, but not Galen Knight. Caleb's mouth or his actions or both would lead him into trouble that Knight wasn't sure he could prevent. So Caleb, convicted of murder, would get a death sentence whether or not the state of Maine killed him.

What to do then? Knight knew that he would not rat on his brother, but neither could he let Chambers go along unaware of the threat. Knight was not a killer and, truth be told, he wasn't sure if he could sit back and let Caleb kill anyone else. He respected Chambers and could not abide the idea that Chambers would die by Caleb's hand, even if Caleb was assured of not being caught. Knight firmly believed that we were all responsible for our actions and that interference was rarely helpful. His guilt about not helping his brother shook that belief. Knowing that his brother might kill an innocent man broke it.

Galen Knight turned to one of the guards and asked if he could have a word with the prison warden.

CHAPTER 61

Warden Stephen Ross called Detective Chambers's cell phone as soon as Galen Knight left his office. When he got voice mail, he said, as calmly as he could, "Dick, I need to talk with you immediately. Call me on my mobile phone as soon as you get this message." Ross left his number and hoped that his friend would call soon.

Dick Chambers missed Ross's call because he was fielding Robertay Harding's complaint against Rendall Kalin. The head of the Rascal Harbor Art Colony and self-defined most important artist in town, Robertay was a far better administrator than human being. She was prickly in that New York City way that rankles Mainers from the first syllable of the word "cawa-fee" to the expression "yous guys." And despite the fact that she'd been in Maine for thirty years or so, Robertay still seemed unaware that she would always be "from away."

Today, however, the issue was less about Robertay's childhood home and more about the size and prominence of her chest. Apparently she'd been about to get into her car, but the driver's side door was stuck. Seeing her straining with the door, Officer Kalin stopped to help. Robertay liked to exercise authority, but she hated the idea in others and so a uniformed member of the local police force set her teeth on edge.

"I can do it myself, Officer," Robertay said brusquely. "Why don't you go on and hassle other innocent people."

Taken aback, Kalin tried to move around her to see where the door was stuck. In doing so, however, he bumped into her chest. Immediately embarrassed, Kalin stammered, "Oh my, sorry Ms. Hard, Miss Hardly, ah Ro-boob-tay." At this last bit, Robertay's temper hit high and she elbowed Kalin in the stomach. Although only his pride was hurt, he quickly shuffled away, still apologizing, but not knowing why.

That might have been the end of it, but Bill Candlewith and Ray Manley had been walking by. They observed the entire fracas and clearly heard Kalin's mishandling of Robertay's first name. Their giggles had incensed Robertay even further and so she had marched over to the police station intending to file a report against Officer Kalin, the two old men, and anyone else she could think of.

It was Chambers's bad luck that he was in his office with the door open. Walking directly past Sergeant Levesque at the front desk, Harding steamed into Chambers's office, put hands to hips, and demanded that he, "Do something with that fascist, Rendall Kalin!"

After getting her settled down, Chambers heard Harding's side of the story. The biggest challenge was biting his cheeks fast enough to prevent the guffaw he felt coming on when Robertay related Kalin's malapropism. Eventually he was able to persuade Robertay to let him resolve the issue with Kalin through some sensitivity training.

Later, listening to Warden Ross's voicemail, Chambers heard the tension in his friend's words and voice so called him back immediately. Ross answered after the first ring.

"Dick, I'm not sure how much stock to put into this, but there's sufficient risk that I thought you ought to know as soon as possible."

"What's going on?"

"Caleb Rimes, or whatever his name is, visited with Galen Knight right after you left. And right after that, Knight asked to see me."

"Oh? That's interesting."

"It's a lot more than interesting, Dick. Knight didn't come right out and say it, but he heavily implied that Caleb Rimes is going to try and kill you."

"What?"

"He was very cryptic, very vague. He said things like 'There's a strong likelihood of an attempt on Detective Chambers's life' and 'I hope Detective Chambers will exercise every caution.' When I pressed him, he either went silent or he'd give some variation on those two lines. It was eerie, Dick. I've been directly threatened before and I was less unnerved than I am right now. I don't know anything about this Rimes character, but if Galen Knight is worried about you, then I'd take it seriously."

Chambers was taking in Ross's concern, but he was still processing the idea that Caleb Rimes had visited his brother so soon after his own visit. Had Rimes been tailing him? And what would the two brothers have talked about that would lead Knight to relay this threat? Chambers had left the prison thinking that, yet again, he had failed with Knight. The man had seemed vulnerable for a time, and Chambers had sensed him about to crack. But his steely calm had asserted itself again and by the time that Chambers left the man had willed himself back together.

All of this led Chambers to listen more carefully to Ross's warning. "Did he say anything else, Stephen? Were there any specifics? Did he specifically say to watch out for Caleb Rimes?"

"No, and I pressed him as hard as I could. He might mean that someone else is gunning for you. But if it was Knight who wanted you dead, why would he be warning you? I figure it's got to be Rimes."

"Makes sense, I suppose," Chambers mused. "Do you think it would be worth another trip up to see Knight?"

"No. He was clear about that. In fact, he said he wouldn't see you. He said, 'I'm telling you and only you' meaning me. Then he said, 'I trust you will know what to do.' Like I said, it was eerie. Almost like someone else was telling me all of this."

"Huh… Not sure I—"

"Oh, one other thing, Dick," Ross said. "And this was even more vague. Knight hinted that Rimes, or whoever, might not come at you directly. I took it to mean that anyone close to you might be in danger too." After a pause, Ross continued. "Look, Dick, do with this information what you will. Like I said before, I don't get rattled easily and I don't expect you do either. But there's something about all this that is more than the standard convict threat. I hope you'll take it seriously."

"I will, Stephen. I'm not sure yet what I'll do, but I appreciate the call and the warning."

As the two men hung up, Chambers leaned back in his chair and thought, Jesus, what have I got myself into? But his next thought was, Ah, shit, it's not just about me this time.

CHAPTER 62

Chambers realized that he needed to talk with Chief Miles. He'd planned to put off the conversation until he had some firm notions. He still didn't, but if Caleb Rimes was as off the rails as it appeared, then Chambers needed to let Miles know.

Resolved to talk with the Chief did not mean that Chambers was sanguine about doing so. He'd worked for a range of men and women during his Florida career. Some he'd cared for more than others, but none had earned the disdain that he had for Chief Lawton Miles.

In Chambers's view, Miles was self-important, pompous, homophobic, and probably racist. He was that kind of policeman who was useless on the street, but well skilled in the administrative infighting that characterizes local government big and small. Chambers had to admit that Miles used some of his skill to improve the department—he and the team had well-appointed cars and equipment and the officers had sharp-looking uniforms. These outward signs obscured the more problematic of Miles's management decisions. Chambers knew that overtime requests were excessively scrutinized and often rejected, certain town members were routinely given free passes on indiscretions, and some businesses found themselves more closely safeguarded than others. Moreover, Miles played favorites among the staff. He was particularly fond of Rendall Kalin and Chambers suspected that Kalin reported to Miles everything he heard and saw.

For his part, Chief Miles sensed his detective's disapproval, but didn't know what to do about it. He knew that Chambers was considered a real cop, while that few people in town perceived him that way. Miles knew his strengths lay in administration and political savvy; he used those strengths to keep himself in power and to keep others from effectively challenging him. They may not like me, he would say to himself, but they can't deny me either.

Chambers's distaste for Chief Miles and his approach to leading the department was one thing; his professionalism, however, was quite another. Miles was the chief and Chambers would not openly disrespect him, nor would he snub Miles when the shit was threatening to hit the fan. Chambers didn't expect any real help from Miles, but he would follow protocol and inform him when the situation warranted.

So, Chambers knocked on the chief's office door, went in, and described the situation with Caleb Rimes/Knight and his brother Galen. Chambers was a little surprised that Miles did not chastise him for not coming in sooner. But then he wasn't sure that Miles actually understood all of the lines of inquiry he'd been pursuing. In fact, Miles seemed only mildly curious up to the part about the threat.

As Chambers finished his report, Miles's expression turned to deep concern and he promised to support whatever plan Chambers devised. Assuming Chambers survived the threat and captured Rimes, there would be plenty of time for Miles to conceive of and grab the publicity. He tried not to smile at this possibility.

"You've got my full support, Dick," Miles said in a bravado that sounded fake even to his ears. Still, he could not stop himself from playing the hard-bitten cop: "Let's take this peckerwood Rimes down." Chambers tried to smile in agreement, but could manage only a nod.

While he had been briefing Miles, Chambers had been considering the second part of the threat Warden Ross passed along. He knew Caleb Rimes to be no criminal mastermind. Still, Rimes could initiate his assault on Chambers by attacking those around him. Toni Ludlow was the obvious first choice, but Chambers wondered if John

McTavish might be a reasonable second. He decided to talk with both of them.

Chambers caught up with Toni Ludlow in her studio. She and a fellow artist shared a large space over one of the shops in town. Ludlow's friend, Tina Wales, was a watercolorist whose biggest paintings were only five by seven inches. Ludlow, by contrast, painted in oils on canvases sometimes as big as five by seven feet. The two also varied in size and body type—Ludlow's rangy height compared sharply with Wales's diminutive curves. Both, however, had smiles that lit up their faces and ironic streaks that ran deep.

When Chambers came into the studio both women were working while a Bach concerto played softly. After greeting Wales with what he hoped did not seem like a forced smile, Chambers asked Ludlow if she'd like to have a cup of coffee with him. A little annoyed that he hadn't called first, she nevertheless agreed and they walked down the stairs to the village street.

Instead of turning toward Lydia's, Chambers steered Ludlow toward his car. "Let's drive out to Clayton's," he said, still trying to maintain an evenness to his voice that he did not feel.

"Okay…" Ludlow said, with a hesitation in her own voice. Then deciding to question that hesitation, she asked, "What's up?"

Once in the car, Chambers said, "We need to talk, and I didn't want Tina to hear."

Not sure what to expect, Ludlow turned toward him and nodded. Chambers told her the story of Warden Ross's call and his meeting with Chief Miles. As usual, Ludlow listened intently and without interruption.

When he finished, Ludlow said, "Jesus, Dick, that's scary. What are you going to do?"

"A couple of different things. The first is that I'd like you to consider leaving town for a couple of days. If there's anything to this threat against people around me, you'd be the first target. I can't protect you and chase down Caleb Rimes too. I'm hoping you'll consider taking a short trip—maybe a drawing excursion?"

"I'm not thrilled about that idea."

"I didn't expect you would be and I'm not thrilled to have to ask, but to be honest, I feel like if you stay, my attention just isn't going to be as sharp. I'm gonna need to focus to see what this guy is up to and frankly I'll do that better if I know you're safe."

"Damn that Caleb Rimes," Ludlow said sharply. "I'm tightly centered on that piece you just saw and I'd hate like hell to step away."

"I know, Toni, I really do, but…" Chambers said.

"Okay, I'll do it," Ludlow said suddenly. "I know that's not what the girlfriend says in the movies, but this real-life stuff is a whole lot scarier. And the idea that I'd be a distraction to you seals the deal for me. Do I have time to pack a bag and my gear?"

"You do if you can go now," Chambers said with relief in his voice. "Thanks, Toni."

Ludlow looked intently at Chambers before responding. "Get that fuckhead," she said simply.

Ludlow packed silently. Chambers tried to help, but it was clear that she needed to do it herself. Once she finished, he carried her bags out to her car while she called a friend in Castine to arrange a visit. Ludlow started to protest when Chambers told her that he'd follow her out of town. When she saw the resolve on his face, however, she nodded and got into her car.

Chambers saw no sign of Caleb Rimes's truck as he followed Ludlow until she turned onto Route 1. He would not be able to draw a full breath until Rimes was arrested and Ludlow back home, but he knew there was little else he could do to keep her safe.

On the drive back to Rascal Harbor, Chambers tried to think of any other friends and colleagues who would need warning. The only name he came up with was John McTavish. They weren't really friends, but given Rimes's attack on McTavish and the fact that Galen Knight might have told Caleb about McTavish accompanying Chambers, the detective felt it prudent to warn McTavish. He tried calling the artist, but got shunted off to voice mail. He left a message asking McTavish to call him.

Chambers watched the traffic as he came back to town, trying to be vigilant, but not obsessive. He drove to the police station, pulled Sergeant Andy Levesque and Officer Artie Long into his office, and explained the situation. Levesque said that he would bring Rendall Kalin up to speed once he came in from patrol. Good luck with that, Chambers thought.

After checking his side arm and putting an extra magazine of ammo into his jacket pocket, Chambers sat down to clear his desk with the thought that it might be a day or two before he sat down again. Twenty minutes later, he realized that he'd not heard back from McTavish. He called again and got the same voicemail message. He decided to drive over to the artist's cottage.

CHAPTER 63

Caleb Rimes watched Noah McTavish drive away in his father's car. He had grown cold and stiff watching the McTavish cottage over the last hour, but his brain was working fast now. "Push into the cottage, kill that prick, and then go after Chambers. Finish this thing," he said to himself over and over.

Standing up and working out a kink in his left leg, Rimes heard a car coming down the driveway. Fuck, he thought, the kid is coming back. Rimes knew McTavish to be a faggot lover, but he would not kill the man's son. It was McTavish he wanted dead.

Then he smiled. Instead of McTavish's boy, it was Detective Chambers coming down the driveway. "Two for fuckin' one," he said to himself.

Hiding behind a large oak, Rimes waited until Chambers was parked and out of his car before he revealed himself. "Put your hands in the air, you prick," Rimes said in a low growl and put the muzzle of the gun against the back of Chambers's head.

Raising his hands, Chambers's brain buzzed. Goddamn it, he thought. Then his mind filled with anger at getting trapped, worry about McTavish, and relief that Ludlow was far away. "Caleb," he said as calmly as he could. "We can talk this through."

Rimes didn't hear him, however, for he had seen McTavish emerge from the cottage. "If you don't want to see your friend here get his brains splattered, then get your ass over here," Rimes called out.

McTavish, who had had his phone off while he was working, tried to make sense of the scene unfolding. He thought he was coming out to see why Noah had returned. Instead he saw Detective Chambers's car and Caleb Rimes holding a gun to the back to Chambers's head. "Jesus, not again," he said to himself. To Rimes, he said, "What are you doing here, Rimes?"

"I come to kill you, you faggot, and I got a fuckin' bonus," Rimes said, indicating Chambers.

"Caleb," Chambers repeated. "We can work this out. Put the gun down and we'll go inside and talk."

"Talk is all you fucks ever do!" Rimes said, his voice rough. "You don't serve no one." Then pushing the gun hard into Chambers's neck, he said, "Get over there with that faggot lover." Chambers and McTavish now stood in front the latter's woodpile.

Still trying to engage Rimes on the assumption that a talking gun-holder is not a shooting gun-holder, Chambers tried to get McTavish out of the picture. "C'mon, Caleb. I'm the one you want. Let John go."

"You got that right, Chambers. You're the one I want. I'm gonna blow your fuckin' head off. But I'm gonna kill this bastard too." With that threat, Rimes shifted the gun to the center of McTavish's chest.

"I don't get it, Caleb," Chambers continued, voice calm and steady even as his insides churned. "You've got me. I'm the one who's been talking to Galen. I'm the one who thinks you were involved in Walter Simpson's murder. John's got nothing to do with that."

"You don't know shit," Rimes suddenly screamed. "You don't know a fuckin' thing! This guy is just like all of 'em with the boys!"

"What boys?" Chambers asked.

"He's the one," Rimes said in a softer, but more menacing voice. "He's the one that did that Bradley Little kid. We all know what the Park kid was, but this fuckin' guy, he's the one that turned that Little kid. Turned him into a faggot. And for that, he's gonna die. He ain't gonna hurt no more boys." As he said these words, Rimes eyes started to redden and his gun hand started to shake.

An insight flashed and before he could take it back, Chambers said, "It was Simpson wasn't it, Caleb? Simpson hurt you."

"You don't know!" Rimes screamed, despair echoing through his voice. "You don't have a fuckin' clue… That fuck, what that fuck did…"

Taking a chance, Chambers said, "It's over, Caleb, it's over. What Simpson did to you…he can't do anymore. He's gone, his evil is gone. But let me help you, Caleb. I can help you…"

"The fuck you can, Chambers," Rimes spit. "None of you assholes helped me or my sister then, and you ain't gonna help me now."

"That was wrong of us," Chambers said, following Rimes's lead. "We were wrong not to help you and Susan. But let us help you now. Let me help you tell your story. People need to know."

"Tell my story? Who wants to hear my fuckin' story? Everyone'll just think I'm a faggot too, that I deserved it—"

"No, Caleb, no. People will understand," Chambers interrupted. "I'll help you make them understand."

"They'll never understand," Rimes said, his voice weakening. "And now they won't have to because that fuck Simpson is dead." Now looking directly at Chambers, Rimes said, "And I killed the fucker. I stabbed him right in the fuckin' heart and if Galen hadn't stopped me, I'da cut the thing right out of him." Rimes said these last words in panting fashion as if he couldn't get enough breath to speak them. As he did, his face and his gun arm drooped toward the ground.

Chambers took a breath. If they were where he thought they were, this stand-off was almost over. He just needed to bring Rimes around to hand over the gun.

"Caleb," Chambers said softer than ever, knowing that Rimes would have to pay attention to hear his words. "Caleb, let's…

Rimes raised his gaze, locked onto Chambers's face, and in a steady voice said, "So now you got what you wanted, Chambers, you got it. I confessed right here. Now you go get my brother out." And with that, Rimes raised the gun and shot himself in the temple.

CHAPTER 64

At the sight of Rimes slumping to the ground, Chambers and McTavish both fell back against the wood pile. Their eyes remained focused on Rimes's grievous wound and the awkward position in which he lay.

"You okay, John?" Chambers asked eventually.

Looking over at the detective, McTavish said, "Are you kidding? Jesus, Chambers, are you kidding?"

"Sorry, John, just instinct," Chambers said, pushing himself away from the wood pile, checking for pulse at Rimes's neck. Detecting none, he extended a hand to McTavish. "C'mon, John, you can fix me a drink while I call this in."

"We may have to drink from the bottle. I think my hand's shaking too badly to pour."

"Then that's what we'll do," Chambers said.

Chambers chewed a mint when he went out to greet Chief Miles and Officer Kalin. He knew it wouldn't disguise the whiskey on his breath, but he didn't really care. Sergeant Levesque had called for a state forensics team to come down; they'd be there in an hour. In the meantime, Chambers directed Kalin to seal off the area while he and

Miles went inside McTavish's cottage to discuss logistics.

Not sure what to do with himself, McTavish poured a few more fingers of Bushmills into a tumbler and told Chambers he was going for a walk.

"Don't go too far, Mr. McTavish," Chief Miles said officiously. "You'll need to give a complete statement." McTavish glanced at Chambers then told Miles he'd be back in ten minutes.

While he walked along a wooded trail, McTavish considered calling Noah. But he knew his son's job kept him busy. And then he remembered that he'd left his phone on the kitchen counter. Maybe Noah will be happy enough to see me alive so as not to chew on me too hard, he thought.

Realizing that he was still shaking, McTavish sat down on a stump and nestled his drink into the moss at his feet. Putting his head down and drawing several deep breaths, McTavish said, "Jesus, Maggie, I don't know what's going on. In a year, I've been threatened with a knife and then a gun. I'm supposed to be retired, for Christ's sakes!"

Softly chuckling in his ear, Maggie said, "Who knew how exciting you were, John? And how dangerous becoming an artist was. Maybe you better go back to the university where nothing ever happens."

"Maybe, Mags," McTavish said wearily. "Lord knows, I've had enough excitement to last me several more years."

McTavish looked up as he heard someone coming up the trail. "Who are you talking to, John," McTavish heard Chambers say.

"Just the wind, Detective," McTavish said getting to his feet. "Just the wind."

"Does it answer?" Chambers asked seriously.

"Sometimes it does."

News of "something" happening over at "that artist's guy's house" swelled the crowd that stood in McTavish's driveway and in the woods

outside the police tape Officer Kalin had strung. Huddled inside the tape, the forensics team took pictures and gathered evidence, the ambulance crew stood ready to take Caleb Rimes's body, and Rendall Kalin told the on-lookers near him that he'd have "A hellava story to tell" once the scene was cleared.

Once he'd given his statement, McTavish wandered around his cottage. He knew he wouldn't be able to work and he didn't want to drink any more until he could talk with Noah. He tried to read a magazine, he tried to imagine his next piece of art, he tried to hear Maggie's voice. He failed at each.

Eventually, the crowd inside and outside began to leave and Chambers offered to give McTavish a ride down to Lane's Wharf so that McTavish could talk with Noah. As they drove, McTavish asked Chambers what he was going to do.

"I'll give Toni a call…if she's still talking to me," Chambers said dryly. "Then I think I'll drive up to the prison so I can talk with Galen Knight before he hears it through the prison rag line."

"That's going to extend a pretty trying day. Do you want company?" After McTavish had given his statement back at the cottage, Chambers had filled him in on his visits to the prison, Knight's reaction, Rimes's visit, and Warden Ross's call relaying the threat.

"No, I'll take this one on my own. If I'm too tired to drive back, I can sack out on the Warden's couch."

As they pulled into the Lane's Wharf parking lot, McTavish said, "You saved my life today. Thank you."

"I'm tempted to say it's all in a day's work, but if I had too many more days like this…"

"Well, I thought you were masterful and pretty damn brave," McTavish said. "You kept pulling Rimes's attention away from me and back to yourself. I kept thinking you were like the rodeo clown who keeps the bull from charging the cowboy who's lying there dazed and confused."

"Interesting analogy, but I did what I did in hopes of distracting him so that you could use your splint to bop him on the ear like you did Bradley Little." Chambers smiled. "I was trying to give you the glory shot, but Caleb…well, you know."

"Glory shot? Hell, I was so scared I'da probably hit myself in the head."

"Anyway, glad you didn't," Chambers said, as McTavish got out. As he walked toward the restaurant, Chambers called out, "You know, John, it was the figure-ground thing you told me about that finally helped me see what had been staring at me the whole time. So, thank you."

McTavish smiled, nodded, and said, "Be careful on the drive, Detective."

CHAPTER 65

Detective Chambers made two calls as he drove to the state prison. He first called Toni Ludlow. He began by assuring her three times that he was okay, that Caleb Rimes was dead, and that the saga was over. He offered a relatively short account of the stand-off, promising to give a more complete version when she got home.

Chambers gave that more complete version to Warden Ross. He knew that his visiting in the late evening was unusual and probably violated half a dozen protocols. Yet Chambers also knew that once Ross heard the story, he'd acquiesce to allowing Chambers to speak with Galen Knight.

As usual, Chambers tried to create a game plan for talking with Knight…and, as usual, he failed. *Guess I'll figure it out when I see him,* he thought.

Given the time of night, Ross ordered Galen Knight to be brought to his office. Chambers had suggested that Ross stay. He had no idea how Knight would respond to the news of his brother's suicide so he thought it only right that Ross be there to assess the man's reaction.

Waiting for Knight's arrival, Chambers willed his face not to give away the news. He needn't have bothered. On entering the office and seeing Chambers, Knight said quietly, "You have bad news for me, Detective."

"I do, Galen," Chambers said, equally quietly. "Caleb is dead."

"I see," Knight said, little emotion in his voice. "Would you tell me how it happened?" So, Chambers did. His straightforward account spared no details, but neither did Chambers fluff up or tone down any elements of the encounter. When he got to the part where Caleb talked about his abuse by Walter Simpson, Knight lowered his head and clenched his hands tightly enough that they lost color for a few minutes. Chambers stopped his description until Knight looked up at him again and nodded for him to continue. When Chambers relayed Caleb's admission about stabbing Simpson and trying to cut out his heart, Knight looked down and shook his head a couple of times. When he saw Knight raise his eyes again, Chambers told him about Caleb's last words—the demand that, with Rimes's confession, Chambers now needed to work on setting his brother free.

Knight blinked, shook his head a couple of times, and then his eyes filled. "I didn't save him, Detective," he said in a whisper. "I didn't save my brother and he can't save me."

Chambers was almost home when he took a call from Warden Ross. With voice cracking, Ross said, "Dick, we just found Galen Knight dead in his cell."

"Oh, goddamn it, Stephen!" Chambers gasped, as he pulled to the side of the road. "How the hell did that happen?"

Ross waited a beat and then explained. "We were worried, so I had a guard walking by every ten minutes. He saw Knight back to his cell and get himself ready for bed, all without a word. Next time the guard walked by, Knight was sitting at his desk writing something. After that, the guard saw him lying in bed seemingly asleep. The last time he saw the blood pooling on the floor. Knight had pulled his razor apart and slit the vein in his left arm from his wrist to nearly his elbow. He tried cutting the other one, but he must have passed out before he could finish. He went quickly and quietly."

Chambers didn't know what to say and wasn't sure that his voice would have worked anyway. Ross interpreted his silence as reason to continue.

"Dick, the note he was writing, it was addressed to you. Do you want me to read it?"

"Please," Chambers croaked.

"Okay. It says, 'Dear Detective Chambers. Thank you for your kindness in delivering the news about my brother. You now know all or most of the story of our family and of Caleb and Susan's desperate experiences on the Simpson farm. I will offer no excuses for Caleb's actions, but neither will I condemn him. I could not save my brother, Detective, and now I cannot save myself. Yours truly, Galen Knight.'"

"Thank you, Stephen," Chambers said. He closed his phone and wept.

CHAPTER 66

It doesn't take much to set a gossip fire in small town America. News of Caleb Rimes's suicide quickly took over all the rumor channels. Most folks were relieved. Rimes had cut a narrow, but nasty swath through Rascal Harbor and his presence, even among some of his friends, was not missed. Still, some felt something for the man, especially when they learned of the circumstances of his abuse.

But it was a tangled story—murder, abuse, suicide. Sarah McAdams tried to capture it all in her *Gazette* story, but ended up just reporting the basic facts—the vicious murder of a child molester, a silent murderer who turned out not to be, a damaged family and a disappearing father, the suicide of the real killer who had been abused as a child, the second suicide of the innocent brother.

McAdams did an admirable job of untangling the various threads. What mystified her and most Harbor residents, however, was simple—who was the good guy? Certainly, it wasn't Walter Simpson, the man who abused Caleb Rimes and his sister. But then the man did take in, feed, and shelter two children who were not his own. Certainly, it wasn't Galen Knight, the man who could have saved the town and the police a lot of trouble if he'd simply told the truth. But then the guy went to jail to protect his damaged brother. Certainly not Caleb Rimes, a brute who terrorized others and committed a violent murder.

But then he was abused in the worst kind of way and, well, everybody knows how that can create a monster.

In the end, common sense suggested that the only way to put a good face on the situation was to heap praise on the detective who wouldn't let it go, who kept working the leads until a clear picture formed. So, Detective Dick Chambers became the hero, facing down a crazed and gun-wielding nut job. People congratulated him on the street, bought him cups of coffee, and wrote letters to the editor citing his bravery.

Chief Miles fumed that his detective got most all of the accolades. But then he realized that reflected glory was still glory. After all, wasn't he the one who hired Dick Chambers? And so, he basked in the dim light of that decision.

With the exception of Rendall Kalin, the rest of the Rascal Harbor police force got back to work chasing down under-aged partiers, checking out broken-into summer cottages, and directing traffic around car accidents. Kalin did all his assigned work, but worked every detail of the case into a narrative in which he played Robin to Chambers's Batman. Most folks knew that it was bogus and that Kalin was more pretender than defender of the town's virtues. Still, he told a good story and he didn't drink much, so for a price of a single beer, an evening's entertainment could be had.

For his part, Dick Chambers tried, he really tried, to accept the hero's mantle. He acknowledged the greetings and accepted the cups of coffee, though he ignored the letters to the editor.

"What kind of hero lets the guy he's chasing kill himself right in front of him?" Chambers said to Toni Ludlow on her return to town. "Oh, and then lets an innocent man kill himself, too?"

Ludlow knew that Chambers was not really looking to her for answers. He needed to talk, he trusted her, and so she let him talk. Sometimes she just held his hands, other times she brought him coffee or beer, still other times she just held him. The other side of being a hero, she thought.

Knights Disarmed

Back on the job, Chambers tracked down and resolved the last lingering question. After establishing that she was home, Chambers drove out to Dorothy Simpson's home.

Welcomed to sit at the kitchen table and have a cup of coffee, Chambers skipped the condolences about her father—that ship had sailed and sunk. Instead, he got directly to his question—why had she been silent about Caleb Rimes?

Chambers tried to ask the question neutrally, but the emotions of watching one suicide and contributing to the conditions of another infused his voice. If she noticed, however, Dorothy Simpson ignored it.

In a detached, but straightforward fashion, Simpson described her abusive father, her battered mother, and her own nightmare. She described the arrival of the Knight children and the respite she and her mother realized once her father had new victims under his roof. She described her father's anger when first Susan and then Caleb escaped the Simpson farm and how he revisited his cruelty on his family.

"So you see, Detective," Simpson said flatly. "I didn't give a shit who killed the bastard. What mattered to me was that he was dead. Caleb or Galen, whoever really did it only did what I didn't have the nerve to do. I will always celebrate them."

Chambers had read about and experienced enough victimology to know that he would never be able to understand the deep complications. "Why do people do the things they do?" he said to no one as he left Simpson's house. "Damned if I know."

CHAPTER 67

In many ways, Nellie Hildreth's dual obituary for Galen and Caleb Knight spoke to and for the Harbor townsfolk rattled by the events surrounding Walter Simpson's death:

Galen Knight (aged 42) and Caleb Rimes/Knight (aged 34) died by their own hands in separate incidents a week ago Tuesday.

There are a lot of miserable characters out there and many of them probably deserve to die. Walter Simpson seemed to be one of them. It's a little less certain whether Caleb Rimes was another one; it's a lot less certain that Galen Knight was.

The thing is that death has a way of both clarifying and confusing the lives we lead. Some elements come into sharper focus, others recede. We condemned Galen Knight only to learn that his actions may have been a misguided attempt to protect an untethered brother. We condemned Caleb Rimes only to learn that there might have been good cause for his untethering. And we now condemn Walter Simpson, but we have to wonder whether we might change our minds if we knew more about him.

None of this means that we ought not denounce evil when it presents itself. After all, we're more than the product

Of course, no set of ideas ever gains universal acceptance, so the Letters to the Editor predictably included a range of perspectives. Mae Parton took the brightest path: "Our brave police force with their fine Chief have, once again, acted in a way that serves and preserves the best of our town!" Lois Wren worried about a lingering effect on the tourist trade: "I can only see heartache for our lovely town on the tourist front. Why would any sensible out-of-towner come to a place where people are killing each other?" Jerry Glenville put the matter more simply: "Two guys from one little town commit suicide? Pathetic!"

Although his name may have come up in side conversations, John McTavish seemed to escape any overt attention. Still, his name was mentioned in the state newspaper accounts of the case. And that led to a barrage of email from his sister Ruth and brother Mark.

Ruth started the group exchange with a plea for McTavish to re-think his decision to move to the "cesspool of violence" that Rascal Harbor had become. "Please, John," Ruth wrote, "please consider moving away from those 'people' who cannot seem to control their most animal urges."

Mark took a slightly different tack: "Jesus, brother, you move to town and the whole place goes to shit. Maybe the townsfolk ought to leave you!"

McTavish considered responding immediately to these notes, but didn't. And then a couple more days passed and his impulse to write back weakened further. Then brother Danny chimed in from Chicago: "Holy smokes, John, Rascal Harbor is becoming the Chicago of the east coast! Do you need me to gun-up and come over as your body-guard? Just say the word, brother, and I'll be there!"

Before McTavish could even think of a response, Ruth jumped in to support "Danny's excellent plan" and Mark seconded that notion. McTavish suspected that, although Mark was joking, Ruth was quite serious. Both, however, would support any plan to bring the youngest McTavish back to the home state womb.

Hoping to avoid being labeled "rude," by Mark and Ruth, McTavish finally responded. "I'm fine everyone. By rights, Rascal Harbor has reached its crime threshold for the next twenty years so I expect to walk the streets unscathed. That said, if you'd like to come back for a visit, Danny, we'll all help you carry your Chicago 'heat.'"

"Think your note will quiet them down?" Noah asked after seeing his father's response.

"Doubtful. I'll catch hell the next time we all gather, but it'll likely die down after that."

"I don't know, Dad. That family of yours seems to have long memories for some things."

"Ayuh."

Noah smiled. Then, more serious, he asked, "What does Mom think about it all?"

McTavish looked over at his son before answering. Since his admission that he and Maggie "talked," he and Noah had skirted the topic. McTavish suspected that Noah had wanted to bring it forward a couple different times; he, by contrast, was content to let it go. Noah *was* Maggie's son, though, so he could muster no real surprise at his son's question.

"I bet you can probably guess," McTavish said.

"Yeah, I probably could, but I'd like to hear the particulars."

"Fair enough," McTavish said, conceding. "Well, you know, she's concerned. She wonders if I'm just not paying attention to my surroundings. She called it 'doing that McTavish zone-out thing.'" Both men smiled. "And she's wondering if I'm really up to the task of looking out for you if I struggle so mightily in tending to myself."

"She's got a point there, Dad, but you can tell her that Louise is looking out for me, and for you."

"She knows, Noah. She quite likes the girl." Father and son smiled again. Noah paused, looked down, and then looked deeply at his father.

"Dad, would you ask her something for me?"

Not sure where this was going, McTavish said hesitantly, "Um, okay, Noah. I'm not really sure it works that way…but I can try." McTavish paused and then asked, "What do you want me to ask her?"

"'Would you ask her to come to me?" Noah said, his voice breaking. "Dad, would you ask her to just come talk to me? Just once, if that's all she can do. If she could… If she could just once… Even if she just came and said 'hi'." Though he continued looking at his father, Noah's shoulders shook lightly with his sobs.

Pulling his son close to him, McTavish said softly, "Ayuh."

THE END

# Geoffrey Scott

is the pseudonym of **S. G. Grant**, a professor of history education at Binghamton University. Grant has authored or edited a dozen education-related books and numerous articles and book chapters. This is the second book in his series of art-flavored novels.